# KIT

## A SCARRED HEARTS NOVEL

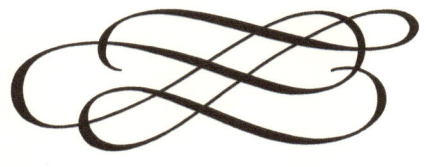

*S.M. WEST*

# CONTENTS

**Cover Design:** *KiWi Cover Design Co.*
**Edited:** *Leanne Rabesa*
**Cover Photo:** *Wander Aguiar Photography*
**Cover Model:** *Zack Salaun*

*"I did then what I knew how to do. Now that I know better, I do better."*
*~ Maya Angelou*

# PLAYLIST

**Listen On Spotify**

*"Old Time Rock & Roll" – Bob Seger*
*"Quitting You" – Arkells*
*"Let You Down" – NF*
*"Never Forget You" – Zara Larsson and MNEK*
*"Lay it on me" – Vance Joy*
*"All of Me" – John Legend*

# CARO

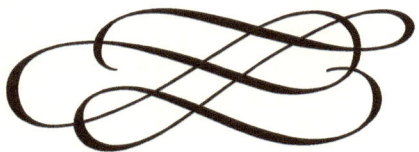

*"That's bullshit. Get Foley, now." A gruff male voice brings the hairs on the nape of my neck to attention.*

*Only feet from the door to the outside, I stop and turn on my heel; all eyes in the clinic waiting room are glued to the two burly men looming over the intake desk. They are a wall of muscle.*

*On the other side, Willow's on her feet back from them when usually she's sitting, pleasant and smiling. She's talking to them, standing stiffly with her shoulders jamming into her ears, but I can't make out her words over the low hum of the ventilation system.*

*Closer now, I'm almost at the counter when her melodic voice wavers, "Dr. Foley hasn't worked here for over five months. But we have several other doctors—"*

*"If Foley isn't here, get Doctor Caroline Archer," the bigger of the two, a bald man, growls.*

*I nearly trip over my feet, now only a foot from the men. "I'm Dr. Archer, how can I help you?" My confident tone hides my trepidation and mounting anxiety.*

*The strange prickling sensation has now spread from my neck to every region of my body. Unfortunately, patient harassment isn't anything new at this walk-in clinic. We're in a rough neighborhood, and despite the signs plastered all over the place noting no narcotics on site, that's usually what all the ruckus is about.*

*This feels different. But what they are after isn't obvious.*

*Neither appear to be bleeding or wounded, no one is clutching at or favoring a body part. And despite how intimidating they are, neither of these men act or look like they are high or in need of a fix.*

*"Come with us." The bald man, who is super intense and scary, grabs my bicep with his thick, sausage-like fingers.*

"Excuse me." I try to pull away, but it's too late. His grip is firm.

Behind us, in the waiting area, someone gasps and another calls out, "Hey, you can't do that."

My free arm juts out to the side, palm down in an everyone relax gesture, and I struggle to remember my self-defense training. What am I supposed to do when grabbed?

Nothing. I can't remember anything.

I'm a doctor, dammit, and worked in the ER for years, no less. I perform exceptionally well under pressure. Yet now, when I'm faced with potential danger, I'm… useless.

"Let her go." Willow holds up the phone and her gaze mirrors my concern. "I'm calling the police if you don't leave right now."

The other guy, the mustached one not manhandling me, reaches across the counter and snatches the phone from her, slamming it into the cradle.

She jumps back, afraid he'll grab her too, but undeterred, she scrambles to pull her cell from the front pocket of her scrubs. This woman is awesome.

I've worked with Willow for a few years, and she's proven to not only be an outstanding nurse and office manager, but also a good friend.

"No one gets hurt if Dr. Caroline comes with us." The guy at my side tightens his hold, trying to drag me to the door.

"I'm not going anywhere." I muster all my courage into a calm and controlled tone, briefly glancing at the many faces around the room, some worried, some bewildered, and some fascinated. A few even have their phones out. Terrific.

"Like I said, maybe I can help you." Trying to satisfy them might be foolish but it's all I have right now. "What is it you need? I just finished my shift here but if you want me to take a look at whatever is wrong—"

"Where can we talk privately?" The hostile Mr. Clean dude scans the room, and I point to the door to his left that leads to the examination rooms.

Going farther into the clinic isn't smart, but I'm not leaving this building with him. And this way, Willow can call the police and we're *away from the people in the waiting room, who may get hurt if this goes south.*

*I stop at the first room, close enough to the front of the clinic, and enter. "Leave the door open."*

*They ignore me and one guy shuts the door while the other still has me in his grasp. My heart rockets into my throat.*

*"Where the fuck is Foley?" The bigger one leers at me with eyes as black and toxic as tar.*

*"We already told you. He no longer works here and hasn't in months, but he's still a doctor and you should be able to find—"*

*"Shut up." He pinches my arm, crowding my space. "We've fucking looked and can't find him. So we've come for you. Where the fuck is it? You give us the goods and this'll be over."*

*The door opens and Willow's there with two male doctors from the clinic flanking her sides. "I've called the police."*

*"You fucking bitch." Moustache guy curls his fingers into bowling-ball fists, all his fury aimed at her.*

*The guy in front of me snarls and releases me. He taps his buddy on the shoulder, and the three in the doorway quickly scatter, making room for the two giants to storm out.*

*"You okay?" Willow is the first to my side, rubbing at my arm, and it's the first time I register it's throbbing.*

*"Yes, just a little shaken."*

*"What did they want?" She rolls up my sleeve and examines the red welts in the shape of fingers on my arm. "Oh my God."*

*"It's okay." I pull from her grip and straighten my shirt. "I'm not sure what they wanted. They said something about looking for Elliot, and they couldn't find him so they came for me. They asked for the goods but never said what they were."*

*"The goods?" She wrinkles her brow. "I wonder what that means. We should call Elliot—hopefully he'll explain this to us."*

*"Yes, but I'll call him."*

*"You sure? I mean, I'm glad you want to call him and I don't have to, but you had to deal with those guys." She's sincere and caring but I can't help but chuckle while nodding.*

*Elliot Foley is her least favorite person among the staff who work, and have worked, at this clinic. Sadly, I also dated him. Not something I'm particularly proud of, and not because of him but more because I don't know why we were ever together.*

*I broke things off five months ago and around the same time, he found another job at a hospital. Scrolling through my contacts, I hit his number and it goes straight to voicemail.*

*"Dr. Foley. You know what to do." Even his recorded voice leaches arrogance. Just one of many reasons why we didn't work out.*

*"Elliot, it's Caro. We had a…an incident at the clinic today. Two guys, um…big guys, scary even, came in looking for you. When told you no longer worked here, they asked for me. They are looking for 'the goods,' do you know what that is? I hope things are okay. Please call me when you get this."*

*While our split was amicable, we haven't spoken since. Those guys are intense, and if Elliot is mixed up with them, he might be in trouble. We'll never be friends and we're both okay with that, but I don't want harm to come his way.*

*Two uniformed cops arrive nearly an hour later, and by that time, we've isolated the incident on the security system. The police set about taking statements and in addition to Willow and me, a few patients stuck around, more than eager to chime in with their account of how things occurred.*

*No surprise, the police don't promise anything since no one was hurt and no damage was done, but they'll get back to us if the images of the guys on the security tape lead to anything.*

*"Hey, Willow, do you need me to stick around?" Everything is back to normal, and once again, I'm on my way out.*

*I was supposed to be at Léa's Home nearly two hours ago. The Home is a private facility I own with my brother, Nick, for people suffering from acquired brain injuries.*

*"No, no. You go." She smiles. "I'll talk to you later."*

*By the time I get to the Home, it's a little past five and I'm already exhausted. I've been juggling two jobs—the clinic and the Home—for almost two years now and my energy is near depleted.*

*When Nick first came to me with his plan to build the Home as tribute to our dead father and older sister, Léa, I jumped at the idea. Both of them suffered brain injuries as a result of two different incidents which altered their lives and eventually led to their deaths.*

*I left my ER job, but it didn't take long to realize every dollar we could put into this endeavor only improved its chances of success.*

*The Home is a not-for-profit, and like Nick, I didn't want to need a salary so I took on more hours at the walk-in clinic. This way, the Home didn't have to pay me and those funds could go back into the Home.*

*Of course, Nick didn't like the idea and told me we'd make it work, even though it was all right for him not to take a salary. Two years later and I was fine with the fact that we haven't had another discussion regarding my salary. I wouldn't take it anyway.*

*This was finally a way for me to give back to my brother and sister. I'm the youngest, and without our parents, they always took care of me no matter the cost or impact to them.*

*My double duty helps, but the back and forth and spending every waking moment working is taking its toll on me. The sooner I can walk away from the clinic, the better.*

*And there is hope. We're hosting an investor reception the day after tomorrow in support of the Home. If it's a success and we sign on new donors and raise more funds, my last day at the clinic will be closer to becoming reality.*

*After spending a few hours in Nick's office, I take a quick walk around the floors, checking on our patients, and finally reply to Willow's text that came in when I was on a phone call.*

**Willow: All good here. The men didn't come back and the clinic is closed.**

**Me: Good.**

**Willow: Have you heard from Elliot?**

**Me: No, I'm going to send him a text now.**

**Willow: Jerk. Someone needs to teach him manners.**

*I shake my head, coming out of the last room. She never passes up a chance to take a shot at him and the feeling is mutual. Willow and Elliott sling words like swords as if they are mortal enemies.*

Me: He'll call. I remembered earlier tonight, there's a box of his things at the clinic. Just stuff he left behind and never picked up.

Willow: That's right. Why didn't I think of that? It's either in the front closet or the bin behind reception. Or maybe the medical supply closet. Sorry I'm not sure where it is.

Me: I'll swing by on my way home and find it. There may be a clue as to what the men are looking for.

Willow: No, go home. It's late.

*The thought of going home is tempting, and I will be at the clinic by seven in the morning. I could deal with this then.*

Me: I guess. It's just bugging me. What are those guys looking for? And since Elliot hasn't called, this could give us some answers.

Willow: True. But whether we get answers tonight or tomorrow doesn't make much difference.

Me: OK. Thanks and I'll see you tomorrow.

Willow: Night.

*Phone back in my pocket, I round the corner and stretch, aching for a hot bath. I can't wait for Nick to get back; I hate paperwork. He runs the administrative end of things and together with Maggie, his partner, they secure the investors and donors. I, on the other hand, run all medical operations.*

*"Everyone is settled for the night," I say through a sneaky yawn, covering my mouth as my cheeks redden.*

*Trudy, the night nurse, a plump, older woman, swivels from the monitor to face me, and her round, ruby cheeks and thin lips curve upward. "Good. Now go home. You look like you're about to fall asleep standing up."*

*"Wow, thanks. Remind me never to look to you for a compliment." I tuck an unruly curl back into the tie holding my mass of hair, suddenly conscious of my appearance.*

*She shoos me with a hand. "Shush, you. You don't need compliments. We should all be so lucky to look like you. Go on, drive carefully, and get some rest."*

"Yes, ma'am." I mock salute the kind motherly woman who runs the night shift at Léa's better than some administrative staff in hospitals.

"You know, normally I wouldn't say this to the boss—it's not my business." She stares at me and I want to smirk at her blatant lie.

This woman doesn't know how to hold her tongue and has never not spoken her mind. I lean in, elbows on the table, as if showing her she has my rapt attention.

"Caro, we have a schedule for a reason. At the young age of thirty-four, you've got a lot on your plate. On top of owning and managing this place, you also work the floors." She rests her hand on top of the very schedule she's talking about. "And as if that isn't enough, you're also putting in hours at the Jane Walk-in Clinic. You're going to run yourself ragged."

My phone pulsates with a near-silent buzz in the pocket of my scrubs and I ignore it.

"Point taken, and I am seriously thinking about cutting back my time at the clinic…" I trail off and she clucks at me, her tongue kissing the back of her front teeth.

"You need to cut it out altogether. I know you're superhuman or something, but not many people could go on for as long as you have working two full-time jobs with the hours and stress that come with both." Her warm green eyes stare at me over the rim of her glasses, and she rubs her hand tenderly over mine before sliding the chair toward the now ringing phone. "Good evening, Léa's Home. Trudy speaking."

I wave at her and grab my bag from under the desk, then my winter coat from the rack in the corner. Before I head for the exit, I mouth good night to Trudy and pull my phone from my pocket.

**Unknown: Tell us where it is or else.**

Is this a wrong number? Or some kind of hoax or scam?

**Me: Who is this?**

I stop only feet from the exit to the building because a response pops up.

**Unknown: We can't find Foley. You're all we've got. Give it to us and no one gets hurt.**

*Icy fingers curl around my insides. Not this again. Even through text, it's threatening.*

**Me: Tell me what you're talking about.**

**Unknown: Don't play stupid. You're a doc, supposed to be smart. Give it to us or else you'll regret it.**

*Why won't they tell me what it is they're after? One of the men called it "the goods"—what goods? Furiously I type out another response.*

**Me: I'm trying to cooperate. I don't know what you're talking about.**

*Sixty seconds pass and nothing. No response. The wait feels like eternity but nothing comes in. I'm not giving up yet.*

**Me: Tell me what you want.**

*A jab of pain slices through my bottom lip and the taste of copper hits my tongue. My teeth withdraw, relinquishing my chewed flesh.*

*Biting my lip is a nasty habit I picked up in med school when most of my hours were spent worrying about studying, my grades, and ensuring I didn't kill anyone.*

*I try one more time to get a response, already knowing it's futile. They have gone silent.*

**Me: Hello?**

*Not bothering to wait, I dial Elliot's number for the second time today and without even a ring, it goes to voicemail. Doesn't that mean his phone is off?*

*"Elliot, it's Caro. Again." My bite will not get him to call me any sooner.*

*He's the type of man who needs his ego stroked and often. He's the perfect example of that old adage that you catch more flies with honey than vinegar.*

*I lay it on thick and sweet. "I really need your help and would really appreciate it if you called me back as soon as you get this. I don't care what time it is, anytime day or night. Please."*

*Ending the call, I drop the phone into my jacket pocket. Well, I can forget about going home.*

*Sleep will elude me with all the questions I have and a threat of bodily harm hanging over my head. I need answers, and the box at the clinic is my only chance of getting any tonight. This can't wait until tomorrow.*

# CARO

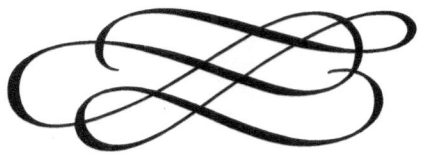

*A blast of wintry air slaps at my face as soon as I step outside. Tucking my chin into my chest to block the unforgiving wind, I hurry to my car. Every breath, thick and frigid, burns my lungs on the way in and billows from my mouth in puffs of icy smoke.*

*February is the worst of winter in Toronto. Months into the season, we're fed up with temperatures well below freezing, and snow has long lost its magic. Every snowflake feels more like a prison sentence with the harsh reality that winter isn't near done with us and the end isn't in sight.*

*My pocket vibrates and I still. Did they answer my texts? I jump into my car, get the engine going, and crank the heat before fumbling with gloves and chilled fingers to get my phone.*

*There's a text from Nick to call him, which I do once I'm on the road.*

*"Caro, you good?"*

*My heart rate evens out and I start to feel more levelheaded as his gravelly voice booms through the car speakers.*

*"I've been better." I can't lie to him and yet I don't want to worry him. "How's the weather?"*

*Nick and Maggie are at our family cottage in Quebec. He stole her away for a long weekend—Valentine's Day of all days. The corners of my lips tip up at the thought of Nick Archer all heart eyes, overflowing with love for a woman.*

*The image of a cartoon character with a huge red heart thumping right out of his chest comes to mind. And he loves not just any woman. He loves Maggie. A true force of nature. She's the perfect match for my stubborn-ass brother. God help her.*

"It's been snowing for two days straight but no complaints. We're hunkered down by the fire, keeping ourselves busy." His sly grin flashes through my mind as I hear it in his voice, along with the innuendo of how they're keeping busy.

I roll my eyes, slightly uncomfortable thinking of my brother getting it on—ick—and a little saddened, not for him but for me.

Wallowing isn't something I do, but right now I'm feeling particularly alone and a little unsettled. I don't have a special someone to share stupid days like Valentine's with or even to talk to about stuff like these maddening texts.

But I won't let any of my crap take away from how happy I am for my brother. Stuck with Maggie, no matter where, is Nick's dream come true, and snowed in at the carriage house is even better. No one and nothing to intrude on them.

I hit the blinker to signal the upcoming left turn, shaking my head wryly. "I'm sure you are."

He chuckles, and just as quickly, his humor vanishes. "What's got you sounding glum?"

"Ugh, I didn't hide it very well, did I?" I pause—how do I tell him about the texts and incident at the clinic without causing him to come home early?

"No. What's going on? And don't tell me it's work or something like that. This sounds like something more."

I scowl, grateful he can't see my face right now and loathing how good he is at reading me, even through a damn phone line.

"Caro, come on." He senses my hesitation, and like a dog with a bone, he's going to chew on it until satisfied.

I've always admired, envied even, his uncanny ability to pick up on the things people don't say or do. It's one of the many reasons he was so good at his old job.

No, job isn't an accurate way of describing my brother's role in helping unsavory characters fix their problems.

But even with his skill, I wish he wouldn't use it on me. He makes it really hard to hide things from him, especially when I was a teenager and wanting my independence.

"Caro?" He's insistent.

*Shoot. I don't know how to say this without causing alarm. I don't want him to cut his time away with Maggie short. He's already given up so much for me.*

"It's been a strange day." *My exhale is long and waning, like that of a deflating balloon.*

"Strange how?"

*There isn't any point in holding back. Nick always figures things out eventually, and in the meantime, he won't give up, so I recount both the texts and the altercation at the clinic.*

"And you don't know what they're looking for? And you haven't heard from Elliot?"

"I really don't know and no, I've tried Elliot twice and nothing so far. I guess if he's in surgery or on duty, it would explain why I haven't heard from him. I'm on my way to the clinic right now."

"Why?"

"There's a box of Elliot's stuff, things he left behind, and I figured there might be something there. So I'm going to check things out."

"Now? By yourself?" *He doesn't give me a beat to answer.* "Like hell you are. No way."

"Stop worrying." *Aggravation scratches at my throat. I also hate him being right in how he's responding.* "I can take care of myself."

"Yeah, but it isn't a good idea. Let me call Ki—"

"No. Don't call him." *A strange, curious little hitch lodges in my chest at just the hint of Kit, and like a razor's edge, my words cut him off.*

*His best friend and my ex... ex-lover? My ex-best friend? Kit's my ex-everything. Everything aches—head, heart, and body—at the mere thought of him. He's the last person I want to see... No, that isn't true.*

*I want to see him but know better than to crave someone I pushed away. He's better off without me. I've done enough damage.*

"I'd feel better if Kit went with you."

"I'd be wasting his time, and besides, I need to find whatever it is these guys are looking for. They already tried the clinic so it isn't like they'll go back there."

"You're not helping—" His intensely anxious tone causes me to envision his molars grinding into dust with how tight he must be clenching his jaw.

"I promise to text you once I've checked things out." I turn into the plaza where the clinic is located, holding my breath as I wait for him to tell me he's backing off and not bringing Kit into this.

"Caro—"

"Nick, please enjoy your last day. When you guys get back, you're going to wish you were away again with the investor reception that night. What time are you planning to arrive on Friday?"

"In enough time to get ready. Why? We can leave earlier."

"No, that's fine. I was just curious. Do you need any help with any last-minute preparations?" Maybe if I get him focused on the reception, he'll let the Kit thing go. Nick loathes event planning, almost as much as I do.

I also don't like attending these things, but it's the least I can do considering I'm hands off with this end of things. Nick manages the events, or more accurately, Maggie does.

"No. We're good."

"Okay. Don't worry about me and say hi to Maggie for me."

My car swings into a spot at the front of the clinic. I usually park in the back when it's open, but it's night and the lighting is better in the front. The white neon sign atop the front door is bright.

I'm both anxious and optimistic to go inside and get my hands on that box. I recall finding some medical journals back when he left, but I wonder what else might be in there. Hopefully, answers.

"I will." His tone is more agreeable and with any luck, he accepts that I can check out a box of Elliot's belongings on my own even if he doesn't like it. "Caro, text or call me."

"Yeah, yeah. Night, Nick. Love you."

"You too." He ends the call and his worried tone nags at me.

My brother is a protector and before Maggie, safeguarding me was his lifelong purpose. At times, his hovering and cautious attitude was smothering, but it's also why we're so close. Nick is so much more than a brother to me.

*He went to great lengths to make sure my dream of being a doctor came true, sacrificing his future for a life of crime. It was never for himself, but more for the money it afforded him. It was to give me a life I never would have had without it.*

*A familiar pang of guilt strikes my chest—it never goes away. No matter what I do, I can never truly repay him or Léa for what they sacrificed for me. My sister paid with her life.*

*And among other reasons, this is why, daily, I'm thankful for Maggie in so many ways. Since she came into his life in the wild and crazy way that she did, nearly two years ago now, he's no longer in that life.*

*He's a legitimate businessman, some might even say a philanthropist. Léa's Home is his life, and all the thugs, guns, and violence are behind him. My relief is palpable.*

*A long life isn't a sure thing for any of us. I get that. But before, it was almost guaranteed Nick would die young. Now, I'm beyond thankful. Those sleepless nights and the sickening worry are behind me. And according to Nick, the same can be said for Kit. He's supposedly out of that life, too, and yet I severed all ties.*

*Kit.*

*My palm hits the steering wheel in frustration. Why'd Nick have to mention him? It's been months since he's crossed my mind. Shit, why am I lying to myself? I think about him all the time. We haven't seen each other in nearly a year even though we've been broken up for much longer. All of it is my choice.*

*Yet my reason for not being with him—the crime—is no longer a factor. Does that change things?*

*I shake my head, truthfully afraid to consider what Kit's more mundane and definitely safer lifestyle might mean. No obstacles between us.*

*I can't think about him. Not tonight. Not ever.*

*The sooner I get in there, the sooner I can get home. What is it with tonight and my exes?*

*Elliot and Kit are so vastly different. Kit was and still is the only man I've ever loved. The danger and violence are what drove me away.*

*And then there's Elliot. There's no denying he's safe, albeit boring and overbearing, and that's what appealed to me the most. I overlooked his inflated ego and sense of self-importance for safe. But was he safe?*

*If so, who are these guys after him? And what is it they're looking for?*

*Engine off, I zip my jacket up to my chin, preparing for the chilly night air, and get out, locking my car. Bracing for the cold whip of the wind, I jog the short distance to the front door of the clinic.*

*Strangely, the door is unlocked but the alarm is set. Wary, I enter the alarm code into the keypad, and my finger hovers over the light switch. I'm not going to turn them on.*

*If someone is here, I don't want to alert them to my presence. With my phone flashlight now shining into the blackness, I scan the beam around the waiting room.*

*Rows upon rows of plastic chairs with square tables on the ends, some cluttered with outdated and dog-eared magazines, fill the large open space. Nothing is out of place.*

*The more I look around the front and nothing is awry, the more my nerves settle. I then spend about twenty minutes, if not more, digging through the front closet.*

*It's a mess and I come up empty, but being the Type A that I am, I can't leave this clutter and quickly rearrange things to my liking.*

*Next is the bin Willow mentioned behind the reception desk. That's worse than the closet and Elliot's box isn't there either.*

*I've already been here way longer than I intended and I push through the door to the exam rooms, medical supply closet, and washroom. All eight examination room doors, four on each side of the hallway, are shut.*

*My feet stutter, and a sharp, icy panic grips the back of my neck. The door to the medical storage room, at the end of the corridor, is open. It should be locked.*

*We lock the supply room at all times, and it's off limits to anyone but staff given its contents. We may not have narcotics, but there are medical supplies, some drugs, and samples that could cause damage or death in the wrong hands.*

*Why did I get sidetracked up front? I spent countless minutes cleaning up the clutter and organizing things when there could be an intruder in the building?*

*The lights are off inside the room and, even with the beam of my phone, I can't see much except that the glass pane insert of the door is shattered.*

*The thickness in the air clogs my throat, and my knees lock, keeping me firmly rooted in place. That's how they got in there. Someone smashed the glass and reached in to flip the lock.*

*Jagged spikes rise like mountain peaks from the edges of the pane, and some are coated in a dark substance. Blood. Whoever did this cut themselves.*

*Could they still be here? Hurt. I want to call out, see if anyone is here, but I don't know what I could be walking into. None of this makes sense.*

*How did someone get in here? The front door was unlocked but the alarm was set. Usually if the alarm went off, I'd have been notified by the security company.*

*I should call the police, but I stand there for a few more seconds, straining to detect any movement or sounds. Nothing. Only spine-chilling silence.*

*Quietly, I slip back into the front of the clinic, closer to the front door, eyes trained to the back of the clinic just in case someone is here. In hushed tones, I call the police and explain the situation.*

*Tonight must be a busy night. Given I'm not in danger, I'm told they'll get there when they can. I push for a better sense of timing and reluctantly, I'm told it'll be close to forty minutes or more before a cruiser can come by. And of course, if things change on my end, I'm to call them back.*

*The operator advises me to wait in my car and I almost do but then it hits me. The fog of fear, brought on by the day's events, clears. The clinic has been broken into before.*

*Mostly, it's the homeless seeking a place for the night when it's freezing outside. Tonight is well below zero and expected to get colder before dawn. What if this is what has happened now? And it has nothing to do with those awful men and those texts?*

*Maybe Willow forgot to lock the door? It's possible. And now I've unnecessarily called the police.*

*If someone is hurt and only looking for somewhere warm for the night, I don't want to turn them out into the cold. I'd rather find them a shelter for the night and avoid the police hassle.*

*I grab a toy truck from the play area. It isn't much of a weapon, but it might be all I need to get away if someone is here and ready to attack. While I make my way past the four sets of doors on either side of the hall, my insides churn. I should stop and check each room, but for some reason, getting to the supply closet feels urgent.*

*I pass the cutoff to a short corridor where both the lunchroom and bathroom doors are closed. My breathing is still the only sound.*

*The flashlight shines brightly into the room, no shapes or movement so far, and shards of glass crack and pop under the sole of my boot. I pause, flashing my light onto the broken fragments littering the tiled floor.*

*The familiar smell of antiseptic, sterility, and chemicals fills my nostrils, and for a brief moment, it brings calm. This is my domain. I know every nook and cranny of this place.*

*But my composure is soon lost when a loud smack, like a door slamming, comes from the front of the building and grips my insides and twists.*

*I'm not alone. Someone's here.*

# KIT

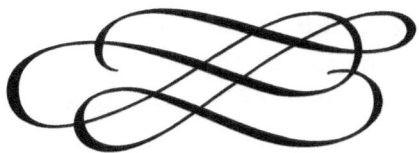

BOb Seger rasps about the days of old, and I tap my big foot to the catchy tune. His rough voice fades in and out, mingling with the whirs, bangs, and clanks of the garage. A raucous noise, that's what it is, and one I'm all too familiar with and I can't say I don't like.

The Phoenix is my home, where I'm most comfortable under the hood of a car or searching for our next classic to be restored. This is Maggie's place, but since day one, I've worked my ass off and tried to pull more than my weight.

She did me a solid by taking me in and giving me a job. I intend to pay her back and then some. To date, most of the business at the garage is word of mouth, and while the work is steady and she's making a healthy profit, it could be better.

The woman and her crew are talented, among the best in the restoration business, but she doesn't go looking for the business. I want to change that and do my share to grow the revenue and reputation of the Phoenix.

It took a bit of convincing, but she finally agreed to let me take a proactive approach to sourcing and buying cars we could restore to their original beauty. The plan is to then sell them either privately or at an auction.

That's where Pinter comes in, and tomorrow, when I meet with him, I'll be closer to making it a reality. To bring my master plan to life, we need our first car. I just need to close Pinter.

But that's tomorrow.

I've already got a lot going on. We're closed for the day, but a couple of the guys are still working, trying to finish a job or get a head start on tomorrow's work. I'm almost done with an El Camino; tonight's work puts me ahead of schedule. Then, well, I have a date.

*Tightening the last of the screws on the back tire, I pause, popping my head up to listen. Did someone call my name?*

*"Yo, Kit. Call for you." Manny saunters toward me with an outstretched hand, fingers blackened with oil and grit from the day. He's holding out the office cell phone.*

*"What?" I step from the 1979 El Camino.*

*"Nick's on the phone. Wants to talk to you." He hands it to me and walks back the way he came.*

*"Damn. Miss me already?" An easy chuckle tumbles from my mouth.*

*"You wish." Nick's laugh is tight and not at all sincere. "I have a favor to ask."*

*"What's up?" I try to ignore the tension riding its way up my back.*

*"Need you to check in on Caro."*

*Like a kid just hit while playing freeze tag, my body immediately stiffens. At the mention of his sister, my ex, a white-hot knot forms between my shoulder blades. Throbbing and growing.*

*I prop the phone between my ear and shoulder, grabbing a rag from a worktable to wipe the grease off my hands, and really, to give me something to do.*

*"What? Why?"*

*Caro hates me, and he knows better than to ask me, of all people, to go anywhere near her.*

*"She went to the clinic to check something out, but I don't have a good feeling about it. I don't want her alone."*

*He explains the events of the day and how his sister had a run-in with two intimidating muscle men and then got some threatening texts. And of course, how her asshole ex is ignoring her.*

*Finally he pauses, and this is where I should alleviate his concerns and accept the task.*

*My chest constricts. A heavy, cloying sense of guilt blends with the never-ending desire to protect Caro. There was a time, not too long ago, when no questions asked, without hesitation, I would have done whatever Nick asked, especially where his sister was concerned.*

*Despite our differences, Caro was the one person I cared about the most in the world. If I'm being honest, she still is, even more than Nick, and that's saying a lot because the guy's my best friend. The brother I never had.*

*But none of that matters. I promised her I'd stay out of her life. Something tells me she won't understand if I just show up because Nick asked me to.*

*"She doesn't want to see me." I sound like a pussy, too scared to face her, and that isn't it at all. "It'll be bad."*

*I drop the greasy rag and lean my ass against the table, concentrating on easing my now shallow breaths.*

*"Shit, I wouldn't ask..." His voice peters out, and shame eats at my gut.*

*Why am I fighting this? Fuck. Self-preservation. But Nick isn't one to overreact, and his instincts are generally on the money. If he has a feeling something isn't right, he's got reason.*

*"If I had someone else to do it..." Nick starts again, and there's only one other person he'd trust with his sister's safety.*

*Logan, and he isn't here. He's on the road once again and not due back in town for another week. That's if he shows up.*

*No, I'm the only one he can ask, and if something ever happened to her... fuck, I can't not help.*

*"Fine. I'll do it. She's at the clinic?" It isn't exactly around the corner, so I'm going to have to get a move on. It will take me about half an hour to get to that shitty part of the city.*

*"Yeah. Thanks. I owe you."*

*"Shut up. I'll call or text once I've checked it out." Ending the call, I trek through the garage toward the office.*

*And now Caro is back, front and center in my thoughts, where she's been for most of my adult life. I don't do drugs or alcohol—I can take them or leave them—but she isn't someone I can kick. No matter how I try.*

*Shit, I'll have to cancel the date. Or maybe I can still make it work? It's close to eight, and Sally will be at my place in thirty minutes for dinner. It was my big idea to grill steaks. A big step for me and one I'm not so sure I'm ready for.*

*I haven't been on a date since Caro.*

*Shit.*

*Nope, I'm not cancelling. At thirty-six, I have to move on and get a life. Sally is a nice woman, a friend, and maybe that's all we'll ever be, but I want to give it a try. If I don't, I'll stay stuck like I have been for years. Hung up on a woman with no chance of a future together.*

*I pull up my texts with Sally.*

**Me: I'm running behind. How's 9:30?**

*Worst case, if dropping in on Caro takes longer than expected, I'll order dinner. She replies almost immediately, and my lips curve upward at the corners. Was she waiting and hoping I'd text her?*

*Even if I don't take this any further, Sally is good for my ego, for reminding me I could have more with someone else. Again, another reason to have tonight's date.*

**Sally: You getting cold feet? Afraid I won't like your cooking?**

*I snicker, shaking my head. We always have fun, poking at each other. That's how this dating thing started.*

**Me: Not a chance.**

*Three dots dance on the screen, and while waiting for her response, the urgency of making sure Caro is fine flies at me full force. Yup, she's always on my mind, even when I'm doing something else and especially when she shouldn't be.*

*As much as I want to volley back and forth with Sally, the sooner I go to the clinic, the sooner it'll be over.*

**Sally: 930 is good.**

**Me: See you then.**

*"Guys, quittin' time." I trudge to the back room to wash up. "Five until I lock up."*

*They murmur agreement, and as I clean up, Caro continues to mess with my mind, edging out any other thoughts.*

*Memories of the two of us back in high school, inseparable and complete, war with more recent ones where our interactions were stilted and brief. My need to get this over with forms a tangle of knots in my belly.*

The guys amble out of the Phoenix, muttering their goodbyes. With my hand on the keypad, I enter the code to lock up, just standing there for who knows how long.

After the breakup when she was in med school, we only saw each other occasionally and that was because of Nick. Her brother pulled back, not wanting to put her in danger, and we practically never saw each other.

But recently, two years ago, once Maggie came into our lives at the same time Nick and I went legit, Caro was once again in the picture. Then one day, she told me to stay out of her life. She didn't want to be friends.

Foolishly, I'd hoped getting out of the illegal shit might have changed things, but nothing did.

Shit. I stare down at the keypad. Did I lock up? I double-check all entry points—the main, side, and bay doors, to make sure things are secure. Get a grip.

I hustle to the warmth of my restored 1967 Aston Healy, tempted to call Caro instead of going over there. That's if she'd even answer. And then what? She'd tell me she was fine, and it isn't like I'd argue with her. Nah, a call isn't what Nick wanted.

Before I talk myself out of this, here I am, in front of Caro's parked car. My heart skips a beat. In only a few minutes, we'll be face to face. This isn't going to end well for me.

I pull in a few rows back, surveying the dark, desolate parking lot. Most of the businesses, like the bank, dry cleaners, and dentist in the strip plaza are closed for the night. The only place hopping is the pizza joint in the far corner, and cars fill the spots in and around the restaurant.

Across the street, teenagers hang around the gas station lot, and on the other corner of the intersection, a small group of men—or maybe they're teenagers too—conspicuously gather in the shadow of the apartment building. They're looking to score.

Satisfied with the harsh realities of this area, nothing out of the ordinary, I give the clinic another once-over before going in.

*I don't like her working in this neighborhood but it isn't like I have a say. This is why Nick asked me to check things out. Despite our differences, I'm always going to want Caro happy, healthy, and safe.*

*If it were up to me, she wouldn't work in this area. But Caro's not in the least bit fazed by the sketchy neighborhood or the thankless hours. She jumped at the chance to work here. She loves a challenge.*

*I flip open the glove compartment and grab my gun just in case, although I don't want to use it. Sprinting from the car, I head to the clinic, desperate to get this over with. I'm anxious to see her, more like yearning to, and even if it is in my best interest to turn around and walk away, I can't.*

*But I need to focus and bury any emotion. Yeah, right. Not possible. And for some reason, I don't see tonight ending well for me where Caro is concerned.*

# KIT

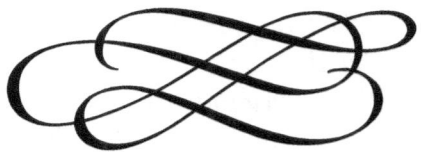

*Hand curled and ready to knock on the door, I try the knob and it opens. Shit, why is the door unlocked? Caro knows better than this. Frustrated, I slam the door shut, shattering the silence.*

*The walls reverberate, and I rush in like a mad bull, giving in to my emotions, which get the better of me. If Caro is inside and in danger, I've just announced my arrival. Talk about knowing better. What if my loud entrance leads to something disastrous for Caro? Nick would kill me. I might even help him.*

*Chest heaving, shoulders tight, and gun at the ready, I force myself to slow down, steady my breath before I do something rash. Focus.*

*Careful not to draw any attention, I turn on my phone flashlight. Nothing is disturbed in the empty waiting room, and there's no sign of Caro, yet I sense I'm not alone.*

*Not ready to announce my arrival any more than I already have, I won't call out her name. Let's find out who's here.*

*Flashlight in one hand and gun in the other, my steps are measured as I move through the doorway into the corridor at the back of the clinic. Another beam of light flickers from inside a room at the end of the hall.*

*It's fleeting, and the light goes out. Someone is here. Is it Caro? I'm not close enough to do anything if she's in danger. And I need to know what I'm dealing with if I'm to help her.*

*"Show yourself." My order is a boom and my steps quick, rushing toward the room.*

*"Who's there?" Caro's shaky voice, coming from within the dark room, triggers both a wash of relief and a chill of dread.*

*Is she okay? Hurt? Held at gunpoint? Who the fuck knows what I'm walking into?*

"Caro, it's Kit." I edge into the room, noting the broken glass on the floor and jagged edges to the insert of the door. "Are you hurt? Alone? What happened?"

"Kit." She shines a brilliant white light in my face. "I'm okay."

I wince, bringing a hand up to shield my eyes. "Can you point that somewhere else?"

"Sorry." She lowers her phone. "You can put away the gun." The prickly edges of her tone sting, and I tamp down my need to defend the use of a weapon.

She's in the dark and there must be a reason. I turn toward the hallway and take one more look, making sure no one has jumped from the shadows. All is quiet, no sound or movement.

Then I face her and shove my gun into my waistband. I'm here to make sure she's safe and then I'll leave. That's it. In and out. Piece of cake.

"Did you cut yourself?" My light shines in her direction, making sure not to hit her face. "And any reason why the lights are out?"

"Did Nick send you?" Her wild, dazzling array of lush brown curls causes my breath to still.

It's been a year since I've occupied the same room as her. Staying away was nothing short of torture, not only because of our history, but also because her brother is my best friend. This rift, or whatever it is between us, is a strain on everyone.

Shit. I can't do this. It's one thing to be consumed with thoughts of her when there's no chance of coming face to face. And it's another kind of hell to be this close to her. I can't get lost in Caro. It's a slippery slope.

"Yeah, he was worried about you and asked me to come by. Why'd you leave the front door open?"

Her brows pinch, lips mashing into a thin line. "I told Nick I was fine and that I'd call or text once I'd checked things out." She huffs, pushing away from a corner of the room. "And I didn't leave the door open."

"Yeah, you did." I try to keep my tone neutral, not accusatory. "How else do you think I got in?"

"Sorry." Her tone is softer now. "I must have forgot with all that was going on."

"What happened?" I flick the light on since she hasn't answered my question and blink, gaze roaming her body for any injuries, but I quickly get lost in her tall, slender form.

I was once the lucky bastard who got to worship every inch of her. Shit.

"I found it like that." She's tense. "I'm sorry Nick called you. I've called the police and—"

"You called the police?"

"Yes, you can leave." Her voice is flat and she comes toward me, nudging me to the door. "They're on their way."

Her touch still does all kinds of things to me, and my pulse spikes, skin heating as a want I've tried to kill and bury starts to unfurl inside me.

"I'm not going anywhere." I don't budge. "Let's not do this."

She drops her hands, looking up at me. "Do what?"

"You're pissed, frustrated, or both, and you want to take it out on me. Fine, but now isn't the time or place. Save it for later." I brush past her, scanning what looks to be a storage room. "Tell me what happened."

She sags against the wall, head down, and I wonder if I'm going to have to ask again. But I don't have to.

Starting with why she came to the clinic in the first place, she goes over everything from her arrival, when she found the front door unlocked but alarm set, to now.

I bend to further inspect the broken windowpane, then down to the scattered pieces of glass on the floor. Mixed in with the debris are drops of blood, splattered in no discernable pattern.

"They stemmed the bleeding at about there." She points to where the blood splotches end and then the unraveled bandage roll and scissors on the counter.

Was the person careless in getting cut or clueless? Either way, they figured they had time to bandage themselves up before leaving.

"And you found no one inside the clinic?" Even as the question leaves my mouth, her reluctant gaze sends my gut into a flip.

"I haven't looked into any other rooms but this one. You arrived at the same time I came into this room." Her awkward whisper matches her regretful regard for the dark corridor just outside.

All is quiet, but that's no comfort. We can't assume we're alone, and depending on what we find, I may have to use my gun after all. If so, that'll be another strike against me in Caro's mind but I'll do whatever it takes to protect her.

"We need to check this place out. You have security cameras, right?"

She turns to me, and a few more strands of her wavy hair fly loose. "Yes, the recording system is in the lunchroom."

"Good, we'll find out who was in here." I stride into the hallway, feeling the heat of her at my back and my strong desire to keep her there, safe. "You stay here."

She grabs my bicep, attempting to stop me. Caro is strong, but I've got more than half a foot and about eighty pounds on her. And while she used to, and most probably still does, take self-defense classes, if I don't want her to, she can't stop me.

"Let me help you." She forces a thin smile.

"It's safer if you stay here."

She tenses, face twisting in irritation. "I can help. It'll go faster."

I never liked fighting with her and more times than not, being at odds wasn't worth it. I never had a burning need to be right, and as the saying goes, I pick my battles. "Fine, but we do it together. You stay behind."

She bites at her lip, likely forcing the urge to not argue with me, and nods as I say, "Okay, we'll check the rooms along the hall, but let's clear these two rooms first." I point to the doors adjacent to the storage room. "What's in there?"

"That's the lunchroom and the washroom."

We work our way through the clinic quietly and efficiently, and like I figured, we come up empty. We're alone, but there's still the matter of the broken glass and the storage closet. Someone was here, and they came with purpose.

33

"The police should be here soon." She frowns at her phone. "Or not."

I step back into the medical supply room, not commenting on the cops. We need to find something before they arrive, because once they do, we'll be shut out of the intel.

Getting involved isn't what I intended, but something bigger is going on and I can't leave her to deal with this on her own. And when Nick comes back, he's going to want details so we can get to the bottom of this.

"Someone wanted something in this room. What could it be?"

"Maybe whatever is in the box of Elliot's things?"

"Where is that?" I scan the room and she grabs a small box on the floor in a corner.

Placing it on the counter, she opens the flaps and removes each item: a small stack of medical journals, a navy blue hoodie, a pair of glasses, a stress ball, and a ratty copy of Elmore Leonard's The Hunted.

"That's it." Her tone is dejected. "Nothing that would make someone go to the trouble of breaking in."

"Okay, let's assume whatever they wanted isn't in the box but it's in this room. Any ideas?"

"The only thing I can think of are the pain meds." She looks to a locked glass cabinet against the far wall.

Shelves are lined with rows upon rows of bottles. Drugs. Some liquid, some pills. Moving closer, I inspect the unit, and there's no signs of damage or an attempt to break the lock or glass.

If it's drugs, nothing here looks like something you couldn't easily get. Definitely not something worth harassing a doctor and nurse in front of witnesses and then coming back to break in for and risk getting caught.

On the same wavelength, Caro interrupts my thoughts. "But there's nothing stronger in there than what you can get over the counter in any drug store." She rakes a hand through her hair, securing the tie.

"Can you tell if there's anything missing?" The beam moves slowly across each row of the cupboard.

Caro's now at my side, concentrating and shaking her head. "Nothing looks out of place."

I grab at the handle, checking to see if it's unlocked like the clinic door was.

"Kit, you shouldn't touch that. You're contaminating any evidence."

"And you touching the box,"—I dip my chin to Elliot's stuff on the counter— "isn't?" I give her my best nice try smirk.

Her look, a cold, hard stare, is sadly all too reminiscent of our final days together. This very topic—the law—was another sticking point in our relationship and why she broke things off.

I can no longer twist myself in knots about it. For the most part I'm law-abiding, and sure, some things are slightly gray, but a little variety isn't a bad thing.

Caro is a rule follower, always doing things by the book. Not me. Much like her brother, I want to be in control and would rather take my chances on my own. The cops, or those on the side of law, haven't always had my back.

"Good point." Her shoulders deflate. "So now what?"

"You've had break-ins before, right?" I recall from conversations with Nick in the past as I bury the surging frustration and anger that came every time I heard she might have been hurt.

"Yes..." Her gaze scans the room and then the hallway behind her. "This feels different."

"How?"

She doesn't say a word, and I sense her reluctance to share any information. The idea of partnering with me must drive her mad. As much as she may not like me here, too bad. I'm not leaving her alone no matter how uncomfortable it makes her. I care about her and will do what's needed to get her out of harm's way.

"The other break-ins had been for shelter. A homeless person looking for somewhere to sleep for the night. And no one ever came back here or damaged anything."

"What about for drugs?" I look to the locked cabinet again.

"Sure, some people came in demanding opioids, but we don't have any."

There's an island in the middle of the room, and three of the four walls contain shelves of medical supplies. She rifles through each shelf, taking inventory.

"Besides, that stopped once we put up the signs saying we didn't have narcotics and we don't give out prescriptions for opioids. Patients have to get them from their family doctor or a hospital."

Illegal prescription drugs are a thing. A booming market, not just in Toronto but globally, and annually tens of thousands of people around the world die from opioid overdoses.

"Then there's also the texts," she mumbles more to herself, and at the same time, a phone buzzes. It isn't mine.

"Can I see them?" The hair on the back of my neck prickles. Is this another one coming in?

She pulls her phone from her jacket, staring at the screen for what feels like an eternity. Finally, she lifts her head and I'm hit with her troubled expression.

"It's the same private number. Again." She holds up the phone so the screen faces me.

I read the most recent text and then the ones before. All of it is ominous, and my insides coil with apprehension.

"It looks like your last text, the hello, prompted this latest text. Do you think it's the guys from earlier today?"

"Maybe. I don't know." Caro's rattled, moving closer. For what? Protection?

We both stare at the text once more.

**Unknown: This isn't a joke. Where the fuck is it?**

# CARO

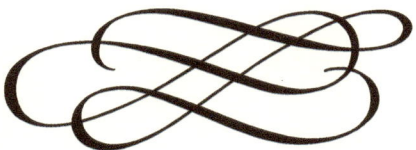

My heartbeat thunders in my ears, and I'm only filled with gratitude to have Kit by my side. When he first appeared in the doorway with a gun aimed at me, I'd been a ball of confusion.

Part excited, since my love and desire for him is still alive and kicking, and part annoyed at Nick for not trusting me to do this on my own. And my warring emotions are even directed at Kit for killing my silly hope.

He's never far from my mind, but I've been thinking more about him lately. I'd been considering reaching out, seeing if maybe he could forgive me. That maybe things could be different—better—now that we had both grown and his life was different.

But the gun in his hand only reinforces all the concerns I'd had when we were together. Violence is still part of his life.

But now, with these mysterious texts and their subtle threats—some not so subtle—I don't want to be alone. I won't lie—I'm scared, and if I have to have someone by my side, I want Kit.

He's my ex, but not just any old flame. I was with him the longest, loved only him, and I dreamed of settling down with him.

The last time we talked was awkward and tense. I said some horrible things, and I told him to stay away. Never talk to me again. And until today, he has respected my wishes.

Sometimes I still struggle with how things ended because a part of me hadn't expected him to give up so easily, and when he did, I didn't know what to do.

Finally, I came to grips with reality. I'd lost him and I couldn't fault him for disappearing from my life. So the fact that he's here now is huge. I've always wanted Kit, even when I told him to leave.

"Caro, are there any more texts?" His somber tone pulls me back to the present.

I shake my head, handing him the phone. "No, just these, and they started today."

"Do you have any idea who these people are?" Concerned brown eyes bore into me.

"I don't know who they are or what they're talking about. Until today, I'd never seen those men. The police said they'd let us know if they're able to identify who the men are from the video."

"Okay. And still nothing from Elliot?" He hands me back my phone and then starts to roam the small room, examining the rows upon rows of supplies with renewed interest.

"Nothing." I want to yell at Elliot if he ever calls me back.

Yes, he likes to keep people waiting, show how busy and important he is, but this is ridiculous.

"Call him again." His order sparks a burst of annoyance, but I have to remind myself he's here and trying to help me.

He squats onto his haunches in a corner where two boxes rest, a recent delivery of medical supplies, and proceeds to open them with a switchblade he fishes from his pocket.

Always with a weapon. Do things change? Does it matter anymore?

My fingers rake through my hair, curling at my scalp and lightly tugging. Hopefully the slight pain will incite a new thought or banish any frustration.

"Caro, call him now." Kit snaps his fingers in front of me, and I'm taken aback, not remembering him being so bossy.

Or more like forgetting he can be demanding when he's concerned. He's a kindhearted man, and despite his large, muscled frame that has people shaking in their shoes upon first sight, he wouldn't hurt you unless you're a threat. He isn't that kind of man.

"Fine. Relax." I make the call, not holding out for an answer.

"Voicemail," I say to him and then leave another message, following it up with a text to the same number.

"So you two are no longer together?" He runs his hand against parts of the wall, curling his knuckles and rapping ever so often.

"We broke up five months ago." The prickly heat of embarrassment creeps up my spine at admitting this to him. After all, Kit always said Elliot wasn't right for me, and he wasn't wrong.

"What are you doing?" I ask, pushing any more thoughts of both my exes from my mind.

"I'm trying to figure out if anything is behind these walls. Does Elliot still work here?" He's still walking the perimeter of the room, lightly knocking on parts of the wall.

"No." This time my frustration slips out and it isn't at him, but more the situation.

"Do any of these shelves move?" He grips the sides of a shelving unit and lightly tugs.

"No, they're screwed into the wall."

Nodding, he stamps his foot a few more times and stops to listen, repeating the process over and over. He's methodical, working from the outside in, and it isn't long before the now-familiar thud shifts to a hollow thunk.

"Wait. Did you hear that?" I inch closer, now very intrigued.

At first, his actions seemed pointless, but something might be there. He's in front of the island with his boot half-on and half-off the black anti-fatigue mat. The toe of his boot nudges the mat a few inches, revealing the corner of…a door?

What on earth? Is it a secret compartment? Or an exit from the building?

Kit bends and shoves the black rubber out of the way. There's a square door, about four feet by four feet, with a metal ring in the center. There isn't any kind of lock.

I drop down beside him and he looks to me. "Did you know this was here?"

"No. I've never seen this before, and it wasn't there when the clinic first opened. I don't know how or when…"

I've worked at the clinic since day one and even toured the place during construction. This door, hatch, or whatever you call it, leading God knows where, wasn't here.

"This looks newer than the rest of the floor." He presses on the tile. "Was any work done on this room?"

"Yes." A memory slashes at me like a whip. "It was Elliot, right after he joined the clinic. That was around the same time Léa's Home had just opened."

Like now, my days are split between the clinic and the Home, but things were moving at a snail's pace at the Home. A day here or there wasn't working. At that rate, it would have taken us years until we were fully operational.

"Go on." Kit slides his finger into the metal ring.

"I took two weeks off from the clinic to focus on the Home. I had to train staff and put processes in place. Elliot ran things for me at the clinic during that time. There was another woman here at the time, Flora, and she was in charge of doing most of the office manager type things. Willow, the nurse here, was only part-time then and I remember she was the one to tell me work was being done on the storage room." The words tumble from me like water from a tap.

I'm rambling, trying to keep up with all these snippets of things that happened in the past. Things that at the time seemed insignificant but now feel like they hold such meaning.

The door leading under the floor opens easily, and it looks like a metal containment space. It isn't very big, but it's dark and only a portion of the space is visible from the opening.

It appears to be empty and I want to scream, annoyed and exhausted. So what if we found this vault under the floor? If there's nothing in it, that's all we have. Nothing. Another dead end.

"Do you think whatever was in here was what those guys were after?"

"Maybe. Tell me more about when Elliot could have had this built." Kit takes out his phone again and then gives me his full attention.

"I remember thinking it was strange that Elliot never said anything to me and when I called him about it, he said it was a surprise. I even remember him getting upset with Willow for telling me."

Mentally, I'm back all those months ago and recall that was the first of many disagreements Elliot would have with Willow. He never liked her, and that should have been a sign that we wouldn't last.

"There'd been so much going on at the Home that I never gave it a second thought. And then when I saw he'd put in an island and new shelves..."

"You didn't question him any further," he finishes for me, and while his voice is neutral, there's something in his eyes.

He'd never say it out loud, but I can't help but feel it's an I told you so. At the time, when Kit made comments about Elliot being stuck-up and arrogant, we had been talking, but rarely, and I'd chalked it up to jealousy. We weren't together, but there was no denying we still cared deeply for one another. Always would.

But I should have known better. He isn't the jealous type. He's good at reading people, much like Nick, and his dislike was more about who Elliot was or wasn't than anything to do with me.

What an idiot I was.

"Why didn't I question him more?" I feel my lower back slump into the counter, the weight of everything hitting me at once.

Sure, my relationship with Elliot was new at the time but I wasn't blind to him. We were taking things slow, and truth be told, our relationship never advanced.

With the benefit of time and hindsight, I'd had reservations about Elliot from the beginning. He'd pursued me, and there was something about him that had me keeping my distance. That's why I eventually ended things.

"Don't beat yourself up. It might be nothing." He doesn't believe that and it's clear in his voice, but his attempt to make me feel better brings a small smile.

He jumps into the container, getting onto his knees, and I peer in after him, but it's so very dark and cramped. A vault is the closest thing I can compare it to. He crouches as low as he can go, and given his big, brawny frame, he still takes up almost all the space.

Out of my view, he pulls at something, then hands me an open cardboard box, bigger than a toaster. "Check this out."

"Where was that? I thought there was nothing in there?"

"It was in the far corner, we wouldn't have seen it from the door."

*The box is light, it may even be empty, and the first thing to catch my eye is my name and the clinic address on a label affixed to the outside. Fear grips my insides.*

*"What on earth?" This makes no sense. Deliveries to the clinic aren't personally addressed nor do they come in boxes like this.*

*"What is it?" His voice is muffled with his head inside the container.*

*"My name's on the box label, but most everything about it is wrong. And I've never seen a box like this before."*

*I open the box, and the bottom is covered in popcorn-sized chunks of Styrofoam packaging material.*

*Carefully, my hands swim through the kernels, coming across a wad of paper. I remove it and flatten the edges. It's a page of labels with all but one removed and it looks a lot like what's on the front of the box. Except this label includes a number.*

*"I've got a phone number." I hold out the paper, and Kit calls from under the floor, "Good."*

*Buoyed by this one clue, I want to make sure there isn't anything else, even if I have to take out every single kernel. I dump mounds of packaging onto the counter and there at the bottom, there's a blue tablet, long and cylindrical in shape, enclosed in a small, almost quarter-sized baggie.*

*This could be a number of different drugs, so I look carefully at the capsule for any indication. Prescription pills usually have numbers and letters to indicate the drug. One side of the pill is imprinted with a strange bug-like icon, and the other with the letters OC. Oxycontin.*

*"Kit, look at this." I bend over, holding up the bag as he sits up, curling his hands over the edges, readying to lift himself out.*

*"Damn, there's our reason for someone to break in. That's probably what they were looking for. Is that the only one? Do you know what it is?"*

*"Yes, it's the only one. It's Oxycon—"*

*"Fuck." Kit's staring at something inside the vault.*

*"What is it?" My gaze locks with his, tension emanating from his tense jaw and rigid brow.*

"It looks like opening this triggered some kind of countdown. Here in the hinge of the door." He jumps out of the container and points to tiny red digits counting down. "There's a timer. We have ninety seconds."

"Until what?" Alarms scratch at the darkest corners of my mind.

"It could mean any number of things. We gotta go."

His hand wraps around my bicep and my mind spins, eyes glued to the timer. We now have eighty-three seconds.

My phone buzzes again, and he stops in his tracks as my blood turns cold. I shove the pill and paper into my pocket and remove the phone. It's a text from Elliot.

**Elliot: What have you done? Get out of there. NOW.**

"Shit. He knows we're here and something bad is going to happen. Let's get out of here." His tone and expression are tightly wound, and every word plunges into my dread like a dagger.

"The back exit is closer." The words come from me but I don't recognize my voice.

I wince when Kit yanks my arm, nearly taking it from the socket. Running alongside him, I rush down the hall to the red exit sign.

My heartrate thunders in my ears, panicked tears springing to my eyes. Not knowing how much time we have left and what will happen when it runs out scrambles my thoughts and fills me with a cold and deadly fright.

We both push on the metal bar in the middle of the door, and it swings out into the icy darkness. The shrill emergency alarm pierces the still night.

"Kit, slow down," I cry. Danger and the possibility of death claw at my insides, rattle my bones, and force all the air from my lungs.

The gravitational force hits me first, punching at my back before the earsplitting blast or searing heat registers.

An explosion rocks the ground beneath my feet, and I'm lifted from the pavement as if I'm a Lost Boy and can fly.

Fingers intertwined with his, I cling to his hand, desperate not to leave his side, but it's out of my control. Something heavy whacks the back of my head.

*A white-hot pain shoots through my skull, down my neck, and into my shoulders. My neck cracks forward, sight and sound shifting and blurring.*

*I'm inside Edvard Munch's Scream painting, and my vision tunnels to a dark pinpoint in the distance. My lungs fill, burning, and blackness as dark and thick as tar eclipses everything.*

# KIT

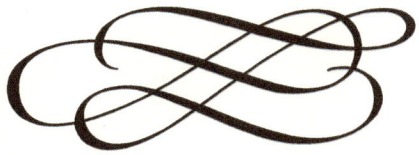

As weightless as a piece of paper, Caro crumples to the hard ground. Her name rushes from my lungs like a roar of thunder. Jesus Christ.

My feet grapple to gain purchase to stop my own fall. I've got to get to her.

The pop of my bones, knees hitting an unyielding surface, jangles everything in me. My open palms scrape along the cold, abrasive pavement, trying to slow or stop me from sailing any farther.

My head bows forward from the sheer force of the explosion, so close I may kiss the ground, and my cheek smacks into the road, skin ripping on impact.

Finally, I'm motionless on my stomach, arms and legs outstretched like a dead starfish. Acrid smoke fills my nostrils and adrenaline kickstarts my brain, numbing any pain and filling me with only one thought.

Caro.

She's three feet ahead of me, on her front, seemingly lifeless. On hands and knees, pure instinct driving me, I scramble to her side.

"Caro." My voice chokes on her name. "Caro." My frenzied tone is nothing like the soft strokes of my fingers, brushing her hair from her face.

I want to take her in my arms, get some help, but I can't move her. There might be damage to her spine.

"Caro." This time I shout, or at least that's what I think I'm doing but I can hardly hear myself. The incessant ringing in my ears drowns out almost everything.

Except for the fear. Like a black inkiness, it spills throughout my insides, darkening and intensifying my senses, tormenting me with the worst.

*The fear the blast may have killed her.*

*Fuck, no. She has to be alive. Though her eyes are closed, blood streams from a gash on her forehead. I can't tell if she's breathing.*

*My trembling hands fumble to find her pulse point on her neck and a rushing, buzzing noise in my head is the only thing I can make out.*

*"Fuck, no," I shout, trying again to find her pulse, a sign of life.*

*My soul collapses onto itself at no sensation where my fingers lie against her clammy skin. I can't...no, I will not fathom a world without Caro.*

*It's only when I detect the faintest pulse that I curl around her, releasing a sob. Gradually my breathing slows and I will my heart to steady. The beat grows stronger, the throbbing of her heart against the pads of my fingers bringing tears to my eyes. Thank God.*

*A leg twitches and her mouth opens on what could be a gasp. I can't hear much from the buzzing in my ears and the hisses and crackles from the fire. She bends her arms and tries to push up from the pavement.*

*"Hey, I got you." All too eager to hold her, I lift her onto my lap and my lips lift into a smile even in this insanity—she's alive.*

*She tucks her head into my chest, arm against my side, and I say loudly, "A bomb." It's as if I need to say it out loud to fully comprehend what happened.*

*Pulling back from me, she wrinkles her nose and looks up questioningly. She's saying or mouthing, "What?" She can't hear me.*

*"A bomb went off." I slowly mouth the words, and she nods once, casting her gaze to the now-burning clinic.*

*The heat from the blazing building wafts through the dense, cold night air and I hold her head in my hands, once more saying the words slowly and loudly. "I'm so sorry, Caro, but the clinic is gone."*

*We were inside only minutes ago, and now it's a charred marshmallow. Whatever she is mixed up in, it's serious shit, and whoever is behind this means business.*

*"Oh crap..." Or that's at least what I think she says as she jerks upright, leans over my arm, and vomits onto the asphalt.*

*I hold back her hair, murmuring words of comfort. She must be concussed. What other damage did her body take in the blast? We need a doctor. Her muscles spasm and she expels the contents of her stomach.*

*"Sorry." She straightens, wiping her mouth with the back of her hand. Again, I'm guessing at what she's saying as there's a five-alarm bell going off in my head.*

*"You okay?"*

*"I'm not sure. What hit me?" Now she's shouting too.*

*Her hand tentatively touches the back of her head, gingerly picking her way through the mass of hair.*

*"Something from the blast. Metal."*

*"There's no bleeding." Her fingers skillfully trace a bump the size of an orange at the back of her skull.*

*"Oh my God, are you all right?" A woman rushes at us and I can just make out what she's saying.*

*I tighten my grip on Caro, scanning the area for more people and potential threats. Where the fuck are the cops? For the first time in my life, I want them here, or at least an ambulance. Caro needs a doctor.*

*"I called nine-one-one. Help's on the way." A teenager is at the woman's side and the sirens cleave the bleak, smoke-filled sky.*

*It's about time.*

*The following minutes or hours are a blur of action. Firefighters are first on the scene, and we're hauled farther away from the inferno. Not long after, two ambulances arrive along with the police.*

*Caro's on a gurney, oxygen mask plastered to her soot- and dirt-covered face with a belt across her legs and middle, securing her.*

*"I want to go with her." I grab at the EMT's arm, and at the same time, someone tugs on my shoulder.*

*"Sir, you need to be examined too," a male voice from behind me says, and at the suggestion, the impact of the blast and many bruises start to throb and ache.*

*"We're taking you to the same hospital. You'll be with her." A paramedic, tall and lean as a flagpole, attempts to steer me in the direction of another waiting ambulance.*

*I don't want to leave Caro. She finds my eyes, and her expression pleads with me to do as I'm asked. Fine. I don't want to cause her any more stress by resisting, and she needs medical attention. The sooner I get in an ambulance, the quicker we can get to the hospital.*

*"I'll see you at the hospital." I squeeze her ankle gently and quietly follow him to the other ambulance.*

*At the hospital, I'm checked out and given the all-clear. As with most people, hospitals are the last place I want to be. I'd rather be with Caro, making sure she's taken care of, and I've got to call Nick.*

*Nick. I'm not looking forward to that call. The guy will jump in his car and come home once he hears what's happened to his sister.*

*With the exception of the minor scrape on my cheek and some cuts on my hands, I'm none the worse for wear. I'll be stiff and sore for the next few days, and there'll be bruises, but nothing I haven't lived with before.*

*Before the nurse leaves the small room I'm in, I ask her for directions to Caro's room. Unfortunately, I don't get very far.*

*Outside of the examining room, I'm faced with a cop in uniform and an older man with a receding hairline. He's in charge, judging by the stern expression he throws at me. This is going to be fun. Not.*

*Despite his day's worth of stubble and haggard appearance—it looks like he's slept in his clothes for easily a day, if not more—he wants me to know he means business.*

*"Mister... er..."—the man pauses, looking at a small notepad in his hand—"Jensen, I'm Detective Holman. I'd like to ask you a few questions about tonight's explosion."*

*It's meant as a question but comes out more like an order, and he doesn't wait for a reply, ushering me into a room across the hall.*

*"I can't, I've got to see Caro." I turn to go the other way, even if it's in the opposite direction from Caro's room, but the uniformed officer steps into my personal space.*

*"We'll be quick. I had a chat with the doctor. Your friend is going to be fine." Once again, he doesn't leave room for anything but acceptance.*

*Holman shuts the door to the small waiting room, leaving the uniformed officer in the hall. "Sorry for the less than private surroundings. I figured it was either here or down at the station."*

*The mention of the police station is meant to intimidate me, but I don't give a fuck. I've done nothing wrong.*

*"Fine. But make this quick, I need to see—"*

*"Ms. Caroline Archer," he says, making an effort to appear comfortable in the hard, plastic chair.*

*"Doctor Archer." My jaw tightens, immediately disliking this guy and how readily he focused on asserting control rather than concern. It's as if he's already decided we have something to hide.*

*"Why don't we start with why you were at the Jane Walk-in Clinic this evening?" Pen poised to take notes, his bleary eyes settle on me.*

*It would be easy to insist on seeing Caro. If he tried to force this on me, imagine the media shitstorm I could bring down on him and the police department when I was a victim of an explosion. But I don't need the attention, and maybe I can spare Caro the ordeal.*

*I recount most of what happened, giving the impression of cooperating but omitting Nick's call, the texts to Caro, and the secret container under the floor. Caro's in danger and that fucker Elliot knows what it's about.*

*If I hand everything over to the police at this stage we'll be told to stay out of things, and even if they assure us that they can protect Caro while they get to the bottom of this, I'm not willing to put Caro's life in their hands.*

*Nick and I can resolve this a lot quicker and easier and without police involvement. We need to get to Elliot as soon as possible. He knows what's going on and should be able to call off the hounds who are after Caro.*

*As for Holman, if he's any good at his job, he'll soon find out about the men who showed up at the clinic today. That's if the police even logged the call.*

*Shit, the security footage. I didn't grab the recording of the break-in before the explosion. So that lead is dead, or in this case, ashes.*

*"Are you a patient of the clinic?" Holman stares intently, expression blank.*

*We've been at this for about twenty minutes, maybe longer, and he's already covered this ground.*

"No. Like I said, Caro's my friend, that's my reason for being there."

"Kit Jensen, you have a record—drug possession at seventeen, a bar fight where you were charged with assault—"

*And of course, he brings out my past. It doesn't matter that I'm a victim in this situation. This is why I don't rely on cops in general. I'm guilty without anything to suggest so.*

"I'm well aware, you don't need to give me a rundown. And none of that is relevant." *I lean forward, resting my elbows on the small table.* "What's your point?"

"I find it hard to believe you have no idea what tonight's explosion was about." *He relaxes into the chair, raising his arms above his head as if he's chilling and has all night.* "Seems to me, Mr. Jensen, you have a knack for getting yourself mixed up in trouble. So let's cut the crap and tell me what's going on."

"Already told you, I don't know." *Fury boils my insides; this guy isn't listening. My hands curl into fists and I force some kind of calm into my next words.* "We were inside the clinic so Caro could grab something, and she saw one of the rooms was broken into. She called the cops and we waited. We got tired of waiting inside and left. Then the place went kaboom."

"Why were you even in the place when the 911 operator told you to stay outside and wait for the police?"

*Okay, maybe he isn't a complete idiot. Good question.*

"We were curious." *I shrug. My response is weak and I wish I had something better to give him. My lame answer will only fuel his suspicion.*

"Why'd you exit from the back of the building when your cars were in the front?"

*He's been busy. He must have already run the plates on the cars in the plaza parking lot to know both our cars were there.*

"We decided to go outside and wait."

*He eyes me skeptically.* "You had to have been several feet from the building when the explosion happened. Or else your injuries would have been more severe." His harsh gaze lands on the bandage on my cheek.

He hasn't asked a question and so I keep my mouth shut, matching him blink for blink.

"How did you just happen to get out in time?" He arches a gray brow triumphantly as if he's got me.

"Already told you. We realized we should listen to the operator and wait outside."

"Isn't that convenient. I'd say you're lucky and you should buy a lottery ticket." He scribbles something on his notepad before lifting his eyes to mine. "Let's take it from the top."

"Already asked and answered." I lean forward, unable to curb my snarl. Even with the table between us, I'm almost in his face. This has gone on long enough. "Unless you're going to arrest me, I'm out of here."

I stand, staring down at him. He has no grounds to keep me, and we both know it. "I'll call you if I remember anything else." I'm quick to add the common wrap phrase cops love to use to keep the door open for future visits and questions.

Briskly, I march from the room, brushing past the bored officer leaning against the wall. Holman doesn't say anything, nor does he follow, but I feel his shrewd gaze on my back as I turn the corner.

Caro is where the nurse said she'd be. Her eyes are closed and both of her hands are bandaged. I tiptoe into the room, an odd sinking feeling ghosting up the back of my neck at the scratches, swells, and bruises marring her pure smooth skin.

Shit, she looks how I feel. No, worse. As if she's been to war and I'm not sure if she won. Most of the blood has been cleaned from her face but some dried patches still remain around her hairline.

My hands ache to touch her but I'm afraid to hurt her, cause her any pain. Dammit, why didn't I get us out of there sooner?

Deep chocolate-brown eyes open, blinking long and slow, trying to focus, and a crooked smile skates across her dry lips. I try to ignore the tightness in my chest, as if her simple smile isn't robbing me of my breath.

*Who am I kidding? Just one look from her and I'm already feeling all kinds of things I shouldn't.*

"Hey, how are you doing?" I clear my throat, sounding way too vulnerable.

"I've been better." Her voice is more a croak.

"What did the doctor say?" I sink into the chair beside the bed, resting my forearms on my dirty jean-clad thighs. For the first time since stepping into the clinic, I feel almost relaxed to hear her voice and see she's mostly okay.

Her complexion is waxen and movements sluggish. "I'm fine. I have a concussion, but the symptoms are mild, relatively speaking."

"Really?"

She nods as if a concussion is just a scratch, no big deal—bullshit, and as if to contradict her words, she winces with the movement.

"To be safe, they took me for an MRI and everything looks okay."

"You know this already?" I'm surprised at how quickly they had her examined and got the results. Usually, people wait hours for those kinds of tests.

Her lips crest at the sides of her mouth into a sad excuse for a smile. "What can I say? Just one of the endless perks of being a doctor. I'm waiting on discharge papers, then we can go. I'll have to take it easy for the next couple of days."

"Good. I was worried. That hit to your head was brutal." I'm still a little concerned, but I'm not going anywhere anytime soon.

I wipe at the back of my neck, and grit scratches at my skin. We both look like we've been through a war. Her hair could pass as a home for a small feral animal and I'm covered in dirt, flecks of debris, and ash from the blast.

We got lucky. A piece of metal whacked her in the head; just the thought sends my stomach into a tailspin. She dropped to the ground like a dead fly, head cracking against the asphalt. I don't know what I'd have done if she... No, she's going to be okay.

I shift in the chair. "The cops questioned me. Has anyone talked to you yet?"

"No. What did they ask?" Her fists push into the bed on either side of her body, aiding in her attempt to sit up straighter.

*I repeat everything I told Holman, and she frowns when I mention we finally decided to go outside like we'd been told to from the beginning by the nine-one-one operator.*

*"Why didn't—" She stops talking when a young woman in scrubs strides into the room.*

*"Here you go." The young nurse hands her a clipboard and turns to me. "Ah, I see your husband is here, good."*

*A strange sensation, a loosening followed by a vise grip, bands my chest at the mention of me being her husband. How long had I wished for that? How long had that been my future?*

*She pats at the bed and from the corner of my eye, I see Caro open her mouth, likely to correct her, when the nurse says to me, "She'll be fine. She's got a nasty bump on her head so keep icing it. The scan shows nothing unusual in the brain. No swelling, bleeding, or fractures."*

*"Good." I'm grateful for the update from someone other than Caro.*

*While she's a doctor and understands all of this and how to treat a concussion, she's also more inclined to downplay it and omit things. She's a formidable force and doesn't like to admit when she needs help or time to get better.*

*"She needs to rest in darkness, no stimulus for tonight. And will need to take it easy for the next week or so, listen to her body when she's had enough. Headaches, fatigue, that sort of thing. As for full recovery, it's likely a few months. It's hard to say because every situation is different, but the symptoms will lessen and fade over time."*

*Caro sighs. "Thank you, Marie. I've got it."*

*Marie purses her lips and glances from Caro back to me. "We all know how doctors don't make good patients. I'm only sharing with your husband so one of you knows what to do."*

*She winks and Caro thrusts the clipboard toward Marie, worry lining her forehead.*

*"Your clothes are there." The nurse points to a pile on another chair beside the bathroom. "You can get dressed in there and then you're free to go."*

*Finally, what I've wanted to hear since we got here. I've got to call Nick, and Caro will come to my place. She can't be alone tonight for many reasons.*

*Holman walks into the room, notepad at the ready, and the man ignites a fire within me.*

*His smile is more charged, putting a little more effort in appearing concerned. "Hello, Ms. Caroline Archer—"*

*"Doctor Archer." I'm deliberate in cutting him off and correcting him, once again. Why is it so hard for him to remember she's a doctor and treat her with the respect she deserves?*

*He pauses, eyeing me warily before turning his attention on Caro. She's sliding out of the bed on wobbly legs.*

*There's a long, superficial scrape along her shin bone and several tiny scrapes or indents along her bare legs from her collision with the pavement. While I hate seeing her gorgeous skin marred and don't want her in any pain, tonight could have been a hell of a lot worse.*

*I grip her elbow to help steady her, and the nurse is at the door, standing sentinel.*

*Holman continues, "Doctor, apologies. I'd like to ask you a few questions."*

*Concern clouds Marie's friendly demeanor. "Dr. Archer, please take it easy and remember to see your family doctor as soon as possible. And Detective..." She pauses, ensuring she has the man's full attention.*

*Holman is slow to face her, pausing to scrutinize Caro, then me, and finally he casts his skeptical gaze at Marie. If I didn't know better, I'd swear he thinks we're all in this—whatever this is—together.*

*"Please, not too many questions. Dr. Archer needs her rest and should be home." The nurse has a firm tone and my smile is appreciative, although I don't hold any hope it will make a difference with this guy.*

*"This won't take long." His forced smile sets me on edge. Marie nods and leaves.*

*"I'm not sure what Dr. Archer can add to what I've already said since we were together." As fast as is possible, I usher Caro into the washroom, wanting to prevent this conversation. Caro needs her rest.*

She hesitates at the door, gaze on Holman. "Please let me get dressed and then we can talk."

Her voice is weak, tired, and I'm not happy at her concession. "Caro, you don't have to do this now. We can go to the station tomorrow and give your statement."

My tone is cutting and aimed at the detective.

"Kit, I can do it now." Caro is insistent. "I just want to get this over with."

"I'll wait. Take your time, Doctor." He nods curtly.

"Do you need any help?" I grab her clothes and hand them to her.

"No, thanks." She's weary, her smile faint and movements sluggish as she shuts the door and I'm alone with Holman. Great.

He ignores me—well, not quite. His gaze is fixed just above my head, but he keeps his mouth shut. I pull out my phone, not wanting to appear free to talk, and I see two missed calls. One from Sally and the other, Nick. Shit.

Sally's been to my place and is wondering where I am, and Nick, well, he's freaking out even though he doesn't even know about the explosion. My throat closes, unable to find any words to tell him how I broke my promise. I was supposed to keep her safe, and while she's alive—thank fuck—she's injured and still in danger.

I can't call him, not now when I don't know what to say and not with Holman here. And texting is better for both of them right now. I'll have to call Sally and explain, but it'll have to wait until tomorrow.

Shit, Pinter is tomorrow too. I have to call him.

**Me: Sorry. Something came up. We'll do dinner another time.**

This time no response comes immediately. I stare at the screen, willing a reply from Sally, something that will say it's okay. That me not being where I said I would be didn't come off as if I stood her up. Shit, of course it would come off like that.

Her silence could mean any number of things. Maybe she's on the subway home? It's almost eleven thirty, and my gut spasms at the thought of Sally trekking over to my place, only to be stood up.

*I should have canceled once Nick called. Even with my reservations about seeing her, I wanted to give us a try and now I've blown it. I'm long overdue on moving on, and Sally is supposed to be that chance.*

*We might never be more than friends, but that isn't the point. Dating Sally is more a chance to have a life after Caro. Or to finally face the reality of a life after Caro.*

*As if she's reading my mind, Caro steps from the washroom, pausing to grip the doorframe. She's pale and frail, so unlike her usually strong and vibrant self. I spring to my feet at her side.*

*"It's okay. I can do it." She pats my arm and shuffles into an empty chair at the speed of a senior with a walker. I've got to take better care of her.*

*"Mr. Jensen, please leave us." Again, Holman isn't asking, even if the words are meant that way.*

*"I'm staying." My fingers grip my phone tightly, anticipating his objection.*

*"It's okay. Please wait outside." Caro dismisses me, and a sharp twinge pokes at my chest.*

*Her hair is wild and crazy, face dirty, and posture nothing but defeated and despite all of this, she will always have my respect. I won't challenge her in front of this guy. I respect her too much, even if I think this isn't a smart move.*

*Holman is all too happy to shut the door in my face, and I try not to dwell on any inconsistencies that will arise from her account of tonight's events compared to mine.*

*There's not much I can do about that, and I have to give Nick an update. I pull out my phone and go to texts.*

**Me: Don't lose your shit. There was an explosion at the clinic but we're both okay.**

*Absently, I stare down the hall with my phone in hand. No rings or buzzes from Nick or Sally. I'm not sure how long I stand like that, leaning against the wall.*

*I try not to think about Caro in the room with Holman and what exactly I could possibly say to Nick that won't cause him to drive home from Quebec tonight, no longer trusting his sister's life in my hands.*

*Caro finally exits the room with Holman behind her. Concern etches her already drained features and she mouths, "Let's go," eyes wide while grabbing onto my arm.*

*Not needing further explanation, I wrap an arm around her shoulder and guide her away from the room and the detective.*

*Neither of us spare a glance at him, although he's clearly watching us. There's no doubt, this isn't the last we'll see of Holman.*

# CARO

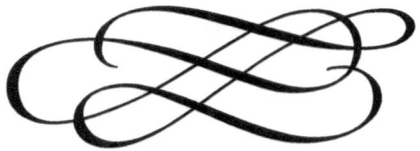

"What's wrong?" His hand presses gently into my lower back, guiding me to the taxi idling at the entrance to the ER.

Like so many times in my life, Kit is one of very few people—Nick is the other—that I want right now. My gratitude swells and threatens to choke me with tears. I don't know where I'd be right now without him.

I may never have found the vault and would be stuck putting together a puzzle with missing pieces. Without that discovery, I'm beginning to think Elliot wouldn't have contacted me. He's definitely involved in whatever this is.

Kit opens the cab door for me, but getting into the back seat of the car isn't easy. Bending, I wince and bite my lower lip to stifle a groan. Breathless pain threatens to knock me out as my muscles cry in agony with each clench or flex.

Bruises, soreness, and fatigue rack my body and my head feels like a smashed watermelon—brains split apart and swimming. "Holman asked me why we went into the clinic and then why we left when we did. He just kept coming back to that."

Kit arches a brow at my comment, taking in the cab driver and rattling off an address close to the Beach, a neighborhood east of downtown on Lake Ontario. His home is my guess. I don't know how to feel about that. It's personal, a little too close, and too fast, but I don't want to be alone.

Since our breakup many years ago, I've made it a point to know as little as possible about him. Foolish since, to this day, I still get butterflies in my stomach whenever he walks into a room. When he first walked into the clinic, even with a gun in his hand, my heart flipped and stomach flopped.

*And my feelings haven't changed. The only thing I accomplished by breaking up with him was to sentence myself to a life of loneliness and regret.*

*Why am I even thinking about this right now? All I want is to lie down and curl into a ball until the pain goes away.*

"What did you say?" he asks, and my back slides down the worn leather to rest my head against the top of the seat.

Just tightening my stomach muscles makes me dizzy. "I told him the same thing you did—we decided to go outside and wait. We look like idiots for not listening to the police, and he doesn't believe that we just left at the right time."

"How do you know that?"

"Because he kept coming back to it." Closing my eyes, I brace for every bump and turn as the cabbie drives from the curb.

"He doesn't know anything for sure. He may suspect we know more but I'm pretty sure he isn't thinking we set off a bomb in the floor of the clinic when we opened the door to that hatch."

"But won't they find the hatch and the timer when they start investigating the fire?" Prying my eyes open isn't easy, and I stiffly turn to face him.

"Yeah. But they won't be able to tell we discovered it or possibly even what or who set it off. They could think it malfunctioned or someone detonated it remotely."

"What? Why'd you say that?"

"Well, think about it. Elliot texted you. He got some kind of alert to the door being opened so there's remote capability."

"He said my car was damaged in the blast and that they have both our cars." My chest hollows out at the thought of the vague answers I gave the detective.

"Not surprised." His eyes, brown with iridescent flecks of green and amber, darken and he lowers his voice, mindful of the driver. "The clinic was blown up, and while we triggered it, the cops are likely going to check our cars to make sure they aren't rigged to do the same."

Breath seizes in my lungs, at first stuck on the possibility of another explosion. I'm unable to fully comprehend the danger at my doorstep. But then I recall the clinic bomb was pre-set, not aimed at us. Still.

"But that isn't possible, is it?"

"Anything is possible, but the bomb was probably planted at the time of the renovations, if I had to guess. Elliot's text is a strong indication of that. Taking our cars is just part of the investigation, although I'm sure Holman will look for anything to implicate us."

"What? Why do you say that?" My headache intensifies, the incessant pulsing now almost unbearable behind my eyes and at the base of my neck.

"He'd be stupid not to be suspicious of us, but the way he talked to me... He already thinks I know more than I said."

"But we do..."

Kit only nods, and I'm suddenly more than tired. Bone weary and wrung out. "Are we going to your place?"

"Yes. I don't want you alone. Besides, you shouldn't be with a concussion."

I groan, remembering I need to be monitored tonight and woken up every few hours. Although the MRI was clear, it's a precaution.

"Also, not to freak you out, but those texts..." He pauses to stare down at me, his expression matching his serious tone. "They have your cell number so we can't rule out that they also know where you live and about the Home."

"No." I clutch at my head, unable to concentrate. "Not the Home."

Sheer pain and fear course through my body and override everything else. I'm frustrated and anxious and, if I'm being truthful with myself, scared.

"Hey." He grips the curve of my neck and shoulder, rubbing my tender muscle, and I bite back a delighted moan—the first pleasurable sensation all night. I wish his touch didn't still affect me. "I texted Nick about the clinic, and I'll talk to him about getting both places checked out."

"Thank you. I can't even think about the Home being destroyed."

"Then don't." His hand falls from my shoulder. "We'll make sure everything is fine."

*I'm torn at the withdrawal of his hand. Bereft at the loss of his touch and grateful for the renewed clarity of thought.*

*"Holman was very interested in how we knew each other." My stomach twists. He definitely had the impression we were together, and while I don't normally care what other people think, I made no attempt to correct the detective's assumption.*

*"He's looking at me for this." He relaxes farther into the seat, neither offense nor worry in his tone.*

*"What?" Outrage sparks tension in my already overworked muscles, setting me on edge. "How is that possible? You had nothing to do with this!"*

*He shrugs, running a hand through sandy, jaw-length hair. "It's fine. Anything from Elliot?"*

*I pull out my phone and the screen is cracked. I'm too tired to care or speak, and I shake my head since there's nothing from Elliot since his warning to get out of the building. I immediately regret the movement, grimacing at the agony in my muscles and bones. I feel like I've been through a meat grinder.*

*As the car slows, I type out a quick text asking Elliot to call me. We need to talk to him.*

*The cab pulls up in front of an old factory-type building that's been retrofitted into lofts, and we ride the elevator to the top floor in silence. Even exhausted, my mind fires with how to explain any of this to Nick. How's he going to take the possibility of the Home being in danger? And I'm staying at Kit's, how did we get here? It feels natural, right almost, even with so much unspoken or unsettled between us.*

*A bottle blonde, average height and build, leans against the last door at the far end of the hall. Our presence, the ding of the elevator, or both cause her to turn toward us.*

*She stares at Kit, not acknowledging me, and her features shift from what looks like worry into relief before forming a full-blown smile. Far too quickly, I look away and ignore the burning anguish hissing up the back of my neck and into my skull.*

The darkened ugly feeling inside of me is more than jealousy. It's also self-blame and disappointment because I know how she feels. I once had him, but I tossed him away.

Laughing nervously, she sprints toward him. "Oh my God, you're okay."

White teeth gleam and tiny lines crinkle at the corner of her eyes. She's so happy and seems as if she can barely contain herself. It's clear she wants to hug him or something.

He stops a few feet short, frowning, maybe even confused. It is late, and who knows why she's outside his loft, but he doesn't reject her when she launches herself into his large, corded arms.

His big hands grip her slender waist, pulling her up and into him. She wraps her arms around his neck, fingers sliding into the ends of his wavy hair, and my insides clench.

Who is this woman? Is she his girlfriend?

The deep rumble of his voice pulls me back to the hallway. "Sally, what are you doing here?"

"Oh my God, when you sent that text, my heart stopped." The words rush from her. "Oh no, you're hurt." Her fingers feather across the bandage on his cheek.

Like a punch to the throat, my neck muscles stiffen, all breath trapped, and my eyes sting with unshed tears.

"What text?" Confusion swims in his eyes and he places her on her feet.

"You said there was an explosion. I thought about calling the hospitals but there are so many in the city and I had no idea where you were. I figured your place was the best place to wait." The woman glances at me and her gaze turns inquisitive, taking me in from head to toe.

I can only imagine what she sees. My face is covered in tiny cuts and bruises, my hair is messy, and my pants are torn at the knees. I must look how I feel, like a battered woman.

"Text? Yeah, I sent…" He fishes in his jacket pocket, bringing out his phone, and the furrow of his brow deepens.

It takes a beat or two while he scrolls through the texts and then his head snaps up, eyes intent on Sally, and it's clear whatever she's referring to now makes sense. But he still finds something unsettling.

"Caro, why don't you go on in?" He hands me his keys, motioning to the door at the end of the hall where the blonde was standing just moments before.

It isn't a suggestion; he wants me to leave. A part of me is all too happy to oblige, to get away from their intimate moment, and another part of me feels like I've been banished.

I nod without introduction and walk as fast as is possible in my condition. The pain rattles through my bones and I grit my teeth, needing a warm bath and painkillers.

"And, um, Caro, give Nick a call."

Again I'm mute, nodding, unlocking the door and walking into his home. As if shutting out the world, Kit and Sally forgotten, a smile leaps onto my lips at the sparse furnishings of this beautiful loft.

He's a minimalist. Open concept, high ceilings, exposed piping and brick, and the floor is gleaming ash blonde. On one wall hangs an obscenely large flat screen TV—Kit loves his sports—and there are a couple of pieces of oversized leather and wood furniture.

This is Kit. Simple and comfy. And some of it reminds me of when we lived together. We were still very much kids and didn't have a lot of money so there wasn't a lot to crowd our space, but it was warm and cozy. Somewhat like this.

Like a slap in the face, Sally is front and center. Did she help him decorate this place? Just how little I know about him now is so apparent.

His life is a mystery to me. The fact he has people, this woman for one, who care about him and know things about him that I don't hurts. He has an entire life without me.

I have a life without him, if you can call it that. It mainly consists of work, Nick, and Maggie. Oh, and Willow. It isn't much of a life. It's an existence.

But this is how I wanted things between us. It's silly, arrogant, and even conceited of me to think he'd be alone, his life standing still without me.

*None of this should come as a surprise, and yet I never consciously allowed myself to think about it. At all. I never once imagined Kit with someone else or even thriving and living a happy life without me.*

*At least he was able to move on. I should be glad to know he's got a life, but why isn't that the case? What on earth is that about?*

*We'd been near strangers after our breakup. While devastating, it wasn't hard to avoid him given our worlds didn't intersect because Nick, too, pulled away because of his work.*

*I was in med school and then a doctor, whereas he ran with dangerous criminals, hanging out in places I can't even imagine. Nick rarely saw me, and Kit made it a point to be around as little as possible.*

*Things changed when Maggie came into our lives, almost two years ago now. At the same time, Nick decided he was leaving his life of crime and going straight. He'd had enough and Kit decided to do the same, even if his decision was more out of circumstance than a conscious choice.*

*Kit tried to reconnect with me then. More as friends than anything else, and it made sense. He started working with Maggie at her garage, and Nick and I were starting Léa's Home.*

*Our reunion could have been easy, seamless even, and all I had to do was accept it. But...I couldn't. It was too hard to have him back in my life and not worry that he'd unknowingly break my heart all over again.*

*I couldn't handle the thought of him disappointing me, going back to a life of danger and crime. Or if he was happy with someone else... I just couldn't. So I pushed him away, told him to stay out of my life. And he did, until today.*

*Was it selfish of me? Definitely. Smart? No way.*

*Just then, a muted buzzing in my pocket reminds me I need to call Nick, and I fumble to pull it out, hoping it's Elliot.*

*Long jagged streaks, much like that of a spider's web, crawl along the screen of my phone. My fall, face first onto the ground, must have damaged the screen.*

*"Hey, Willow, I was going to call you." I try to inject a smile in my voice, disappointed it isn't Nick or Elliot.*

"Caro. Thank goodness. Are you okay?" She's frenzied and concerned. "I heard what happened to the clinic. Were you there?"

"Yes, I was there but I'm okay. How did you find out?" I put the phone on speaker while I remove my jacket.

"A Detective Holman came to my house tonight, and I got a call from one of the board of directors. The police had called them too as their name is on the lease."

"Willow, I'm sorry. I was going to call you. We just got back from the hospit—"

"No, no. Don't worry about me. I'm worried about you. Tell me what happened."

I tell her everything, holding nothing back. I trust Willow. While our relationship is mostly professional, we've worked side by side in some tense situations, like the one today with those men—was that only today? And we're friends.

"Caro, I can't even...and Elliot's text, do you think he set that timer to go off?"

"Yes. It looks that way. I only wish he'd text me again, or call. What did Holman ask you?"

"He wanted to know about my job, about anything unusual, and so I told him about the two guys. Then he asked for details on the clinic staff, and I told him he'd have to go through the board of directors for those details. Then he had a lot of questions about you and someone named Kit Jensen."

"Okay. Kit's an old friend and was with me tonight." Maybe Kit was right and Holman does think he's more involved than he is. This isn't good. We don't need the added trouble of the police looking at us like we're guilty of something.

I take the phone off speaker, putting it to my ear. "I'm going to have to call the board."

Just the thought of the phone calls—yes, multiple calls because telling only one member, the chairman, wouldn't suffice—exhausts me further. Almost all of them will want to be told personally. All those egos.

*While the walk-in clinic feels like it's mine, since I've been there since it opened and give so much of my time and self to the care of the patients, it isn't.*

*Health care in Ontario is publicly funded, and the Jane Walk-in Clinic is owned by a private business with a board of directors who we answer to. They lease the space, and they are responsible for the insurance and all the employees.*

*"No, I've got it covered. And I also called all the staff to tell them about the clinic. They know not to go in tomorrow morning. And they'll be contacted by someone in administration once the board gets things rolling for insurance and all that."*

*"Thank you. You're amazing." Some of the tension in my neck diminishes, grateful for Willow but also worried about all she'll have to deal with. "How did the staff take it?"*

*"You know, most of them were shocked, worried about you, but they all go with the flow. They'll be placed at another location soon so they don't have to worry about their jobs."*

*It's true, and that includes me. I'm saddened for the neighborhood and the future of the clinic—who knows how far they may have to travel for medical care? But none of that is within my control. I'm an employee and out of a job right now. Maybe this is a sign to focus solely on the Home and finally let my second job, working at the clinic, go.*

*"You need to take care of yourself and let me know how I can help," Willow cuts through my thoughts.*

*My phone buzzes and I check who is calling. "Willow, I have to go. It's Nick on the other line. I need to speak to him."*

*"Of course. Take care of yourself and talk soon."*

*"Thanks. Night." I click to the other call, feeling almost as bad as when I was flat out on the concrete after the blast.*

*How am I going to tell Nick the Home might be next? The possibility is slim, and I hope with all that is good in this world nothing will happen, but what if the implied threat of those texts is to destroy anything important to me?*

# KIT

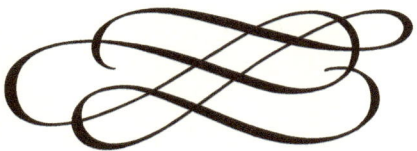

*I screwed up big time. Sally is here, staring up at me expectantly, wanting every detail about what happened to me tonight, and I can't tell her a lot. She isn't supposed to even know what's going on.*

*While it's unlikely—I was watching—we could have been followed back to my place, and if so, Sally can't be seen with me. That's the last thing I want, to put more people in danger.*

*At the hospital, in the wake of Holman's interview and my haste to keep Nick informed, I didn't realize I was still in the text window with Sally. I told her about the clinic explosion.*

*Dammit, and now she's here.*

*I've known Sally for as long as I've worked at the garage, and while she's flirted, I had no intentions of making a move. Then two months ago, she asked me out.*

*At first, I declined, stuttering and blushing like a damn virgin. I'd been caught off guard and truth be told, not interested, but I didn't know how to say so without hurting her feelings. So, I agreed to coffee.*

*Yes, I've been with women since Caro, but not many, and even though I don't do one-night stands, none had been anything more than casual. The smart and gorgeous doctor was still deeply entrenched in my heart and mind, and despite how long it had been, she wasn't going anywhere.*

*Now with Caro back, even if this situation is temporary, this thing with Sally isn't going anywhere.*

*"How do you feel?" She's close and concerned, and her proximity makes me uncomfortable.*

*"I'm okay. I was checked out at the hospital and there's nothing a little rest won't cure."*

She grabs a hand and turns it palm up to reveal my bandage. "Oh my, Kit, what happened?"

"Yeah, there was an explosion and I was a little too close. These will heal." I pull my hand from her grasp, holding each one up to her before dropping them to my side. "I don't know much else. The police are investigating it."

"You're lucky you weren't killed. And you're okay to be at home? Or did you leave?" She arches a brown brow, not to question but more matter-of-fact.

I smirk and shake my head. "Ah, no. The doctor released me."

We aren't close in the relationship sense—we're only just getting to know each other that way—but we're friends. I've hung out with the crew from the garage at her diner almost every day for the past two years. She knows enough about me to suggest I'd challenge the doctor's orders if I wanted.

"Please don't put on a brave face for me. You'd tell me if you were really hurt, wouldn't you?" Pale eyes search my face, looking for something. Maybe a sign I'm being truthful?

"Yes, I'd tell you, and I promise, I'm fine. Really."

She nods. "Okay, but if you need me to stay tonight, just in case, I can crash on your couch."

"No, that—"

"And before you shut me down, this isn't my way of making a move on you." There's a sly twinkle in her eye, more in jest than intent. "I want to help, make sure you're fine."

"Thank you." I grab one of her small hands and squeeze. "I appreciate it, but I am fine. I don't need someone to check on me and I won't be alone." The words jam in my throat as I force my jaw shut and release her hand.

I want to tell her about Caro, call this whole thing off between us, but now doesn't feel right. She's been jerked around enough tonight, first with me rescheduling our dinner, then standing her up and now this.

Honesty is important to me, and I will tell her this isn't going to work, just not right now.

"I'm sorry about tonight. I got a call from a good friend asking me to do a favor for him and it was urgent." Sally knows Nick so I could mention him, but the less she knows, the better. "I should have cancelled our dinner. I thought I'd be quick, but as you can tell, that wasn't the case. I messed up your evening."

"No. No." She leans against the wall opposite me, sliding her hands into her coat pockets. "It's fine. If you wanted to call off our date, you could have just said so. You didn't have to go to all this trouble with an explosion to get me to back off."

She's teasing but there's something in her tone, a slight edge that suggests she senses there's more here. It's as if she's read my mind and knows we're over before we began and she's taking it in stride.

"Nah, I'd have just said so. I was looking forward to dinner…"

"And now?" She cocks her head to one side, trying to appear casual, but her shoulders rise as if bracing herself for my response.

"Now, I need some rest." I inch closer to my door. "Sally, thanks for coming by and for your concern. It means a lot."

I lean on the frame of my door, and she pushes from the wall, now several feet from me. "Do I get a raincheck on dinner?"

"Let's leave things the way they are for now." The downward curve at the corner of her lips, subtle but there, causes me to pause. I'm a shit. "I promise to call and we can talk some more."

Now she nods, forcing a small, artificial smile. "Yeah, sounds good. Good night, Kit, and take care of yourself."

"Night, Sally." I turn the knob and she walks briskly to the elevator.

I wait until the doors open, and when she's in, now facing me, she calls, "And please call me if you need anything. I mean that." The doors close.

Regret is a cold, hard stone in the pit of my gut. I should never have agreed to dating her. As much as I try to move on from Caro, all it takes is a few hours with her, even with bombs, cops, and bruises to show for it, and I'm back where I started.

"Hi, Nick." Caro's voice is tense and a little wobbly.

"Caro. Holy shit, you were supposed to call or text me after you checked out the clinic." Nick's on speaker as I slip into the loft. "I tried

Kit but nothing. Did the asshole even come by?" He's incensed and Caro frowns, not knowing about the text mix-up.

"I thought I had texted you but there was a mix-up. Sorry." I stroll up to Caro, standing in the middle of the room. Has she not moved since entering my place?

"Oh." Her gaze lands on me, both puzzled and relieved. We stare at each other and my concern for her grows; she's as white as snow with black circles under her eyes.

"Would someone tell me what the fuck happened?" Nick's bellow breaks our trance.

Caro bites her now trembling bottom lip and she needn't say anything. This is hard for her, and the events of tonight are more than taking their toll. I guide her to the couch while I take Nick through the events of the night.

The recounting is slow going and painful. Nick interrupts me every three words with some kind of outburst, either to curse, fire a question at me like a drill sergeant, or do both.

"Hang on, you triggered a bomb and the fucking clinic blew to smithereens?" Nick is speechless for the first time since we started this conversation, and I want to relish the silence, catch my breath, and organize my thoughts, but the stillness doesn't last for long.

"Yes." Caro is the first to speak. "We're fine but there was an explosion. The clinic is gone." She swallows hard and with difficulty, as if the words grow tenfold in her throat.

Tears spring to her eyes and she clutches my hand, keeping me at her side. "Kit saved my life."

Air whooshes from my lungs, heart cracking at the agony she's in. I wrap an arm around her and she's now rambling, all her worries tumbling from her shaky lips.

"Elliot set the bomb...the timer...the pill...the Home might be next." Tears come as fast as her words. "We need to check the Home... God, Nick, we can't lose the Home. And if Kit hadn't been there..."

"Shhh." Nick's pained attempts at comfort through the phone mingle with her sobs.

I cradle her in my arms, and the way she melts into me makes me almost come undone. There are several attempts at stringing my *words together coherently before I finally take Nick through what we know.*

*Caro in my arms is both surreal and grounding, and the longer I talk with Nick, the more I'm bolstered in my resolve to see this through to the end. To make sure no one is after her and she's out of danger.*

*I fill him in on our conversation with Holman, how Elliot isn't making this easy, and all the things we still need to do.*

*"We're coming home tonight," Nick says once I'm done.*

*"No," Caro and I say in unison.*

*Wild espresso eyes stare at me, pleading to get through to her brother. But there's something else in her gaze. As I talk Nick off the ledge, because jumping in a car at midnight and then driving six hours plus is insane and it won't help anyone, she looks at me as if she sees no one else, and it does strange and crazy things to me.*

*"You need to arrange for a search of Caro's place and the Home to make sure it's bomb free."*

*"Consider it done. We'll be home tomorrow then."*

*"No." Her voice is raspy from the crying. "Nick, please stay the one more day. Don't worry about me. I'm here with Kit and we're okay. Please do this for me. Stay and I'll see you day after next."*

*He exhales a long, tortured sigh. "Fine. But don't do anything foolish. And if you find out where Elliot is, we're going to pay him a visit."*

*"Don't worry, we'll find him," I reassure him as much as myself. "Okay, Caro needs some rest, and you need to end this call before you wake up Maggie."*

*He grunts on the other end and we say our goodbyes.*

*"I do need some rest," she mumbles into my shoulder, unmoving. "Oh, and I meant to tell you, I still have this."*

*Her hand slides into the pocket of the jacket beside her and she pulls out the tiny plastic bag with the tablet and piece of paper she found in the box.*

*We may have lost the security footage from the break-in, but we still have the pill and telephone number on the label. It's better than nothing.*

*I can't help but smile and she does the same. "Come on." I stand and gently pull her by the hand. "How does a shower and bed sound?"*

# CARO

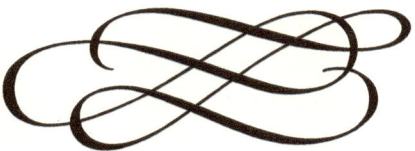

Kit hands me a glass of water and two pills for my headache, then he beckons for me to follow him through the door at the far end of the loft.

"Bathroom's through there." He points to a doorway once we're inside the bedroom, complete with a king bed and dresser.

There's only one bedroom. One bed. A very big, comfy bed but only one. Images of the blonde in the hallway cause my stomach to cramp.

Has she slept in his bed? Have there been other women over the years? Of course there have. What am I thinking?

No. No. No. I will not do this.

He opens a drawer and pulls out a shirt. "You can wear this."

I suck in a breath as he hands me a plain navy blue T-shirt, one I'd know anywhere. It's my T-shirt.

Well, not mine—it's his, but it's the very one I always wore when we were together. I would sleep in it, especially during those jobs where he'd been gone for nights at a time. Without thinking, I bring the cotton to my nose and inhale.

"It's clean." His tone is flat but his nostrils flare and eyes narrow. I've insulted him.

"I know." I straighten, my voice rising in defense.

Lemony fresh laundry detergent surrounds me. Gone is any scent of him or me, and my tongue ties and mind empties. What can I say to excuse my silly, insensitive move without revealing the truth? I was yearning to smell him. For the very reason I loved, no, love, this shirt.

"I wasn't—"

He cuts me off. "Do you need help with the shower?"

"Ah, no." I'm too quick to respond and his features shutter. Damn, I'm doing this all wrong. "I'm sorry. I don't understand what you meant."

"Your hair." His eyes travel to the top of my head. "I can wash it for you so you don't get your stitches wet. And I've got waterproof bandaging that we can put on it while you wash."

"Oh, yes." My hand goes instinctively to the cut by my hairline. I'd forgotten all about it. "Yes, please."

With the precision of a machine, Kit sets up a chair, towels and a few pillows inside the shower stall. The washroom is big, with both a shower big enough for two and a bathtub. Inside the shower, there's a long wand-like faucet head so he can get my hair wet while keeping my face and body dry.

"Make yourself comfortable." He pats the chair and then strolls from the shower.

Through the glass wall, I stare, mesmerized, as he drops his jeans, pulls his long-sleeved shirt over his head and drops that to the floor as well. This leaves him standing there in only plaid boxers.

Mother of all that is holy.

He's a beautiful man.

Always has been.

A perfect body, as if carved from stone, bronze skin smooth and firm.

My stomach flutters and my mouth opens, releasing a small, contented sigh. It's been way too long since I've feasted my eyes on his wide, sculpted chest, abs you could easily wash laundry on for life, and the colorful dragon tattoo running along the left side of his rib cage.

I was with him when he had it done. It took hours, too many to count, and many sessions. For him, the mythical creature symbolizes strength and wisdom, both natural traits of Kit.

Captivated, my gaze tracks the intricate swirls and lines of ink as they disappear into the waistband of his boxers. The glorious sight of him short-circuits my brain.

It's only when I get the odd, wired sensation of someone watching me that I snap out of my stupor.

Kit's hazel eyes bore into me, a funny look crossing his face when my guilty, caught-red-handed gawk locks onto him.

"Can I help you get settled?" His chin dips to the chair, a crooked grin skating across his mouth.

"Um, ah, no, I'm good." My cheeks flush. "Are you sure you're okay to do this?"

I'm talking about his hands as I watch him remove the clean bandages only put on about an hour ago.

"Yeah, they're fine."

As I get comfortable, he bends to get something in the cabinet underneath the sink.

"Do you still use this?" He holds out two familiar bottles—specialty shampoo and conditioner for curly hair—as he saunters toward the shower.

It's the kind I use. The only brand I've ever used.

"Yes. Where did you get those?" My voice is hoarse, words caught as my brain scrambles, not knowing how to react and where to look.

I stare at his toned thighs, covered in tiny golden hairs, as I watch his muscles cord and release with every step towards me.

"I had them from before."

I rip my gaze from his leg, springing higher and higher to his face, just in time to take in the flush spreading across his cheeks. He shrugs, and I sink my teeth into my lip, unable to find the words to express how blown away I am by something as mundane but also significant as him holding on to my hair supplies.

He nears me, and the heat of him and how his stomach muscles flex and ripple with every deep breath he takes is overwhelming. Electricity trills through my veins, and sitting still is near impossible.

"You okay?" He rubs his lips together to hide a grin and I'm almost embarrassed. He knows what he's doing to me.

I urgently shove my hands under my thighs, rubbing my legs together to lessen the pulsing need building in my core. My hands twitch, wanting to boldly touch his hot skin, to traverse the ridges of his defined muscles.

"Tilt your head back." One hand cradles my skull like I'm fragile, special. "Tell me if the water is okay or if it's too hot."

*My tongue dead, or near to it, I nod, flames of desire licking up my neck, and the only thing to do is close my eyes. Warm breath and light stubble caress my cheek and I tremble, eyes popping open as his soft, full lips hover a pinch from my ear.*

*"Relax." The word is a caress against my skin.*

*His fingers sink into my hair, gathering all my strands in his large capable hands, and bolts of pleasure fly through my chest. I can hardly draw air into my lungs.*

*"Breathe." He soothes a hand down the side of my face as warm water soaks my locks. "Is this okay?"*

*"Uh-huh." My skin pricks and heart squeezes.*

*I'm going to have a heart attack. Not because I'm scared or stressed but because I'm turned on. I might combust.*

*His fingers stroke down the length of my hair, working the shampoo into my scalp. Deep, steady circles, calming and kneading like a balm, erase all the aches and pains from the blast.*

*I love when someone washes my hair. When my hairdresser does it, I'm putty and would agree to even a mohawk or full-on shaved head with her fingers in my hair. Now, my body tingles, alive and his to do with as he pleases.*

*The entire hair washing is an experience I will never forget. When he rinses my tresses for the final time and wrings out the excess water, I feel like a limp noodle and no longer have the capability to move.*

*"Okay, all clean." He rests a dry towel over my shoulder. "Let me get those stitches covered so you can take a shower."*

*I spring upright a little too fast and everything is dizzy. He rushes to my side, crouching to look me in the eye. "Easy. You okay?"*

*"Yes." My voice is a squeak and I clear my throat. "I think I've got it from here. You've already done so much. Thank you."*

*He straightens. "Okay. Everything's on the counter."*

*"Great, thanks." I wrap my wet hair in the towel and he leaves.*

*I stare at myself in the mirror and while far from the truth, I look like I'm freshly fucked. I wish.*

*My eyes are glowing, cheeks a dainty pink, and my lips are plump and swollen. What the...? And all this from washing my hair.*

Not allowing myself to dwell any longer on how Kit makes me feel—still makes me feel after all these years—I get into the shower. It's slow going with the aches and pains but it's just what I need.

When I step into the bedroom, Kit's waiting for me. "You can sleep here." He motions to the bed and flicks his gaze to the door. "And I'll be on the couch."

He scratches at the dark scruff dotting his chiseled jawline, and my palms burn, remembering the delicious roughness of it against my skin. Despite the temptation and my weakening resolve, he can't sleep out there.

"The couch isn't going to fit you. You won't get any sleep."

Sure, he's used to catching a few hours of sleep anywhere. Just like me. He had to in his line of work, but he's been through a lot tonight.

Just like me, he needs his rest. And even though the couch is oversized, there's no way it'll fit his six-foot-five frame comfortably. His feet will hang off one end.

"It's fine. I've slept in way worse places." He edges toward the door. "Once you fall asleep, I'll grab a shower."

"Kit." I grab at his forearm, his hard muscles flexing beneath my fingers, and I squeeze in a silent plea for him to listen. "You must be dying for a shower. Go have one now and I'll wait in the living room. And as for sleeping, the bed is big enough for the both of us.

My breath catches as his eyes hold mine, and when his sharp gaze rakes down my body and then back up again, I'm painfully aware of every inch of myself. Once again, with only a look, I'm ready to explode.

Heat flickers through me at the thought of sleeping next to him, of being able to smell him, touch him, hear his steady breaths.

I will my breathing to slow down and the flush to vanish from my cheeks, saying more to myself than anything else, "We're adults—it's no big deal."

I'm such a liar.

# KIT

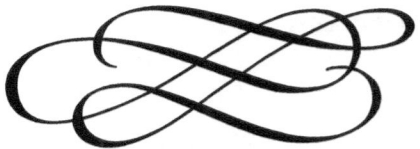

My pulse pounds like the heavy, incessant drums of a sacrificial rite. How the hell am I going to sleep with Caro next to me?

Showered and in a pair of sleep pants, I pad into the living room. Caro's in my T-shirt, staring at the black-framed photographs along one wall. The fabric falls to a little above mid-thigh.

She's tall, about five foot ten, with legs that would bring any man to his knees. The highway of creamy, toned flesh makes my balls tighten. She's sexy even casual and ready for bed. Damn, I've missed her.

I clear my throat to let her know I'm there, and she spares me a brief look before fixing back on the images.

When I moved into the loft, Maggie helped decorate the place. I don't have a lot of things of sentimental value. She insisted on adding a touch of something personal to my place.

Rather than argue with her, I went through my pictures online and got some printed. Ones that meant something to me, reminders of people or places I never wanted to forget. She got them framed and designed the layout.

Unable to stay away, I stand at Caro's back, remaining silent. Aware of my presence, there's a slight shift in her demeanor as she inches in my direction, soaking up the warmth created by her back to my chest.

Only an inch or two separates our bodies, and it feels right. We are both where we are meant to be, and no words are needed.

Nick and Maggie are in a couple of the pictures, and there's an awesome snapshot of Nick, Logan, and me on our bikes. Caro took it.

*A smile coasts across my mouth. We were twenty-one and thought we were badasses with our leather jackets and Harleys. We're such goofs.*

*And of course, there are several photographs of Caro and me in high school, when she was in university and in the early days of med school, when we were still together.*

*Her long, elegant fingers trace the lines of my youthful, happy features through the glass. "I love this picture. Do you remember that day?"*

*Over her shoulder, she looks up at me, and suddenly I'm overwhelmed with the fresh clean scent of her. As if travelling through time, I'm immediately transported through the years and back to where and when that very image was taken. It's an image of us with boxes all around us, and we're smiling like we just won the lottery.*

*"I'll never forget it. We'd just moved in together." I latch my hands onto my hips.*

*No touching.*

*No matter how tempting.*

*I'm lightheaded at the mere thought of her silky skin beneath the pads of my fingers and in turn, her quiver and flush at my touch.*

*Not going to happen.*

*"Yes. That place was horrible." She laughs and her damp curls bounce, taunting me. "But you'd have thought we'd moved into the Taj Mahal or Buckingham Palace."*

*"Yeah, we were crazy." My fingers itch to reach for a lock of hair.*

*She whirls around to face me, and there's suddenly a vise grip on my lungs, squeezing every last bit of air out of me.*

*"Crazy in love." Her chest bumps into the upper half of my torso as she steps into me. I shudder, unable to hide my reaction to her.*

*We're touching.*

*Chest to chest.*

*She isn't playing fair.*

*"How are your hands?" She doesn't wait for my response, grabbing both with hers and turning them palm up to examine the cuts. "I could bandage it up again, if you want. It's already healing."*

"No, it's fine." I pull my hands from her hold. "Besides, the air will be good for them."

She places a hand on my shoulder, staring up at me. Her gaze is loaded with…with what? Love? Gratitude? Or is it just desire? That was never our problem.

"Caro, you should get some sleep." My heart twists in my chest, an unimaginable ache, but I can't torture myself like this.

Her smile crumbles and hurt flashes in her compelling dark eyes as I step away, turning my back to her and walking to the kitchen.

It's an eternity before the bedroom door clicks closed, and my hands, balled like fists, and forehead press into the unforgiving wall.

My eyes squeeze shut as if to erase all trace of Caro.

Impossible.

With a racing heart and raging erection, my body pulses, throbs in near misery, and I can't control my rapid, shallow breaths. I'm not getting any air into my lungs.

I battle the urge to pummel the wall. No doubt I'd lose the fight, but the pain would distract me from how much I want to storm into the room and take her. Lose myself in the only woman I've ever loved.

It's hard to say how long I stay like that, hanging my head and resisting the innate need to love her, be with her. I wake her up in about two hours as instructed by the nurse and she wakes easily, which is a good sign, and she readily tells me her name before going back to sleep.

And I wake her up one more time, wait ten minutes to ensure she's back to sleep, and then I climb in bed, under the covers.

Even exhausted and in the early hours of the morning, sleep is elusive and restless. Caro remains asleep when I finally get out of bed, fed up with tossing and turning. My body's tight and sore, and it takes a bit to get moving.

Last night's blast left its markings on me as on Caro, I'm sure, and I suppose that explains why she's still sleeping. Usually she's an early bird, up well before the sun. She's one of those people who doesn't need a lot of sleep to function well.

Barefooted, I make my way to the kitchen, and with each step I slice through the buttery pink and orange sunbeams streaming in *from the floor-to-ceiling windows. The sky is a clear, cloudless blue and it looks like it'll be another chilly day.*

*While the coffee brews, I call the police station to inquire about our cars. We're not going to get them back anytime soon. Then I call the garage and arrange for a vehicle to be sent over so I have something to drive.*

*Then I sit and take inventory of last night's events with Caro once we got back from the hospital. Nick's baby sister didn't always hate me, and there were times last night that it felt like old times.*

*No, for many years, Caro's feelings for me were the exact opposite of hate. We shared a bed and a life. At eighteen, I met her the same week I started hanging out with Nick. She was sixteen and fucking beautiful.*

*Strong, confident, and intelligent.*

*Irresistible and a bit intimidating.*

*Nothing has changed.*

*I didn't believe in love or even marriage, but she tested those beliefs, made me question everything I'd ever thought about relationships.*

*And then everything changed.*

*My lifestyle wasn't a secret. I worked for bad people, took money to make their dirty secrets and nasty problems go away. Caro knew all of this and had been cool with it. Until she wasn't.*

*One day, I became a thug in her eyes. It happened almost overnight, or at least that's how it felt to me. I suspect it had been longer for her, her changing emotions, but she hid it well.*

*At some point, in med school, she no longer wanted me in her life. Her growing dislike of my life choices became hard to ignore.*

*Growing up poor with a crackhead mom, who I loved even if she wasn't always there for me, made life difficult. I learned to take care of her...us...from a young age and found the promise of a life with drugs.*

*Yeah, ironic, I know. In high school, I fell in with the wrong crowd, surprise, surprise, and turned to drugs. Not using but dealing. I don't touch the stuff—toxic to not only your body but to your relationships and life.*

*Some people might think I should have run in the other direction. I mean, why would I knowingly contribute to the millions already addicted to drugs and the senseless overdoses? Especially considering my mother.*

*It isn't as if I wanted any of this. After my father was killed, gunned down like a dog in the streets before I was even six years old, my mother changed.*

*We were never well off, living hand to mouth even when Dad was alive, but he was a good man and didn't deserve to die the way he did. He was in the wrong place at the wrong time.*

*His death killed our little family. Mom was never quite the same after that, and looking for solace or escape from life she turned to drugs. She lost her job, then the apartment, and pretty soon I was fending for myself.*

*Caro knew all of this. When we met, when Nick took me under his wing, she knew I was dealing and then teamed up with her brother, leaving drugs behind and joining him in his business fixing problems.*

*Foolishly, I thought she understood I'd had no other choice. I couldn't get a legit job to cover rent, pay the bills, put food on the table, and allow me to finish high school. I didn't care about an education but I was a minor. If I'd disappeared from high school, social services would have come looking for me. I didn't need that kind of trouble. Drugs enabled me to make ends meet and get my diploma.*

*Working with Nick was better. We were our own bosses, but we were both doing shady, dangerous stuff to make a living.*

*Shit, Caro benefitted the most from Nick's line of work and she never objected, so stupidly I believed she was good with it. She was all I had until I lost her too.*

*At the time, when we broke up, I didn't understand her. I tried to get through to her, and walking away wasn't something I easily accepted. Those early days were hard—talk about beating your head against a brick wall. It was only with time and age that I started to understand her reasons.*

*We grow and change, and sometimes in relationships, people don't grow in the same direction or no longer want the same things. I didn't think that would be us, but Caro has a lot of stuff from her childhood* that she's never really faced. I thought I could help her with that but I never got the chance. My lifestyle only pushed us apart.

"Morning." She shuffles into the kitchen, yawning and raising her arms over her head slowly, frowning with each move.

"Good morning. How are you feeling?"

"Like roadkill." She takes the coffee from my hands, a look of awe blanketing her still sleepy features. "It'll get better, especially once I get some of this into me. Thank you." She gestures to the mug, inhaling. "And I'll take a few more painkillers, which should help me feel somewhat human. How do you feel?"

"I'm good. You should eat something with the meds."

"I'm not hungry." She rests a hand flat on her stomach and grimaces. "Not yet, thanks."

Sighing and not wanting to argue, I say, "I called the station about our cars and they're going to be there awhile. They said yours was damaged in the blast."

"How bad is it?" She rests her hip against the counter, studying me over the rim of the cup. "Is the Aston Healy okay?"

"I'm not sure how bad it is. The officer didn't say. As for my car, I'd be crying if it wasn't okay. I don't think any damage was done to it."

A ghost of a smile creeps over her mouth. "Well, I'm glad yours is okay. Mine was old and doesn't owe me anything. Although, having to get a new car..." She worries her bottom lip.

"You don't have to think about that right now. I also got a loaner car from the garage, and it should be here soon so we'll have wheels."

She nods. "Anything from Nick about the Home?"

"He texted an hour ago to say he had people in there right now. Your place is clear. He had someone go in last night."

"What? He did? In the middle of the night?"

"You know your brother. Besides, he doesn't want you there on your own no matter if it's safe. He'll let us know about the Home as soon as it's done."

"Gah, I can't even think about what we'll do if...our patients...the potential dama—"

83

"Hey, don't go there." I lower my tone. "Not unless you have to, and if they find something, we'll deal with it. Make sure no one gets hurt."

"Yes. Yes. So what am I going to wear today?" She glances down at what she slept in. "I can't stay in your T-shirt all day, and yesterday's clothes aren't an option. They're dirty and reek of smoke. They're ruined."

My gaze drops to her lean body draped in my shirt, falling to mid-thigh. Long, honey bare legs, knees scraped and bruised, and toes painted blood-red tempt me.

A pulsing sensation, hot and heady, unfurls inside me, starting at the top of my spine and rippling down my body, straight to my groin. Fuck.

"What's wrong with what you're wearing? I kinda like it," I tease and cringe inwardly at how slow my mind is at getting ahold of my tongue.

"Funny." She crosses her arms over her chest. "I'm serious. I need clothes and I'd rather not have to go shopping if I can avoid it."

She smirks and I mock-shudder. Caro hates shopping—she'll do anything to avoid it. "Well, we're not going to put either of us through that."

She laughs and warmth spreads through my chest as my phone rings. I snatch it from the kitchen counter, freezing when I see the name on the screen. Shit, I totally forgot.

It's the guy I'm supposed to meet today, Mr. Pinter. I'll have to reschedule. This isn't good.

I don't want to delay as Pinter's been hard to nail down for an actual meeting. He's had the paperwork for over a week now and agreed to the terms verbally. But I can't see him today—I've got more urgent things to do. Namely, track down Elliot, and I want to be available in case Nick finds anything.

"I gotta take this." I amble to the bedroom. "Kit Jensen," I say, answering the call.

Before fully shutting the bedroom door, my gaze locks on Caro's wary one, watching me. Who does she think I'm talking to? I could take the call in front of her, but this guy is an odd duck.

*Pinter is ninety-three, paranoid, and reluctant to talk about his car, and that's even with him wanting to sell his father's 1934 Ford 3-Window Coupe. From the pictures he emailed, the car needs work, but it's rare and once fixed, we'd have no trouble selling the classic.*

*I can't lose this deal. I've been trying to secure him for weeks, and while I have a few other potential cars lined up, this would be a coup for the Phoenix.*

*Maggie and her garage, the kind of work she does, would grow exponentially. Really cement her already good reputation, and I want that for her, need to show her I'm a partner not a leech, even though she'd tell me she doesn't see things like that.*

*While Caro is my main priority, I have to keep this deal alive and won't be able to push this out much longer.*

*The call is brief, and he isn't pleased to hear I can't meet with him today. Fortunately, he agrees to reschedule, and it renews my conviction in the deal being the best way to see results fast.*

*When I return to the main room, Caro is in the kitchen where I left her.*

*"Was that..."*—she swallows with difficulty, averting my gaze—*"the woman from last night? Sally?"*

*"No. Just work."* I shove the phone in my back pocket. *I'd expected her to ask about Sally last night and was surprised when she didn't. There isn't much to say, but a part of me is thrilled she cares to ask.*

*"Oh."* Now she stares intently, and it's written all over her face—*she has more to say. I wait her out.*

*"About last night."* Once again, her eyes land anywhere but me, and her fingers trace a pattern on the countertop.

*My mind goes to washing her hair, the photographs, and the electric tension that sizzled between us.*

*"Who's Sally?"*

*"Just a friend."*

*"A girlfriend?"* Her watchful eyes burn into me and I avert my gaze and shrug, unable to answer.

*I don't want to talk about other women with Caro. I'd never wanted anyone but her, never pictured myself with anyone else. And the reality of being without her is only more intense and painful if I have to discuss it with the woman I want.*

"I'm sorry if I messed things up for you...with her."

*She's fishing but I don't take the bait.*

"You didn't. Now, about your clothes. We could swing by your place, although it isn't smart. Whoever's behind this knows a lot about you, and it's safe to guess that they most probably know where you live. But..."

"But what?"

"It might not be a bad idea to go by your place and check things out. We could go drive by once or twice first, make sure things are quiet and normal. And if so, we'll go in."

"I'll be quick, I promise. I just need to grab something for a day or two. Once Nick's back, I'll go stay with them, and I have clothes there."

*A crushing weight slams into my chest. She's already got one foot out the door, counting the time until she can leave me. Again.*

"Okay. Then we'll go find Elliot." *I choose to focus on getting her out of danger. Funny how I feel more in control of that than my relationship with her.* "I'm guessing Elliot hasn't responded?"

"Yeah, still no reply." *She frowns, taking another sip of the coffee.*

"This isn't much of a stretch, but he's acting like he's hiding from the goons. But he did the decent thing and texted about the clinic bomb, so he's got his phone, and if I had to guess, he isn't too far." *I don't bother to mention he's thrown her into the mix, and it's his fault she's in it. It's the only logical explanation.*

*But no, I'm not saying anything yet. There's no point getting into a disagreement if she chooses to defend Elliot when I have no proof right now.*

"And any more texts from the unknown number?"

"No. Nothing." *She grimaces and fear wades in her gaze.*

"Okay. Let's focus on Elliot. He can ignore a phone call but we're going to make it really hard for him to ignore us. While you were sleeping, I was thinking we show up at his work."

"I hate this. I'm in the middle of something, but I don't know what or why." *She's frustrated, twisting her features.*

"Hey, we're not completely clueless." Wanting to comfort her and lessen her anxiety—she's been through enough already—I remind her, "We'll talk to him, and we have the telephone number and pill."

"I suppose."

"After Elliot, when we know a bit more, we'll call that number. And we need to find out more about the pill." I'm thankful as fuck we got both of those out of there, otherwise we would be in the dark and our only hope would be Elliot.

"Sounds like a plan."

"You were saying last night that you thought it's oxy?"

She stalls, taking another sip of the coffee and leveling me with her deep brown eyes. "If I had to guess, yes. It looks like OxyContin based on the tablet imprint, OC on one side. But typically, the other side of the tablet would contain the dosage. This one doesn't."

"Yeah, it's got some kind of insect. Can't say for sure if it's a spider or—"

"It could be a June bug," she offers.

"Yeah, or maybe a beetle. Some drugs come with markings or symbols because the chemist, supplier, or dealer wants people to know it's theirs." I snort and add dryly, "Believe it or not, marketing exists even in the drug world."

She frowns but quickly schools her reaction to my mention of my old life. "I have a friend at a lab that can take a look and let us know for sure if it's oxy and what dosage."

I nod. We could assume it's oxy, but there have been instances where one drug is made to look like another. It's best we know what we're dealing with, as it'll help with knowing who may be involved or who to ask from my old world of contacts.

Back when I was rubbing elbows with the likes of thieves, druggies, and dealers, heroin in pill form, which at that time was unheard of, first appeared on the streets of New Jersey. It made quite a stir on the streets, and of course, in the media. And to make things even more interesting, the H had been made to look like oxy.

"Can you have it checked without raising any flags? If not, I can get someone to look at it."

*While she's connected, we don't want people getting curious or talking to the cops. Holman is already suspicious, so any more ties he can make between us and anything illegal will only fuel his conviction.*

*"What? Someone off the street? Was that who you were talking to just a moment ago?" She tips her chin toward the bedroom and my throat dries. "I thought you'd left that life and those people?"*

*The unspoken accusation is spiked like the tip of a spear, piercing into my chest. Does she think I'm lying?*

*"I left that life." My growl causes her to still.*

*I won't justify her question about the phone call. It isn't any of her business, and I told her the truth. The call was work-related, and I'm no longer into drugs or running with criminals or any of that.*

*My phone buzzes and it's Manny; he's downstairs with the key to an SUV. I sigh, dumping the remainder of my coffee in the sink. The normally pleasing liquid leaves a bitter taste in my mouth, and it's got nothing to do with the coffee and everything to do with Caro.*

*"The car is here. I have to go get the key downstairs. You can wear some of my sweatpants to your place. Help yourself." I leave, slamming the door harder than is necessary.*

*Disappointment and something akin to annoyance flood my veins. She still doesn't trust me. I'll always be nothing but a thug to her.*

# KIT

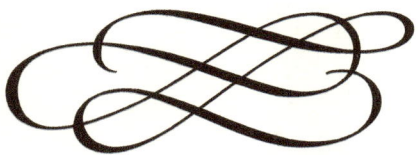

*The drive to her place is tense and silent. I won't leave her while Nick's out of town, but he's back tomorrow, at which time I will walk away. It won't be easy. I care about Caro and want to help, but this way is best.*

*Even if I understand her reasons for ending things with me, it's clear nothing I've done since then—get out of a life of crime, get a job with Maggie—changes anything.*

*We circle her street and some of the surrounding area several times, looking for anything out of the ordinary, or a car parked with one or more people inside. Nothing.*

*Finally, I park the car in her driveway and her phone chimes. We both glance down at the device sitting in the cupholder and then she holds it between us and clicks on the text.*

**Unknown number: We've been more than patient. Don't make this hard bitch. You've got 48 hrs to hand over what's ours or you'll regret it.**

*"Shit." The timing of the text doesn't feel random. What did I miss? Are we being watched?*

*I study the surroundings but there's nothing. No random utility van or another type of service vehicle in the area, no car parked with someone in it, or even a neighbor peeking out of a nearby window. And there's no sign of a camera set up outside her house.*

*Caro's gaze is one of helpless surrender. "Now we've got a time bomb over our heads. Do you think they know we're here?"*

*"Maybe. We have until Saturday to figure this out." It isn't a lot of time but what's the point of stating the obvious, and she nods solemnly. "Do you have a camera feed with your alarm system?"*

*That could be how they were able to detect our arrival...if they know we're here. We need Elliot more than ever. We need him to end this.*

"Yes. Inside the house and outside, front and back of the house."

"Okay, I'll check it out. They might be watching us so let's make it quick." *I squeeze her hand, and she isn't quick enough to hide her skepticism before looking away.*

*I can't walk away just yet even if that's what's best for the both of us. Nick is going to need my help, and truth be told, I want a part in ensuring her safety.*

*She angles her head forward, shoulders rigid and hands clenched at her sides as she peers through the windshield.*

"Someone's broken into my house." *Her voice is hoarse as her gaze lingers on her front door, which is kicked in.* "Why didn't the alarm go off?"

*I'm as puzzled as she is as I jump out and peer back in at her.* "Stay in the car."

*Shutting the door, I curse under my breath. How did we miss this when we drove by? Because the open door is subtle, easy to miss from any real distance. First things first, what happened to the alarm?*

*Before going in, I stand at the door, staring back at Caro in the car. She's holding up her phone and motioning as if to call...who? Nick? No. The police.*

*I shake my head and dial her number with my own phone.* "Don't call the police just yet. I want to take a quick look around and tap into your security feed."

*If we can get some information on the guys threatening her, it'll be one more piece of the puzzle and then the police can have at it.*

"Kit, the intruder could still be in there, and if—"

"Oh, and that didn't cross your mind last night when you went into the clinic alone?" *I cut in before she can say more.* "Where was that logic then?"

*I'm on edge and being an ass. The yo-yo of my emotions is exhausting and getting to me.*

"You're right. Sorry." *Her voice is small and remorseful, and I feel like even more of a dick.* "Can you please do me a favor and stay on the line? I want to know you're okay and this way, if I have to call the cops, I can do it right away."

"Okay."

"Hey, Kit, be careful." I don't miss the tremble in her voice. "And you know this, but try not to touch anything."

"I'll be fine and I know." My snippy tone causes me to wince. "Shit, I'm sorry." I push through the door.

"I only meant because Holman's got his sights on you. We don't need to help him implicate you." Her soft tone and the state of her home nearly cause me to trip.

The house is ransacked. I've seen worse, but this is Caro's home. Her sanctuary. My gut knots at the thought of her reaction when she sees it. There's no way I can keep this from her. And once I tell her, she'll want to come inside the house.

Still on the phone with her, I ask for directions to the alarm system. After what happened at the clinic, I want the tapes first. It's in the laundry room, and it doesn't take long for me to get there and figure out the trip was useless.

"Fuck."

"What is it?" She's panicked.

"I'm okay. It's the alarm system. Someone cut the power. That's why the alarm didn't go off, and most probably it was done from outside."

"Oh. What's it like in there?"

"Not good. Listen, let me just quickly check the house to make sure no one is here and then we need to make this quick."

"Okay."

I run through the house as fast as possible, making sure not to disturb anything. No one is here and I tell her so, waiting for her at the front door.

"Listen, it's bad so brace yourself." I grip her shoulders and stare into her eyes. "If you don't want to go in, I can get some things for you. All you have to do is tell me where they are."

"No, I want to go in. I'll be okay." She nods, nibbling on her bottom lip.

She gasps upon entry, and every shallow intake of air or stifled sob is a nail hammered into my flesh. It's agony watching her try to contain her anguish, and I'm helpless to do a fucking thing about it.

Her fingers curl and uncurl with every step she takes through the plundered house. The urge to touch things, right tables or chairs, sweep up the dirt and broken leaves of an overturned plant...is overpowering.

"Oh my God." She struggles to restrain herself. This is a crime scene, and maybe more than me, she wants the bastards who did this caught. I hate to tell her the chances are slim without witnesses or something as significant as a fingerprint.

Her eyes glisten, lips trembling as she stops in her bedroom. Drawers of clothes scatter the carpet, and shoes, scarves, handbags, and belts spill from her closet. Items are discarded in every direction, leaving her small wardrobe a barren wasteland.

"It'll be hard to know for sure but at first glance, is anything missing?" My insides thrum with rage. Thank fuck she wasn't here when this happened.

"I don't know." She shakes her head vehemently. "Did you see what the back of the house looks like?"

She's referring to the state-of-the-art examination and operating rooms Nick had built many years ago.

"No. I'll check."

The installation of those rooms wasn't at her request, and I'd never dared ask why she agreed to it, given her abhorrence of crime. While Nick stayed away from his sister, not wanting any harm to come her way, the mini hospital he had developed was an insurance policy, of sorts.

Should Nick, me, or anyone else in his crew need medical assistance, he and Caro had a kind of silent understanding. She was a doctor and she'd help if needed so as not to draw the attention of the cops. It's only been used twice, one time more dire than the other.

I leave Caro to pack a bag and still at the sight before me. The rooms are destroyed. Cabinets kicked in, walls busted wide open and shredded to reveal the beams and studs—the framework of the room. Pills, gauges, tape, and other supplies are strewn about the floor.

"It's ruined. The entire house is a mess. So many things destroyed." Her troubled, water-filled eyes slam into me like a runaway train, and my heart stops. Unable to keep my hands to myself, I wrap her shaking body in my arms.

"Hey, it's okay." I gently glide my hand down her silky curls, rubbing small circles along the tight muscles of her back. She buries her face in my chest, the anguished heat of her cries seeping into my body.

Eventually, she lifts her head. "Do they think I have more pills?"

It isn't much of a leap to think the box we found in the clinic at one point in time had been filled with small baggies of pills.

And thanks to Elliot's text and the fact he had the compartment under the floor of the medical supply closet built, odds are he's behind those shipments and the clinic was a delivery destination. From there, the pills were smuggled out by staff, patients, or both. Or the clinic was used to deal drugs.

All of this is speculation, no proof. I've filled in holes and jumped to conclusions based on the little we have, yet sharing my theories at this point won't bode well for me.

She's too raw and unsettled, and when she discovers the clinic was used for drug trafficking, she'll lash out at the messenger. Unfortunately, that poor bastard is me.

There's still a lot I need to figure out before I share any of this with her. Besides, for the risk, effort, and trouble someone is willing to take on, as shown by last night's inferno and now tossing Caro's home, we're not talking about small change or a few drugs.

This is huge. And they're willing to go to great lengths.

Elliot is the key to all this. We must find Elliot fast.

# CARO

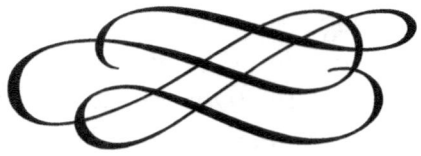

*"You should leave." My hand, secure in Kit's, rests on his muscled thigh.*

*I quickly changed while in the house, stuffing his shirt and my torn pants into a plastic bag inside a small suitcase I took with me.*

*We're in his SUV in my driveway with warm air blowing from the vents, waiting for the police to arrive. And that's why he shouldn't be here, because I don't want him implicated. But I'm more than grateful that he is. I can't imagine doing this alone.*

*"Not a chance." The intensity of his voice matches the fierce look in his eyes.*

*It's more than determination; a protective and animalistic stare drills into my soul, destroying the wall around my heart.*

*I don't deserve his unwavering protection and endless compassion. At one time, I could have included love into that mix but...I made sure to kill his love for me.*

*Fool.*

*Through the years I've been nothing but distant, and yet, this man's loyalty, his concern for my well-being has never faltered. He's been there time and time again when Nick's asked and even when not asked.*

*Reluctantly, I slip my hand from his. "You said so yourself, Holman's looking at you for this."*

*We called the police twenty minutes ago and their arrival is imminent. As much as I want to tell them everything, about the pill and vault in the clinic and even about Elliot, it makes us look like we can't be trusted or have something to hide.*

*"We're in this together." He grabs my hand again and squeezes before laying it back on his leg. While comforted by his touch, my*

stomach roils. I'm unworthy of his devotion. I was so wrong to ever leave him.

Detective Holman is the first to step from the entourage of cars and vans pulling up to the curb. They descend upon my home like you'd see in a scene from any TV crime show.

We're told to stay in the car, a cop standing sentinel, while the detective goes inside. Many minutes later, he exits, beckoning us to meet him halfway.

Holman's in the same bedraggled clothes from the night before and as surly as he was when we first met. He isn't impressed to find us involved in another incident in less than twenty-four hours. He emits a sour odor from his mouth and carries the same spiralbound notebook he had before.

"You two can't stay out of trouble, can you?" The tip of his pen scratches at his weathered face, covered in the beginnings of a gray beard. "Take me through what you found when you arrived, why you were here and so on."

His benign tone bothers me. I'm tired of his fake boredom, as if his lack of interest will get us to reveal more than if he was engaged and pleasant. Idiot.

I lie about how far into my place we went, and the sad truth is, it's getting easier to leave out details. Holman doesn't instill any kind of confidence. I'm not even sure he's competent at his job.

"Dr. Archer, you'll have to come down to the station and give an official statement. About both last night and today." He scribbles something in his notepad, and from this angle it's illegible to me, looking like chicken scratch.

I'd rather not go to the station but it doesn't sound like we have much choice.

"Mr. Jensen, you too." His once lethargic regard is suddenly laser-focused on Kit, as if trying to unnerve him.

The man beside me is wound tight, his muscles tense and bunched, and as much as Kit may want to object to or delay Holman's order, he doesn't. My respect for him grows even more, not reacting to this annoying man.

95

*I watch as the detective motions for an officer to escort us to the police station where he'll meet us. What? Does he think we're going to make a run for it?*

*As we drive to the station, Kit says, "Remember, it's better if our recall of the events or some of the details from the clinic explosion differ. If we say the exact same thing, it'll sound rehearsed."*

*I nod. I'm not worried. I've already given my account last night at the hospital and this is more of the same. He turns into the lot, parks, and meets me on my side of the vehicle.*

*"Don't stress about how you say things." He smiles, trying to reassure me. "Just keep it simple and as close to the truth as possible."*

*"I'm okay, really." I pull my jacket around me, heading toward the police officer waiting for us by the door.*

*As expected, Holman carries on his little games and power plays, leaving us in separate rooms. I wait for nearly two hours before I'm interviewed, and during that time, Nick sends a group text to Kit and me.*

**Nick: The Home is all clear. Nothing. Any word from Elliot?**

**Me: Nothing. I just called him again and got voicemail. Again.**

*My fingers hover over the keyboard, hesitating to mention the break-in at my house. Nick's already itching to come home, and I feel awful because I'm sure the last day of their vacation is anything but peaceful.*

**Kit: We're at the police station. Giving official statements.**

*I wait, wondering if Kit will say anything else, and then another text comes in from my brother.*

**Nick: OK. Kit, Paddy's going to text or call about Elliot's phone.**

*I gave him Elliot's number earlier today so they could try and locate it based on its signal.*

*Kit sends a thumbs-up emoji and that's it. They're silent for the rest of my wait. The interview is as expected. Holman asks almost the same questions from last night and asks me to write it down and sign.*

Then I'm told to wait in the front of the station while Kit's statement is taken.

"You okay?" Kit's expression is neutral but worn as he leads me to the exit of the station several hours after we arrived.

Holman watches us, scrutinizing how close we stand to each other, if we linger or anything else, as if our movements can tell him anything.

I wait until we're in the car to say anything. "I'm fine. You?" I buckle my seat belt and he nods. "Now what?"

"We pay Elliot a visit."

I never thought I'd be anxious to see Elliot, even excited, but I am. The sooner we talk to him, the closer we'll be to putting all of this behind us.

"Okay, and I can drop off the pill at the lab." I'm not sure of the significance of confirming the drug—my need is more curiosity than anything else—but I suspect Kit and Nick will know who to ask for more information based on the drug.

"Where's the lab?"

"Near the hospital."

We head downtown to University Avenue, to a stretch known as "Hospital Row" because, as it sounds, several hospitals are situated one next to the other on both sides of the multiple-lane road. When in med school, I'd interned at one and even picked up extra hours at another.

Elliot works in the ER for one of the hospitals and my friend Sanjay in a lab at another. We stop at the lab first and rather than waste time looking for a parking spot, Kit's going to drive around.

Before I get out of the car, he takes a picture of both sides of the tablet and sends Nick and me a copy of the photo.

Sanjay is alone in the lab and he smiles, expecting me as I called him on the way here. We're friends from med school, where we took pharmacology together. I've helped him out in the past, no questions asked, and he's agreed to do the same for me.

"Hello, Caro, it's been a while." He frowns as I near him. "How are you? What happened?"

Never one for a lot of makeup, I only put on what was necessary in the car while we waited for the police outside my house. But I'm not an expert, and in some spots, you can see faint scratches or bruising.

I lean in for a quick hug and smile. "I'm okay. There was a fire at the walk-in clinic I work at."

"No shit. Did anyone get hurt?"

"Fortunately, no." I hand him the little bag with the pill, sensing he'll ask more questions about the fire if I let him. "Here's the tablet. Can you find out what it is as soon as possible?"

He examines the pill and looks up at me. "First guess, I'd say oxy."

I nod; that's what I'd told him on the phone. "How quickly do you need it?"

"Like yesterday." I'm sheepish, knowing he'll have to squeeze it into whatever else he has on his plate.

"All right, I'll see what I can do."

"Thank you. Call or text me when you have something."

"Will do."

Next, we drive half a block up the street to the hospital where Elliot works. It doesn't take long to find out Dr. Foley has missed several shifts. He called in sick for the first two but as for his third shift, today, no one has heard from him. If he doesn't show up tomorrow, they're going to send someone to check on him.

Normally, this kind of information wouldn't be readily available to just anyone. Fortunately, the nurse I speak to knows me and is under the assumption Elliot and I are still dating. I don't correct her, although I have to do some fast talking to explain why I don't know where he is or why he hasn't been in to work.

Lying is becoming a habit, and I hate it even if it's for a good cause—saving my life.

Kit is where I left him, leaning against a wall in the ER waiting area. I asked him not to come with me so as not to raise any suspicion. I know a fair number of people in the ER from working here years ago, and it's easier to get information on my own.

He's oblivious or ignoring the admiring stares from several women in the waiting area. He's hard to miss, and not only because of his brawny six-foot-five frame and the T-shirt stretched across his broad shoulders.

Rough-edged good looks and just-got-out-of-bed tousled caramel locks would make anyone take a second look. And his face...oh my. Eyes dark and insanely intense. His nose slightly crooked from being broken at least once, a strong angular jaw, and those damn perfect lips. He's my kind of beautiful, and just being near him is messing with my head.

My fingers massage at my temple, banishing my heated thoughts. "Elliot has missed his last three shifts."

"What's that, three days since anyone here has seen him?" He isn't surprised, more confirming a conclusion he had already reached.

"Yes, and they've tried calling him today and nothing." I force my gaze from his defined chest back to his eyes. "We could go to his place and check things out for ourselves."

He nods, pulling car keys from his jacket pocket. "Do you know where he lives?"

"Dr. Archer, is that you?" From behind, a man's smooth drawl skates over me and I shiver, cringing.

Kit's eyes lift to meet whoever is there as I face Victor Walsh, President & CEO of the hospital, decked out in a charcoal bespoke three-piece suit.

His hair, more salt than pepper, sweeps up and off his high, smooth forehead in a classic Cary Grant coif, and his fading tan, from vacationing somewhere warm, seems darker in contrast to the gleaming pearly whites of his smile.

"Mr. Walsh." I shake his hand and force a casual smile of my own.

I'm not a fan of healthcare administrators, and in addition to the ER sucking every ounce of life from me, men like Walsh are right up there among the reasons I no longer work for a hospital.

"I thought that was you. To what do we owe the pleasure of your visit today?" He gives Kit the once-over but it's cursory, his attention squarely back to me.

"I had to drop something off for a friend. How are you?"

"I'm great, thanks. We were in St. Barts, our annual vacation. It's so lovely this time of year. But we made sure to come back in time for

Léa's investor reception. Will you be there?" He oozes fake charm and it pains me to look at him.

Yes, the party…tomorrow night. I hadn't completely forgotten about it, but with everything going on, it felt days away.

"Yes. So glad you'll be there." It takes effort not to choke on my phony words.

The man is a pompous ass and a misogynistic prick. I've heard too many rumors not to believe there must be a grain of truth in all the ugly stories.

Sadly, the success and viability of Léa's Home depends on the likes of Victor Walsh. Not only for his hefty donations, but in our efforts to gain government funding, the Victors of the world carry a lot of clout. He's well respected in the medical community and his word, in support of the Home, would go a long way.

Fortunately, not all hospital bureaucrats are pigs like him and so tomorrow's event won't be one big torture fest. Yet for the time being, I have to play the game for the good of the Home.

"I'm looking forward to it." His hand rises as if about to touch my arm but he thinks better of it, letting it fall back to his side. "Please save a dance for me."

My laughter is unnatural and like broken glass, cutting at my throat on its release. "I'll see you tomorrow night."

The thought of the party reminds me that I forgot to take something to wear when we were at my place. I'll have to call Willow and ask to borrow a dress. We're the same size.

Ready to leave, I prepare to slink away without further chitchat, but no such luck—Victor isn't done. "Caroline."

I cringe, loathing the use of my full name. Only my mother called me that, and she's my least favorite person. I glance over my shoulder at him and his brow is furrowed, scrutinizing my face.

Without any warning, his hand glides across my cheek and I pull back, sucking in a breath as something sours in my stomach.

A growl breaches Kit's tight lips and the heat of him envelops my side. "Get your hands off her."

His order startles the older man as much as it does me, and Victor drops his hand, stepping away from us.

"Apologies." Flustered or embarrassed, his bronze cheeks redden. "I meant no harm. I noticed the cuts on your face. What happened? Are you all right?"

His eyes now narrow on Kit and the accusation hangs between us like the resounding fire of gunshot. Shocking and deafening. None of us speak for a beat or two, maybe more.

"It's nothing." I find my voice, inching closer to my friend. "I just…" I grapple for whether to tell him, as it could mean more questions.

My hand slips into Kit's, seeking his comfort, and in addition to that, butterflies take flight in my stomach.

Victor will hear about what happened eventually. An explosion like that will make the gossip rounds. "There was a fire at the clinic where I work. Fortunately, no one was hurt."

"Oh, that's horrible. I'm glad to hear you're okay." He studies my features more carefully. "Are the pol—"

"It was nice seeing you." I drop Kit's hand, eager to end this conversation, and turn around, my back now to Victor.

"And you too," he murmurs.

I blow out a breath and hustle down the hall. Both of us remain quiet, lost in our own thoughts as we make our way to the car.

"Let me find Elliot's address." I use the map on my phone and enter it. Tomorrow night at the investor reception, it's going to be more of the same—endless questions about my bruises and cuts. I need to do a better job with makeup because I can't handle hours of that.

Kit drives toward the parking lot exit, clutching the steering wheel tightly. "Who was that guy?"

"He's the president and CEO of the hospital."

"Is he normally that touchy-feely?" Irritation rings in his every word.

"No. He's never touched me before." I shiver with the admission, wondering why the man crossed that unspoken line today. I do look banged up, but we aren't friends. Even if he was concerned, it gave him no reason to touch me like that.

"Asshole." He makes a sharp turn onto the highway, causing me to grab the handle of the door.

"Hey, forget about him." I want to ease his frustration. We're both tense and desperate for answers. Kit shouldn't be wasting his time on the likes of Victor Walsh.

"Wish I could." He switches lanes. "Do you have that telephone number from the labels?"

"Yes." I pull the paper from my pocket.

"Let's call it." Suddenly, my stomach twists, not prepared for what to say or what to expect.

By now, I hoped we'd have found Elliot and we needn't make this call.

"What should I say?" I tighten my jaw at the way I sound like a little girl, nervous and uncertain.

"Put it on speaker and I can do the talking." His voice is calm and confident and I relax a little.

While he drives, I dial the number using his phone, which is hooked up to the car's stereo system. On the first ring, an automated voice kicks in. "We're sorry, you have reached a number that has been disconnected or is no longer in service. If you feel you have reached this recording in error, please check your number and try your call again."

No. No. No. Not another brick wall.

"Dammit." He tightens his grip, fingers whitening around the steering wheel.

Bending my neck, I grasp my head in my hands, resting my elbows on my thighs, and sink into the seat.

"It's most probably a burner and has already been dumped. The same guy checking into Elliot's phone..." Kit pauses, looking over at me, and our eyes lock. "He can check this number out too."

The effort it takes to curve my lips into a smile is saddening and makes me all the more grateful for the man sitting across from me. "Thank you. I don't know what I'd do if I was in this alone."

"Well, you're not alone." He squeezes my thigh and his tender gaze warms me.

The sun fades beneath the pinkish-lavender sky and soon we're parking in front of Elliot's multi-million-dollar Georgian style home in Forest Hill, an affluent neighborhood in Toronto.

I've only been here once or twice before and never for too long. While the home is lovely, it's too extravagant and austere for me. Come to think of it, it's a little like its owner, Elliot.

Kit curses with just a look at the house, then gets out of the car. I track him with my eyes from the car, not sure why he reacted that way. The front of the house is hard to see given the time of day and the fast-vanishing light. Then I see it.

Yellow tape, the kind the police use to mark a crime scene and bar entry to a building, is crisscrossed over the door in an X formation. This is another blow to our chances at answers and to my sternum.

Whoever is behind this, looking for Elliot and demanding I give them something—whatever this something is—they are always several steps ahead of us.

I scramble from the car, my brain whirring with endless possibilities and my body prickling with dread.

Kit's already coming back to me, scanning the street before stopping in front of me on the lawn. His grim expression causes my arms to wrap around my middle as if to ward off any further doom.

"What do you think happened?" My pulse drums in my ears and I shiver.

"It's hard to say. It could mean a number of things…either way, it's a crime scene." He stares directly across the road at an elderly woman standing in the window of her home, unapologetically staring out at us.

Without another word, he sprints across the street, motioning to the woman to come outside. She doesn't blink or hesitate, turning from the window with a nod.

"Kit, what are you doing?" I jog after him, my stomach churning as I lower my voice as if someone might hear us. As far as I can tell, we're alone.

"Just going to ask her a few questions."

The neighbor greets us from the top step of her majestic home and the woman looks vaguely familiar. Maybe I've seen her before when at Elliot's—I can't be sure. Or maybe it's because she reminds me of Helen Mirren with her soft gray bob framing her face. She's tall and classy.

*But what's most absurd and triggers a struggle for me not to hang my mouth open, is the floor-length fur coat and chandelier diamonds dripping from her ears. She's dressed as if she's off to dine with the Queen of England.*

*"Hi, sorry to bother you. I'm Al Foley, Elliot Foley's cousin, and this is my wife, Anne." He holds my hand and I smile tightly as he inches us forward. "My cousin lives across the street." He points to the home.*

*"Judy Richardson." Her haughty tone is almost cold but not quite, as if her curiosity prevents her from being downright rude. "I know Dr. Foley. Nice man…or at least that's what I thought."*

*Kit quirks a brow and as much as I want him to delve into her last comment, he doesn't.*

*"Nice to meet you, Mrs. Richardson." He extends his hand and she offers the top of hers.*

*She expects him to kiss it. Without pause, he plays the part, bringing her milky white hand to his lips. "I was hoping you could help me."*

*Seamlessly, he shifts from charming gentleman to concerned relative, fidgeting and worrying a frown as he peers over his shoulder at Elliot's home.*

*"I haven't been able to reach him and we were worried so I thought we'd swing by and check on him. What happened?"*

*The elderly woman softens her gaze at the big guy beside me. "Oh, dear, I can't say for sure what's going on over there. But whatever it is, it's not good."*

*Shit. Is this why Elliot hasn't responded? Something's happened to him?*

*She inches forward, now standing beside us and looking across the street at the dark home with the loud yellow tape marking the door.*

*"I haven't seen Dr. Foley in days. But the other night…" She grips his forearm with her frail, vein-wrinkled hand, and the ruby on her ring finger, the size of an eyeball, winks at me.*

*"I'm no busybody but this neighborhood is my home. It's safe. We're fine upstanding people." She pauses, looking for our agreement, which we readily provide with quick nods. "I've been here since*

marrying my beloved George, may he rest in peace, and I make it my business to make sure nothing untoward is going on, you know."

Her finger waggles and we nod again, wordlessly encouraging her to go on. It's only a hunch, but all this has to be connected to the men at the clinic, Elliot, me...all of it.

I'm concerned for Elliot, sure I am, but I'm more anxious to understand more about these people who are after me. They have already made it clear they aren't afraid to threaten or do harm, but just how far are they willing to go?

"I'm a light sleeper and just happened to be passing the window the other night when I couldn't believe my eyes."

Mrs. Richardson leans in and lowers her voice, looking left then right as if someone might be lurking nearby.

"Three big men, all in black, broke into Dr. Foley's house in the dead of night. They kicked the door in, and at first the alarm caused quite a racket, but it didn't last long. They must have known the code, or guessed at it, or something." Her slight frame trembles and I feel the fear in my bones.

"What did you do?" My words are shaky.

"Well, I called the police. I was worried Dr. Foley was in there." Now she's wringing her hands and staring earnestly at Kit. "Like I said, on that night, I hadn't seen him in two days, which isn't unusual. The man's a doctor, you know, and works all kinds of odd hours, but what if he was home?"

"I understand." He offers a low, solemn response, giving the woman all of his attention. "What happened next?"

"They destroyed the place. All the lights were on. They weren't in the least bit concerned about being quiet. The police didn't arrive in time—they missed them by mere minutes." She tuts her tongue against the roof of her mouth and shakes her head in dismay.

I wrap my arms around my middle, suddenly colder. The woman is visibly distraught and I sense her eagerness to talk about this, to feel like she's doing something. The feeling is mutual. I'm irritated, almost angry with how much effort we've put in and have so little to show for it. This sounds like another one of those moments.

"Did you talk to the police that night?" Briefly, Kit searches my expression, checking in on me, and I put on my best I'm okay look.

"Why, yes. They had me on the phone with the operator until they arrived. Lovely woman I spoke to. So calm and kind. Then they came to my house. It was quite upsetting. This is a good neighborhood. I've never seen such unsavory beasts on these streets. I don't know what Dr. Foley has gotten himself into..." Mrs. Richardson trails off, looking to both of us, as if hoping we can fill in the blanks.

"Do you know who you spoke to from the police? I'd like to be able to talk to them and find out more." He steadies the woman, who's frail and wobbly, while she nods.

"Yes, yes. I have his card right here." One hand slides into the pocket of her fur coat and she produces a business card, shaking as she hands it to Kit.

He holds the card to the light over the doorway. The Toronto Police logo is the first thing to catch my eye, then the bold black letters of Detective Jack Holman.

Shit. This doesn't feel like a good thing.

I don't know much about how the police work, but Toronto's a large city. The precinct Holman works out of is nowhere near here and yet he's working both the clinic explosion and the break-in at Elliot's house? Something isn't right and I don't believe this is a coincidence.

# KIT

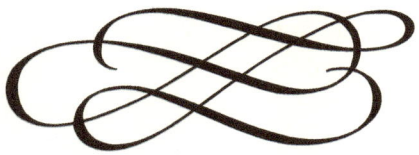

*"All right, call me when you can." I end the call and Caro stares at me expectantly.*

*Today, Friday, is the investor party, and we've spent most of the day waiting around for more information. Finding Elliot is still our best shot but we need a lead.*

*And Maggie and Nick are back today. Then Caro goes to stay with them. I should be ecstatic about that, although I have no intentions of leaving Nick and Caro to figure this out on their own. But I'm not happy about the idea of her leaving. I'm dreading it.*

*"What did your contact with the police say?" She's impatient, pushing from the counter in my direction. We're in a holding pattern until we have something more to go on.*

*"We got interrupted, so he's going to call back. But like I thought, the phone number on the label is a dead end. A burner phone. And as for Elliot's phone, Holman's already on it so Paddy couldn't do too much digging. But what he does know for sure is, they haven't found Elliot. His house was broken into, but Elliot wasn't there so the police don't know if anything was taken."*

*"Holman's all over this."*

*"Yeah, it looks that way. And while Holman could argue we should have said something to him about Elliot, don't you find it telling that he hasn't mentioned Elliot to us? Questioned us about him?"*

*"Yes, why is that?" She cocks her head to one side, puzzled.*

*"Not sure. It's most probably a test." I rake a hand through my hair. "And my guess is we're failing."*

*"A test?"*

"Yeah, he doesn't trust us, and we haven't said anything about Elliot so he might figure we're hiding something, or that we don't know anything at all."

"I know this is ironic to say given we haven't been completely honest with him, but it's hard to trust Holman. So now what?" Her frustration is clear in the way she twists her lips.

"Have you heard anything from your friend at the lab?"

"No, I—" My phone rings and she pauses.

"I have to take this. It's him again."

Padraig Owen is a career cop with only a few years left until retirement, and once upon a time, he was on Nick's payroll. Caro didn't want to know about those kinds of things back then and she sure as hell doesn't want to know now. All she knows is he's with the police, he's well connected, and his information has always been solid.

Nick called him in the day after the explosion. It had been a long time since we'd talked to him. Part of going legit means cutting ties with dirty cops. But this situation called for a reunion.

Paddy helped arrange a crew to check the Home for explosives and he was also looking into tracking Elliot down through his phone. After last night at Foley's place and the neighbor handing us Holman's card, I called Paddy and asked him to look into Holman as well.

If anyone can help with getting answers on Holman, it's Paddy.

The detective is working the Foley break-in, Caro's too, and Elliot's possible disappearance, plus the clinic explosion. Both incidents were in vastly different neighborhoods attached to different police stations in the city. Someone had to have deliberately assigned him those cases, or Holman somehow made it so.

"Hey, Paddy, can you talk now?"

"Kit, my boy, yeah. Sorry about that before. I had to talk to the boss. Listen, where were we? Oh yeah, I've got some interesting stuff. I had to be discreet—nosing around cases and a detective that I have no cause to be isn't good for my health." He laughs and it comes out more like a smoker's phlegm-coated cough.

I cringe at the thought of him hacking up a lung. "Hit me."

Caro's phone rings and she answers, walking into the bedroom, probably so we can both talk without disrupting each other.

"Well, as I'm sure you've already figured out, Holman's approach to things is...let's just say questionable. It isn't clear if he's dirty, but it's safe to say there ain't a loyal bone in his body. His allegiance is to himself and money."

I bite back my laugh at his hypocrisy. He could just as well be talking about himself. As a cop, Paddy's done things he shouldn't for money. "What else?"

Caro stands at the doorway to the bedroom, staring at me. Her call was quick and she doesn't look any more or less hopeful than she did before.

"And you were right, Holman called in markers to get assigned both cases."

"Thanks, Paddy." I rake a hand through my hair, the knot in my chest loosening at what I already suspected, despite having more questions than answers with this news.

"But that ain't all. It's the weirdest thing and definitely cause for concern—Holman's a detective with the Drug Enforcement Unit. It makes no sense for him to show up at the clinic explosion unless there's a known drug affiliation with that location and the same goes for Foley's B and E. I found nothing, although, like I said, I could only dig so far."

"Shit." And the knot is back tenfold. The elephant sitting on my chest makes it hard to breathe.

This isn't enough to say if Holman is working for the bad guys, maybe on their payroll to find Elliot, or working another angle. Basically, we have to be extra careful where Holman is concerned.

"I'm not done. Holman also has a BOLO out on Foley. And get this, you and Caro Archer are listed as persons of interest."

"Why are we being flagged? We aren't hiding." Although maybe we aren't as easy to find as some would think. If Holman is working with whoever is behind this, they'd know how to find Caro, know she's with me. So far, we're safe at my place. This could mean Holman has another agenda. But what?

"Nah, you don't have to be hiding. It's a way to be alerted if your names come up in any calls or investigations where the police are involved. You're entered into the CPIC and if your name pops up, the OIC, in this case, Holman, will get a call."

"Paddy, slow down and speak English."

He full-on guffaws and the sounds spewing across the line make me want to gag. I'm surprised he's still standing with the way he smokes and drinks.

"CPIC stands for Canadian Police Information Centre. It's a database for info on anyone of special interest to or under surveillance by police; all charges and convictions—"

"Got it. And OIC, that means officer in charge?"

"Sure does."

"Okay, so Holman knows about the connection between Foley and Caro. He just isn't sharing."

Great, just what we need, or more specifically what I need. Caro doesn't have a record, I do. And if Holman has a "be on the lookout" for us then he does suspect us of more than being in the wrong place at the wrong time.

"It looks that way." He coughs once more.

"Thanks, Paddy. Appreciate it."

"Sure thing, Kit. Watch your back."

"Will do."

"And say hi to Nicky for me." He's on the cusp of another coughing fit and I end the call.

Caro clears her throat. "What about Holman?"

"Like we thought, he shouldn't be on both cases. Something isn't right."

I hesitate to mention the BOLO. Telling her he's got his eye on both of us will only cause her to worry even more.

"So we continue being careful around Holman." She inches toward the photographs once more. Since staying here, she's stopped there several times, drawn to those images on the wall. "Do you think he'll mention Elliot to us?"

"Yeah. My guess is he's waiting for the right moment to catch us off guard." Like before, I step in behind her and also take in those I care about the most in this world.

"Most probably." She points to my favorite photograph, her tone carrying a faraway quality to it.

The image is of Caro in my lap, cupping my face. Neither of us are looking at the camera. We only have eyes for each other. Not even a second after the picture was taken, I'd kissed her, never wanting to let her go.

"Who called you?" I rub at the stubble on my jaw, dipping my gaze to the floor, unable to linger on the photo or the memory anymore.

Especially with her next to me but no longer mine.

"That was my friend from the lab." She swivels abruptly away from the wall to face me and holds up her splintered phone. "He confirmed it's OxyContin, one hundred and sixty milligrams."

She blows out a breath, glancing back to the pictures. It's brief and then something shifts as if shutters block out the past. I get it, recognize it all too well.

"What do you think it means?" Caro's wicked smart and knows full well what all of this means. She either refuses to accept what's right in her face or she needs someone—me—to spell it out for her.

I'd rather not be the one but I'm not going to pussy out now. Maybe a dose of reality will jog her memory.

"Your clinic was getting shipments of OxyContin, and from the looks of that box and the container under the floor, in large amounts." With one more look at the pictures, the past, I head to the kitchen for water. "This could mean the clinic was a place to hold the stuff temporarily, before it hit the street, or someone was dealing out of the clinic."

"No." She's right behind me and adamant. "I would have known if the clinic was being used to deal drugs."

Rounding the corner into the kitchen, I catch the flush on her face before she dips her head to stare at her painted toes. We both know that isn't necessarily true. She had no knowledge of the drugs being shipped to the clinic, so it isn't a stretch to think there could have been a lot more going on right under her nose.

"Hey, none of this is your fault." My hand clasps her elbow and she lifts her head.

Guilt and shame swim in her eyes. *"Then whose fault is it? I'm the one in charge at the clinic. I should have known about the drugs and the renovations to the storage closet. Damn, Elliot."*

*"Exactly, Elliot's to blame. We need to talk to him."*

*"We have to find him first, and we can't be sure he's a willing participant in whatever this is. You saw his house. He could be in danger or worse."* Her concern hits me in the gut like a sucker punch.

*Is she giving Elliot the benefit of the doubt because she still cares for him? A pall of bitter disappointment falls over me like a shadow.*

*"Caro, he might be in danger, but he brought this on himself."* I step closer, pausing until she looks me in the eyes. *"I'd bet my life he's involved you in his mess. Why aren't you pissed off at him?"*

*She opens her mouth to say something, and at the same time, there's a sharp knock at my door.*

# KIT

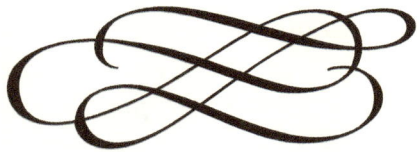

"It might be Nick." I check my phone for any texts as he'd sent one about a half hour ago saying he was close.

Before I even reach the door, it opens and Logan bounds into the room, the key I gave him in hand. "Yo, Boo, I'm back."

He's grinning from ear to ear and his infectious laugh has me doing the same as he pulls me into a bear hug, slapping my back a few times.

"What are you doing here? I thought you'd be back next week?" We pull apart.

I'm glad he's here. The timing is perfect, another man on the job, but it's also curious. He heads into my place, steps faltering at the sight of Caro.

She smiles sheepishly, waving at him, and his eyes widen, blink, and then his light blue irises gleam with what looks like both happiness and mischief.

"Holy shit, I take off for a couple of months and you two get back together again?" He chuckles, rubbing his hands together, and I want to slap my hand over his big mouth.

Before either of us can set him straight, he rushes at Caro, picking her up into his arms and twirling her around. She squeals and laughs, hitting at his shoulder, demanding to be put down.

"You dirty dogs, thank fuck." He places her on her feet. "I thought this day would never come."

She's straightening her shirt and brushing back some of her curls from her face when her expression sobers. "We aren't together."

If ever there's a way to kill a mood, Caro succeeds. Like announcing last call at a bar, his shoulders slump along with his *demeanor. And I'm speechless, not wanting to touch this awkward as fuck topic.*

*"Shit." He saunters to the couch, dropping onto the middle cushion and lifting his feet onto the coffee table. "Nick asked me to get home ASAP. He said he had good news and bad news and needed my help. When I saw you two together, I figured this was the good." His finger points to Caro, then to me and back again before falling to his side.*

*"Nick called you?" This explains the timing and it makes sense. We could use more help. Time is running out.*

*"Good news and bad news?" She's worried, gazing at me. "Do you know what the good news is?"*

*We can both guess at the bad news. There's plenty of that to go around. As for good news, I shake my head, completely in the dark. We could use some good news about now.*

*"They should be here any minute now." He twirls first the ring on the middle finger of his right hand and then the ring on his pointer finger and repeats the sequence again. It's something he does when he's anxious or bored. "I dumped my stuff and came straight here. His text said he was parking."*

*Logan lives in the same building, a few floors down. He's the reason I moved into these lofts, but the bastard's never here. He's a drifter, preferring to spend weeks, months at a time on the road.*

*He wasn't always like that.*

*There's another sharp knock and I open the door to an anxious Nick. He barges in before I have a chance to fully get out of the way. His worried gaze briefly lands on me before skating to his sister.*

*Barely acknowledging Logan, he bypasses any greeting to get to Caro, yanking her into his arms. She lets out a shocked oof followed by an awkward laugh.*

*"You okay?" He combs back her hair and gently rubs a thumb over one of the scratches on her cheek.*

*She nods and I sense Maggie at my side. Lightly nudging my arm, she clears her throat, prompting me to look down at her.*

*Mystical blue eyes soothe my tormented soul in a way only Maggie can. "Hey, how are you?"*

114

My smile for her is weak at best. "I've been better. At least we're still in one piece."

Her smile is rueful and she shakes her head, knowing better than to admonish my twisted attempt at levity. Logan steps up to us, wrapping Maggie into his arms.

"Nomad, it's so good to see you," Maggie calls him by his road name, something he picked up travelling the Americas on his bike.

"You, too, gorgeous." Logan puts her back on her feet.

Caro waves at her from Nick's embrace. Maggie is the only one I've ever talked to about Caro.

Nick was there from the beginning, knows our history, but except for the day he learned Caro and I were an item, he's never said a thing about us.

It's like your parents having sex. Some topics you never want to think about, let alone talk about. That day in high school, when he saw us holding hands, he stormed up to us and ordered Caro to leave. Of course, fearless, she refused.

He threatened to kill me if I ever hurt his baby sister. Funny thing is, I don't think any of us saw what happened coming. His baby sister hurt me.

After the threat, we laughed even though Nick wasn't joking. And since then, he's said nothing despite his opinions. He has them, that much is obvious, but he keeps them to himself.

Maggie, on the other hand, she worked her magic and I spilled my guts without any hesitation. Truth be told, I wanted to talk about my fucked-up relationship with Caro, or lack of it. I just never...I never had someone I could say those things to.

Nick and I are tight, but he was a no-man's-land when it came to his sister. And Logan...he'd rather have a root canal than get real about pretty much anything.

When Maggie came onto the scene, all it took was one look at Caro and me and she knew we had a connection. History. Or as she put it, she couldn't miss the sizzling tension between us, and slowly she got me to open up.

"This must be hard," she whispers once Logan is out of earshot.

She's referring to me being stuck with Caro, worrying about her safety, after a year of no contact.

I nod, the growing lump in my throat making it difficult to swallow much less speak. Nick and Caro are talking and Logan's nosing around.

"Hey, Nomad." Nick shoves playfully at our wayward friend who rests his chin on Caro's shoulder.

Logan chuckles, Caro hip-checks him, and Nick slings an arm around his sister's neck. "Okay, everyone's here. Bring us up to speed."

He turns to me, but Caro starts with her arrival at the clinic the other night and we take turns covering the events leading up to now. Nick and Maggie aren't learning anything new. I've been keeping Nick apprised of the situation every step of the way. Most of this is for Logan's benefit.

The only new information is Paddy's call about Holman and the confirmation of the drug. Once we're done, Logan asks a few questions, nothing we haven't asked ourselves.

"We have the investor party tonight at Casa Loma." Nick's gaze is on Logan. "I need all of you there."

He isn't looking at me and I'm grateful he misses my flinch at the news of attending tonight's bash. Normally, I wouldn't be invited to something like this, mainly because of Caro. The Home is her turf and anywhere she is, I steer clear.

"Are the drinks free?" Logan rubs his hands together and Caro snorts, rolling her eyes.

Nick narrows his gaze and lowers his terse tone. "Yeah, but you won't be having any. I need you on your game. All of you. We are running out of time until who knows what happens."

He's referring to the text with a time limit of forty-eight hours. What happens once the clock runs out is anyone's guess, but no doubt, it won't be good.

"Are you worried something is going to happen tonight?" His sister slips out of his hold, folding her arms over her middle protectively.

"They will strike again, and we can't assume they're going to stick to the time limit they gave us." I walk to Caro's side, gently placing a reassuring hand on her shoulder. "They want something. My guess is drugs or money or maybe Elliot. Or shit, all three. And they think you know something or are keeping it hidden."

"Yeah. They're most probably lying low. The clinic explosion and ransacking Elliot's house brought the cops, or if we got lucky, they may have lost track of you." Nick saunters to the fridge and pulls out a few bottles of water.

He hands one to Maggie. "Anyone want one?" We shake our heads and he takes a bottle for himself and puts the rest back in the fridge. "We have to work on the assumption they know about the Home and so tonight would be a good place to pick up your trail again."

"If this Detective...Holman's dirty, isn't it possible he's in on this?" Logan perches on a kitchen chair and Nick and I nod. "Then, he'd know where Caro is and about Kit's involvement."

"True, but if so, why haven't they made a move?" I ask. That's what I've been mulling over since Paddy's call. "Someone should have paid us a visit here. I'm thinking Holman doesn't know about the texts or isn't working for whoever is behind this, and he's coming at us another way."

Nick nods and Caro paces, her expression tight and closed off. A snarl tears out of me and I clench my fists as eyes land on me. I want to whisk her away from all this. If only it were that simple.

"Or Holman isn't on the inside but he's aware something's going on and wants in on it." Maggie rests her near-empty water bottle on the counter. "Maybe that's why he made it so he was on both cases. He's hoping to find something he can barter with to get a cut?"

That had crossed my mind but none of those scenarios make me feel any better. Holman is an unknown quantity, and while we should be able to trust a cop, we can't.

"Yeah, that's possible." Logan taps his foot on the floor, squirming in his chair. "Kit, have you noticed anyone following you?"

"No. I thought we might get a tail after going to Elliot's but nothing."

"Let's keep all possibilities open until we know more. Holman may just be a dirty fucker and have nothing to do with this. Just looking to seize on the opportunity." Nick dumps the bottle into the recycling and leans against the counter. "Although I'd bet otherwise. That's why we need all of us on the lookout tonight. We're also going to be without Maggie."

I tense, not understanding why Maggie wouldn't be involved. She's capable and Nick knows it. Besides, if she doesn't want to be relegated to the sidelines, Nick doesn't stand a chance of getting his way.

"Nick, we didn't agree to this." She straightens, firming her jaw at the same time Caro wrinkles her forehead and says, "What? Maggie's worked her ass off on tonight. This is more hers than anybody's. What do you mean she's not going?"

"Thanks, Caro." Maggie gives her a warm smile and then turns her sharp gaze back to her man. "I want to be there."

"Not a chance."

Someone knocks on the door, and silence falls upon us. My building has security, and no one gains entry without having their own code or calling someone in the building to let them in.

Whoever's outside my door didn't call to be let in. It could be nothing or they could have slipped in unannounced to gain the element of surprise. The thought chills me. Is this the visit I've been expecting? The guys hunting down Caro.

# CARO

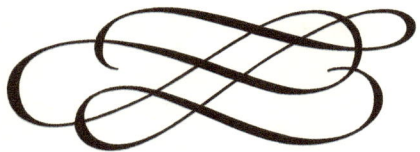

"Are you expecting someone?" Nick lowers his voice, tensing his body, ready for action.

Kit shakes his head and motions for us to go into the bedroom. My brother nods sharply and grabs Maggie's hand and then mine, pulling us to the back of the loft with Logan bringing up the rear.

Nick and Logan make sure Maggie and I are in the room first and then the two crowd the exit to prevent anyone from entering or leaving the room. This is my mess and I hate how it's putting everyone in danger.

A minute passes and Nick whispers to me, "Isn't that woman from the clinic?"

He makes room for me to peer into the room. Kit's at the entrance, back to me, and now standing directly in front of the person at the door.

"Just wait a sec." Nick tightens his hold around my middle as we wait for Kit to shift his weight and reveal who he is talking to.

Kit's deep rumble of a voice carries through the loft. I can't make out what he says, but judging by his tone, it isn't friendly.

A woman responds and something about the voice, though muted, is familiar. Sally? Why would I think about her? I hardly know the woman, and I doubt Kit would talk to her like that.

Like a slap to the forehead, it hits me. Willow. I called her earlier today asking to borrow a dress for tonight's event.

"That's Willow. It's okay." I tap Nick's arm and he lets me go and I enter the room. "Kit, that's Willow. Please let her in."

"Caro, hi." Willow peers around the big man in front of her, relief seeping into her concerned expression.

Kit relaxes and steps aside, letting her enter the loft.

*"I was just dropping off the dress."* She holds up a white garment bag, and in her other hand, she carries a bright pink toiletries case.

Makeup—yes. I'd only grabbed the basics from my house, and I needed more than that to cover up the scrapes and bruises on my face.

*"Thank you."* I take the hanger from her. *"Come in."*

Kit leads the way and joins Nick and the others in the living room.

*"I didn't call up because my hands were full. I was fumbling to hit the buzzer when a woman held open the door for me."* She laughs nervously, casting furtive glances at Kit as her long blonde ponytail swishes over her shoulder.

Her explanation is more for him than me, and I wonder what exactly he said to her.

*"Thank you very much, I really appreciate this."* I hold up the dress. *"You saved me from having to buy one."* With my house vandalized, it's now a police scene and I won't be allowed back for a while.

My arm slides around her shoulders for a quick hug. *"Willow, you remember Nick and Maggie."*

They say their hellos and I cast a glance at Kit, who is still a little wary. *"And this is Kit."* I hold out my hand in his direction.

*"Hi. Sorry about that."* He lets out a ragged breath and his shoulders finally relax.

She smiles but it doesn't reach her eyes, still nervous. I get it although I find it comical. Despite his appearance, large and muscled, and the violence that surrounded him for so many years, he's a gentle soul. It doesn't mean he won't use his strength if needed, but he's the first to try reasoning with someone before resorting to his fists.

Logan clears his throat, and a charmed smile plays along his lips as his blue eyes sparkle playfully. *"Aren't you going to introduce me?"*

*"Relax, I didn't forget you."* Of course, Logan chooses now of all times to flirt. *"Willow, this is Logan."*

He takes her hand, holding it between both of his, and unleashes his megawatt, lady-killer smile. *"Hello, Willow."*

It's a low sexy rumble. She flushes and I tilt my head back, groaning. "Back off, stud." I push at his chest, forcing him to release her hand.

Logan's a great guy, one of the best, but he's always on the run. He's been badly hurt by a woman and because of that, he spends more time on the road than here at home. The last thing I want is for him to hurt Willow when he ups and leaves.

My friend gets control of herself, coercing a tight smile onto her mouth, then turning to me. "I should get going. I know you have to get ready. But before I do, I remembered something about the clinic renovations that might help."

"Oh, what?" I temper my eagerness but Nick echoes my question, more insistent than me.

I glare at him, hoping he gets my drift to back off as I sense Willow's hesitancy. She isn't in the thick of this, but all that has happened is unnerving to say the least.

"It's okay," I reassure her. "You can say anything in front of them. We're working together."

"Well, I don't know if you remember, but the renovations happened around the same time I started working at the clinic. I was volunteering at the Home first."

She's active in the community and was working a few afternoons a week at the Home as part of our volunteer program. We'd hit it off the first day, and when she mentioned she was looking for a job in the daylight hours—she'd be on the night shift for too long at a hospital— I encouraged her to apply to the clinic.

I nod, encouraging her to go on.

"I wasn't at the clinic often, but I remember Elliot stressing to all of us that the back of the clinic, the work that was being done, was off-limits."

An uncomfortable flush climbs up my spine. I wish I'd been more focused on what Elliot was doing back then. This, right here, is reason for alarm. He made a point of keeping people away while the work was done.

"How long did the job take?" Nick asks.

"About two weeks." Willow looks to me. We had already covered most of this in our conversations after the clinic explosion. "I'd forgotten Flora was also working there at the time." She fidgets with her fingers.

Flora is a nurse, and at the time, she worked the intake desk at the clinic. Willow didn't have a lot of interaction with her but even limited, it wasn't pleasant. Flora is a hard person to like.

"Yes, I remember." Or at least now I do. When Flora left the clinic, I gave Willow her full-time position.

"She doesn't work there anymore?" Maggie asks.

"No." Willow looks from Maggie to me. "I don't know why I didn't think of it before, but Flora was the only one allowed back there. Elliot left her in charge, and get this—the construction company used for the job were her brothers."

"Really? Why didn't I know any of this?" The questions are more for myself than Willow but she straightens, her eyes growing round as if I've put her on the spot. "Sorry, I'm not blaming you. It's more that I'm surprised I didn't know this or think to ask at the time."

"You might not remember, but Elliot made it seem like a huge surprise for you." Her tone carries a hint of scorn at the mention of him and in light of what this all means, I can't say I blame her.

We've never talked about Elliot, other than work-related stuff, but I had the impression she didn't particularly like him. She likely held her tongue because I was dating him. I wish I'd asked or been more attuned to my reservations about him back then.

"When he showed me the renovated room, he made it seem like I'd complained about the supply closet or something."

She nods, wrinkling her brow and twisting her lips. "Yes, and while the work was being done, he made a big deal out of it and didn't want any of us to burden you with all of the details."

"What's Flora's last name? And do you remember the name of the construction company?" Kit pulls out his phone, glancing up at Willow.

"Brown," Willow says at the same time I say, "Flora Brown."

*He groans at the common last name and Willow continues, "Off the top of my head, I can't remember the company name, but I'm pretty sure we would have it in our records."*

*"The clinic's gone. The files must be destroyed," Logan says as if needing to remind us. I'll never forget the explosion.*

*"True, but most of our files are electronic. All invoices are scanned and archived," Willow says.*

*"Not only beautiful but smart." Logan winks at her and I roll my eyes.*

*"Okay, enough with the flirting." Nick's patience is wearing thin.*

*"I can't help myself." Logan flashes a self-deprecating smile and Willow looks away, uncomfortable. I glare at him, giving him my best cut it out look.*

*"What about Flora Brown? Do either of you know how to get in touch with her?" Kit moves us right along, now focused on his phone. "You don't want to know how many Flora or F Browns there are in the city."*

*"I can get her home number from our files." Willow shoves her hands into her pockets and I smile, thankful for her help.*

*"That's if she hasn't changed numbers. How up to date are your files?" Nick steps closer to us.*

*"I updated the files just before Flora and Elliot left, and that was five months ago." There's something to Willow's tone that pokes at my insides, and the sensation only intensifies when she avoids my gaze, staring past my shoulder.*

*"Elliot and Flora left at the same time?" Kit's pointed question sucks all the air out of the room like a knife to a balloon as it connects with the strange vibe I'm getting from Willow.*

*"Were Elliot and Flora close?" Logan's now at my back, stepping into Willow's line of sight.*

*"No," I say while Willow says, "Yes."*

*"Yes?" I cock my head to the side and wrinkle my nose, traveling back to that time at the clinic, trying to recall something I may have blocked. It is possible I never noticed anything more between Elliot and Flora?*

"Ye-s-s." She pauses, evading my gaze by looking to Kit. "Flora worshipped Elliot. He could ask her to do anything, and she'd do it without question. I always figured she'd left and gone to work with him but I can't say for sure."

"Okay, let's start there." I try to keep my voice neutral, not wanting her to think she's upset me. She hasn't.

There's something niggling at the back of my mind, but it isn't Elliot and Flora. It's more Willow's reaction to this topic. Why is she avoiding me? Does she think I'm upset she didn't say anything about Elliot and Flora? Does she think she should have said something to me at the time?

I shake my head, trying to let it go. "In addition to getting us Flora's number, can you check where she's working now? Elliot's at—"

She cuts me off. "I know where he is. The clinic still gets the odd call for Elliot and I've had to pass along the messages. I should get going"—she turns toward the door— "and leave you guys to get ready for tonight. If you need anything else, let me know. I'm here to help in any way."

At the door, she spins to face us and rests her eyes on me. Her expression is more like herself, tender and kind, and my heartbeat hits its natural rhythm once again. We're okay.

"Thanks for everything, and I'll call you tomorrow." I give her a hug and everyone says goodbye.

I shut the door and rest my back on the door. "Well, it looks like we have something to go on now. Hopefully Flora will have some useful information, like what the hell Elliot was doing."

It's wishful thinking, but if they were an item, there's a chance. A slim chance but it's something.

"Yeah, I think we should talk to Flora first thing tomorrow, in person." Kit places his phone on the counter. "We've got a couple of hours until the party."

He sounds about as excited as I am for the reception tonight. As much as I'd like to miss it, I can't, and that thought reminds me of our conversation before Willow arrived.

"Nick, what were you saying about Maggie not going tonight?"

*Maggie opens her mouth to say something but my brother beats her to it. "Yes. We've got some good news." He pauses as a face-splitting smile dawns across his face. "Maggie's pregnant."*

*"What?" I bounce on my feet and run to them, pulling them both into a hug.*

*Kit and Logan are next to congratulate the new parents-to-be. I'm laughing and tears spring to my eyes, unable to control the overwhelming sense of joy filling my chest.*

*My brother is going to be a father.*

*"How far along are you?" I wipe at the tear slipping from the corner of my eye.*

*"I'm just three months, so it's still early." Maggie holds up her hand in caution but she's beaming.*

*"That's why she isn't going tonight." Nick wraps his arms around her middle, hand splayed against her still flat stomach. "I don't want her anywhere near this. And Caro, you're going to have to stay with Kit for now."*

*"Okay." I'm not wild about the idea of imposing any more than I already have on Kit, but I agree, it's best to keep Maggie out of this.*

*And truth be told, I want to stay with Kit even with everything that's going on. This feels like a second chance. Like maybe once all of this is behind us, we might be able to try again.*

*I don't know if that's something he even wants. He could be with Sally.*

*"That's cool." Kit's tone is casual, as unaffected as if we're talking about the possibility of snow tomorrow, and it pisses me off.*

*I can't tell if it really is fine or if he's as anxious as I am at the idea of being stuck together. Or maybe it's something else and he's just doing a really good job of hiding it? Am I imagining a hint of heat in his gaze?*

*He has already made arrangements with Maggie to skip the garage until I can return home safely. This means it's just the two of us, with only this situation to keep us busy, all day and all night.*

*My heart thunders and I place a hand over my chest, willing the organ into a steady rhythm. But it's useless. I can't get a hold of this unbridled sensation coursing through me.*

*Smashed to pieces by my own doing, my heart has never felt so alive, and I'm scared. It's as if someone's breathed life and hope back into me.*

*And now, how the hell am I going to keep the few pieces of my heart together as I deny myself the man I love?*

# KIT

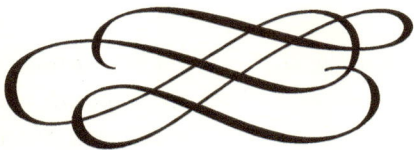

*"I'll be at the party tonight, but after that, I'm not taking the lead on this."* Nick's tortured tone breaks the unspoken tether between Caro and me.

*He's not happy with sitting this out—he never has before—but Maggie and the baby must come first.*

*"Absolutely. I'm on it."* Welcoming the relief at no longer being captive to Caro's pointed stare and also needing to reassure Nick, my tone conveys my commitment to keeping his sister safe. At all costs.

*"Good. And Logan's backup."* Nick rakes a hand through his dark hair. *"I'll be in the background. Throw the grunt work my way. I'll make the calls. I'll do the research, but you and Logan have to be out there."*

*Maggie rubs at his arm to soothe his guilt. Nick's a take-charge kind of person, and taking a back seat when his sister is in danger is difficult for him.*

*"I've got your back."* Logan pats my shoulder and I don a wry grin. *"We better get a move on. The party is in two hours."*

*"Yeah. We're heading home, and I'll see you there."* Nick hugs Caro, dipping his chin in goodbye at both Logan and me.

*Maggie and I hug once more.* *"Congrats, you're going to make an awesome mom."*

*"Thanks, Kit."* She bites at her lip to stop from crying, and Logan, always the one to lighten the mood, swoops in and wraps his arms around the two of us.

*Once we're alone, Caro grabs Willow's things and takes them into the bedroom for a shower. Since there's only one tub in the loft, I gather my tux and other things, preparing to shower, shave, and dress once she's done.*

*Yeah, I have a tux. Dressing up was never my thing, but since working at the garage and dealing with vintage cars with huge price tags, I've had to attend many events and auctions where you need to dress the part.*

*While I wait, I read the text Sally sent an hour ago. She wants to see me, and I'm at a loss as to how to respond. Our ship has sailed, and I'm still ambivalent as to whether I ever wanted a ticket aboard. I have to tell her as soon as Caro is safe.*

*She's a great person, but starting something, or even exploring something, with any other woman feels wrong. That's my problem. Any woman who isn't Caro feels wrong.*

*Not wanting to dwell on this, I check my messages. There's only one, a short terse message from Mr. Pinter about his Ford. I can't help but feel like I'm blowing this opportunity.*

*I dial his number, glancing up at the closed bedroom door, hoping I have enough time to make the call before Caro is out.*

*My work isn't a secret, but Caro has the uncanny ability of seeing through me like glass. One look and she'll know how important this purchase is to me and being able to pull my own weight at the Phoenix. No one has accused me of anything, but I don't want people to think I'm riding Maggie's coattails.*

*The old man picks up on the second ring.* "Pinter."

"Mr. Pinter, it's Kit Jensen."

"Mr. Jensen, I'm surprised to hear from you. From your silence and neglect, I had the distinct impression you were no longer interested." *His disdain laces every word.*

*Shit. Did I just lose this sale? Bile burns its way up my throat.*

"That isn't the case. I'm still very interested, Mr. Pinter." *I amble over to the window, staring out at the mauve sky.* "There's just a lot going on right now and unfortunately my schedule has been upended."

*I flinch at the deep-throated harrumph crackling through the phone line.* "Mr. Jensen, don't ever ignore me or leave me waiting. I have two other offers on the thirty-four that I'm seriously considering."

*I'd like to give him the benefit of the doubt, but he isn't telling the truth. If he did have other offers, he wouldn't be taking my calls, especially if the offers were better than mine.*

*I did my research before reaching out to Pinter, and in addition to all of his other quirks, he's a ballbuster. Before me, a few dealers came close to closing the sale but the old man walked away each time. I can't have that happen to me.*

*When I told Maggie about the car, she was thrilled at the prospect of bringing the beauty back to its original magnificence. And we both know a job like this will only add to the buzz and profile of the Phoenix.*

*"Mr. Pinter, are you available day after tomorrow to finalize the deal?" I've already sent him the papers, and so far, he's said he's good with it.*

*Silence. He likes to leave me hanging—it's one of his quirks. I wait him out, willing to give him an earful of my breathing if that's what it takes.*

*"That sounds fine. But Mr. Jensen, this is your last chance. If you cancel or don't show up, don't call me again." We agree on a time and Pinter ends the call.*

*The mess in my gut lessens and I can't help but smile. I'm going to close this Pinter deal.*

*An hour later and Caro's waiting at the front door. She's in stilettos and a long satiny emerald gown with a side slit, the bronze of her toned leg peeking out. Her dark masses of curls are down and swept off her face.*

*I stop a few feet from her, not trusting that I'll keep my hands to myself. She is irresistible. She's tall at five feet ten, but with her heels, we're almost head to head. I could reach her mouth, kiss her, without having to bend.*

*My tongue gets stuck to the roof of my mouth and I'm unable to say a damn thing. Clenching my jaw, I force one foot in front of the other and grab my keys off the ring on the wall.*

*I barely give her a sideways glance, even more determined not to look at her when scents of jasmine and spice hit my nostrils. Why do I want what I can't have?*

"You look nice." I'm such an idiot. Is that the best I can come up with?

She doesn't seem bothered or insulted by my limited vocabulary or lack of eye contact.

"You always did clean up really well." Her plum-colored lips slide into a lopsided grin, and she steps into my space, running her hand down the front of my jacket.

My heart leaps as if trying to claw its way out of my chest, toward her hand, her touch. Steadying my breath, I go for playful, not wanting to ruin the night before it's even started.

"Well, I'm all for wearing a tux." I flash a wicked grin and she arches a brow, waiting for me to go on. "The first time I wore one, my girlfriend loved it so much, I had one of the best nights of my life."

She barks out a laugh and her head tilts back, exposing the creamy, sensual curve of her neck. Waves of silky dark curls ripple down her back, which my fingers itch to touch.

Her sheer joy, evident in that lyrical, flirtatious sound of hers, strikes low in my belly. Fuck my life, this woman.

Suddenly, she straightens and looks at me. Her cheeks are now pink, a few shades lighter than the color of her lipstick, and she's glowing.

"Oh, what a night." Her eyes darken, heating with what I'm pretty sure are memories from prom night. "It was amazing, wasn't it?"

The desire in her eyes, something I haven't seen in a while, causes my heart to skip a beat.

Not in a good way.

It hurts.

Caro hasn't looked at me like that in years, and there's nothing I can do to keep that look. To make her want to be with me, look at me, like she is right now.

I'm a decent guy and try to do good. Always. Even when I was on the wrong side of the law, as fucked up as that sounds.

But I'll never be the man she wants.

"Let's go," I choke, heart in my throat.

Traffic is heavy on most of the roadways, and the drive is filled with awkward silence. We pull into Casa Loma, a heritage landmark and one of the only true castles in North America, nearly forty-five minutes later.

Luxury vehicles line one side of the entrance, with a few drivers, some who easily double as muscle, mulling around smoking, on their phones, or chatting. A few wear jackets embossed with logos like a padlock, shield, or trident, signifying private security firms, whereas others are traditional chauffeurs. Any way you dice it, the whole set-up reeks of wealth.

Inside the Gothic revival style castle, there's a growing crowd. Women in jewels and dazzling evening gowns and men in tuxedos roam the conservatory where the reception is being held. This is so not my scene, but rather than focus on how out of place I am, I'm on high alert, constantly examining the area for any threats.

The room is centered around a breathtaking stained-glass ceiling and surrounded by windows overlooking the gardens. It must be something to see in the day with the natural sunlight setting the room aglow.

The idea behind tonight is to ply these wealthy socialites with food and drink until they're feeling so good that they'll open their hearts and wallets to the Home.

It's worked before and Maggie's good at partnering with the right people, donors themselves, to help her put together the best invitation list. From what Nick has told me, the Home is doing really well and nights like tonight make a big difference in how much they can help those in need.

Nick and Logan are easy to find, both looking just as uncomfortable as I feel among Toronto's high society. I spend my time observing our surroundings while Caro talks with this or that hospital administrator or one wealthy person or another. She's gracious and relaxed, and I get lost in just watching her.

"How you doing?" Logan sidles up beside me, sipping from a bottle of sparkling water.

"Fine. Good to have you back." I eye him warily. "Are you staying put this time?"

*He shrugs and looks away. That pretty much says it all. He'll be on the move again soon.*

*We don't talk about it, but he wasn't always a wanderer. As an only kid from a crappy home with not much of a family to speak of, he's like a brother to me and a solid friend. Always here. Until Phoebe.*

*He fell madly in love with Maggie's best friend and she broke his heart. She lives here, in Toronto, and that's why he doesn't want to be here. Or at least, that's what I think.*

"Hey, I'm like the wind. Always on the move and hard to say what direction I'll be headed tomorrow."

"Wow. Deep, man." *I grin, mimicking the sound of a pothead.*

"Shut up," *he snorts, bumping into me.* "I'll stick around until Caro's safe. After that, I can't say."

"I'm glad you're here to help out. You know, you could stick around this time. Settle down, Nomad." *I make a dig at his name. It's stupid but I'm making a point. He's got a home and doesn't need to be on the road all the time.*

"Speaking of Caro." *He narrows his eyes.* "How are you two doing?"

*My friend never shies away from the direct questions, despite not appreciating when someone does the same to him.*

"We weren't talking about Caro." *I fold my arms over my chest, staring at the woman in question as she listens with interest to an elderly lady regale her about her prize-winning roses.*

"C'mon, I'm on your side, Kit. Always thought you were good for each other."

"We're fine. Dealing, you know." *It's my turn to shrug, not willing to dwell on how good Caro and I could be if only we had the chance.* "I want her safe. Her asshole ex set her up."

"Elliot Foley?" *Logan's only heard about her ex and I nod.* "You want me to look into that?"

*He isn't a criminal—well, not like Nick and I once were—but he's on the fringes. How could he not be with his best friends up to our necks in that shit for most of our adult lives? He knows how to dip into that world, if needed.*

132

"Yeah, if you could toss Elliot's name out onto the streets and show the picture of the pill around, that would be great." He nods and that's another burden off my shoulder.

"Hey, you two all right?" Caro saunters over to us, holding what is her third or fourth glass of champagne. It's near empty save for a sip.

She's a big girl and I'm not one to count drinks or tell someone what they can or can't do, but she's been downing those babies pretty fast.

"We're good." Logan downs the little that's left in her glass. "Want another one?"

"You're not drinking tonight." I glare at my friend. I don't need two of them shitfaced. "And besides, should you be drinking with a concussion?"

"I'm fine." A silly grin is plastered on her face as she looks to Logan. "I'd love another one."

Great, she's tipsy when she should be alert and ready to react if needed. Logan grabs her glass, walking away without regard for me or what I just said. "I'll be right back with another for you, milady."

My hand snakes out to grab his collar but he's too fast, weaving through the crowd toward the bar or one of the servers carrying a tray full of champagne flutes.

"I think you've had enough." My hand wraps around her elbow to steady her.

"Hey, lighten up. What's the big deal? I'm just trying to have fun..." She glances around the room, her smile briefly faltering, curving down at the corners. "Trying to forget."

"Hey." I lean in close, breathing her in, and my lips brush her warm cheek. "This will be over soon."

Gently, I rub my thumb along the inside of her arm and her cheeks flush, lips parting as she pants. I could so easily take her sweet mouth, taste her honeyed tongue and all that is Caro.

She shivers, flashing me a sloppy smile, and turns into me, chest against mine. My knees nearly collapse out from under me.

*Carefully, I plant my hands on her waist, peering down at her as she gifts me a staggering view of the swell of her perfect tits. Jesus. She slays me.*

*Need licks at my flesh and my chest hitches. Maybe we'll never be together again, but even as I try to accept that, my entire being resists.*

*"I'm fine and it's only a few drinks." Unaware of what she's doing to me or maybe fully aware, her palms cruise up the lapels of my jacket and around my shoulder, fingers tangling into the hair at the nape of my neck.*

*My cock is already hard, alive, but my heart's suddenly heavier than it should be. Why does it feel as if I'm not breathing properly?*

*"One drink is no big deal." I force the words from my mouth, struggling for self-control. The urge to touch her, roam my hands all over her body, pushes and pulls at me. "You've had a few..." I pause and she blinks several times in succession, as if unable to focus easily. She's drunk.*

*"Caro, you need to be alert in case of anything. Don't leave my side."*

*"Kiss me." Her mouth is only inches from mine, and the wet tip of her tongue darts out to lick her lips.*

*It would be so easy to capture her mouth. I'm getting drunk just on the thought and I haven't had a drop of alcohol. Drunk on her. The heady scent and enthralling heat of her surrounds me.*

*"Jesus Christ, Caro."*

*A dark figure casts a shadow over us and I glance behind her— Logan. My mouth tightens, body taut, at the full glass in his hand.*

*I wrap my arms around her waist and shoot him a scathing look. If he knows what's good for him, he'll get rid of the drink. She's oblivious to his presence, one hand now trailing across the stubble of my jaw.*

*It's the sweetest kind of torture, slowly killing me.*

*My body is on fire.*

*Logan nods in understanding and leaves. Air expels from my lungs, but nothing loosens inside me. I'm still battling with myself not to do something I can't take back and it isn't because I'd regret it.*

*No, it's because Caro may regret it once she's sober.*

"Why won't you kiss me?" Her finger traces the edge of my bottom lip and flames of want flicker through me. "I was so wrong to leave you. I've missed you so much. Every day."

She's talking softly, more to herself than anything else and I stiffen, shocked at her words. Is this a confession or drunken rambling?

I've loved this woman for as long as I can remember, and her words are both a balm, soothing a barely-healed wound, and an ache, like salt stinging in the same wound.

Someone steps in behind her once more and I'm half expecting Logan, but it's Victor Walsh. He's staring wordlessly at us and I want to punch him. He put his hands on her as if he had a right to yesterday.

I hadn't missed him when we'd arrived, and I've been keeping an eye on him as he parades through the crowd like some king.

"Caroline, I've been trying to get to you all night." He ogles her silky smooth back, afforded by the low cut of the dress, and I wish I could dig his eyes out. This man's sense of entitlement is galling.

She turns to face him, leaning into me for support, and her mass of brown hair spills onto my shoulder. My heart is going to explode from the feel of her clinging to me. How many times have I dreamed of this very thing?

"Victor." Now rigid in tone and posture, she presses her back into my front.

Finally relenting, my hand glides around her middle, resting on her stomach in plain view of Walsh. Yeah, it's a caveman move, more to stake my claim in front of this creep than feed my desire.

"You're beautiful as ever." His gaze is lecherous. "I've come to collect."

Hard, teeth-gritting anger invades my body as I recall their conversation at the hospital yesterday. There's no way in hell he's getting a dance.

# CARO

*The tingling buzz from the champagne quickly fizzles at Victor Walsh's arrival. Not even ten seconds ago, I was begging Kit to kiss me. I want him, another chance, whether I deserve it or not. And it felt like I was getting somewhere, and now I have to play nice to this pretentious man.*

*"I think you have it all wrong. This party is for philanthropic individuals like yourself to donate to the Home." The heat of Kit at my back is comforting, fueling me with confidence. "So, I'd say I should be collecting."*

*Victor lets out a short burst of laughter but he fails to hide the strain pulling at the corners of his eyes. Something is off about this man. I first felt it at the hospital and now, even more so. He wants something but he won't say what.*

*"Why yes, you are correct and I've made my donation. Just ask Nick." He hooks his finger over his shoulder in the direction of where my brother has been most of the night.*

*"Thank you." I beam and place my hand over Kit's large one, flattened on my stomach. His touch does all kinds of things to me, and I can't shake my hyperawareness of him. A clean, earthy scent wraps around me and his hard, chiseled muscles bring only comfort and security. I want to stay here all night, in his arms.*

*Victor flits his dark beady eyes to where Kit and I are connected. I should move away, be embarrassed at this public display of affection. After all, I am co-owner of Léa's Home and this is a business event, but I can't seem to bring myself to care.*

*"So now that you've collected, I'd say it's my turn. May I please have this dance?" His outstretched hand causes my stomach to flip*

and all the champagne I drank or the bubbles or both bring on a wave of nausea. I did agree to a dance but it's the last thing I want.

"Um." I hesitate and Kit tightens his grip on me.

"I'd prefer it if you didn't." His request is deep, a low rumble aimed at Walsh even if he's talking to me.

"Oh." I peer up at him but his gaze is pinned to Victor. "Okay. Sorry, I'm going to have to pass up your offer. But thank you."

The older man's eyes widen, likely shocked that I dare turn him down, but they quickly narrow into thin slits trained on the man at my back. The hairs on the back of my neck stand at the now familiar feeling of something more sinister simmering under the surface.

"I don't think we've been introduced. Didn't I see you with Caroline at the hospital?"

Kit remains silent and I sneak a sideways glance at him, not wanting to take my eyes off Victor. My closest friend is stoic, staring at the older man with his mouth set in a thin line, a blank look in his eyes.

"Ah, Victor, this is Kit." That's all I allow myself to say. The man has no need to know anything about Kit, and I'm fairly certain Kit doesn't even want him to have his first name.

"Good evening, Kit." The typically overly courteous man doesn't extend his hand for a shake. "I'd usually say it's nice to meet you, but it seems you have the wrong impression of me." He rests his short stubby fingers into the center of his chest as if offended. "I was merely asking for a dance, not to steal her away."

"Yeah, well, we're leaving." Kit flexes his jaw while clenching his teeth and I'm more than happy to leave.

Done with Kit, Victor releases a derisive snort and pins me with his sharp gaze. "Caroline, where's Elliot?"

My heartbeat spikes. Victor and Elliot don't run in the same circles, and while they work at the same hospital, Elliot has nothing to do with the Home, and Victor doesn't know anything about my personal life. Or at least, he shouldn't.

"I don't know. Why do you ask?" I study his features, looking for any evidence of what he's really after, and except for the twitch to his lips at my response, his face is blank.

137

"He's missed his shifts at the hospital for the past several days now and we're worried. I thought you might know if he's okay and where we could find him."

The back of my neck heats and Kit's grip is almost painful. "No. I don't know where he is. Why would I?"

"Aren't you together?" Again, the question is for me but Victor's gaze is glued to Kit.

"No, we aren't." I bristle, hoping I didn't sound as defensive as I feel. "And I haven't seen Elliot in months." I shift to Kit's side, taking his hand. "Is Alma here with you?"

Alma is his wife and complete opposite. She's the most down-to-earth woman, who has not only shown her support for the Home with her money, but also her time. I could talk to her all day.

"Yes. Alma is here." Victor flushes, almost chastised by the question, and that is my intention.

"Please say hello to her for me, and I'm sure she'd love to dance with you. It was nice seeing you and thank you for your donation. Good night, Victor."

"You too." He doesn't wait, leaving immediately.

I lead us across the room toward Nick and Logan to say our goodbyes, eager to have time alone with Kit. My brother's relieved I'm leaving and that the night is without incident.

"You two go." He pats Kit on the back while wearing a strange expression, eyes boring into his best friend.

Logan is less subtle, an enormous smile breaking free as he waggles his eyebrows suggestively. "Yes, you two go home and go screw until you can't see straight."

"Logan." Kit's tone is hard as stone.

"Fuck off." Nick hits the back of his head.

I press my lips together, holding in my laughter as red heat climbs into my face.

On the way out of the castle, I swipe one more glass of champagne from a passing server, enjoying the toasty bubbles sliding down my throat despite Kit's scowl. The conversation with Victor Walsh was near sobering and I want the warm fuzzy feeling I had before.

As we wait for the valet to bring the car, I spot Victor standing at the far end of the entrance with his back to us. He's talking to a man in a uniform in front of a luxury SUV.

Once we're in the car on the way to his house, Kit asks, "Why's Victor asking about Elliot?"

"Well, he is the head of the hospital, so ultimately Elliot's boss. But I'm surprised he'd even know Elliot missed his shifts. Normally, something like that would be handled by HR."

"It does sound strange, and even more so that he thought you and Elliot still had a thing."

"Yes, it is weird because I wasn't aware he even knew we dated. His question threw me. I was going to tell him you were my boyfriend when I introduced you."

I realize what I've just said when he takes the turn sharply, exhaling a harsh breath. Okay, maybe I'm fooling myself to think we might have a chance, given his reaction to even saying we're together.

"Everything about him felt wrong." Kit skips over my comment.

I compel myself to stay focused on the conversation and not how hot he looks in a tux. "I know. It felt like there was more to the conversation but I couldn't put my finger on it."

"Yeah, me too. The way he looked at you, the words he chose, it felt too personal and with purpose." Kit takes the next turn onto the highway. "I'll ask Nick to look into him."

I snort. "He isn't going to like that."

"Why?"

"Victor is a big donor, and Nick is counting on him to put in a good word for us with the provincial government." Something ugly and sludge-like creeps up my throat and makes me want to vomit.

The Home is one small way Nick and I pay tribute to our father and sister by helping others like us, who struggle financially to care for their loved ones with brain injuries.

While the Home is a private facility, we offer subsidizing with the help of private funding and donations, and we're currently in talks with the government to expand our offering. This is where Victor and others like him come in.

*His support is crucial, or more specifically his opposition could end our chances at funding and expanding.*

*Kit grunts and I can't bring myself to continue talking about Victor. All I want to think about is Kit and how to best bring up the possibility of more. If not now...someday and hopefully soon.*

*Once back at the loft, Kit deposits the keys and lumbers to the kitchen. "You want some water? Aspirin?"*

*I chuckle, slipping off my heels. "I'm fine. I could use some water but no to the aspirin. Thanks."*

*While he pours water, I pull the pins from my hair, running my fingers across my scalp to loosen my waves. He rounds the counter, eyes heavy-lidded and smoldering as they roam my body from head to toe. Thoughts of how close we were earlier tonight, how much I wanted him to kiss me, bring my insides to a boil.*

*Given the way he's looking at me now, perhaps he wasn't immune to our closeness back at the castle? When we were pressed against each other, surrounded by people. He felt it too. My body grows hot and heavy with need. He may have denied me a kiss, but he wants me as much as I want him.*

*Heat flares low in my core, flicking between my legs, and for the life of me, I can't think of one single reason why we shouldn't give in to our desires.*

*Water in hand, he stops short of giving it to me, bending to put the glass on the table in front of me. The distance is a cold rush of air between us and I shiver, suddenly empty.*

*He takes a few more steps back and starts to remove his jacket. I meant it when I said he looked good. Damn, good isn't even enough of a word to truly describe what he makes me feel.*

*The longer I stare at him in his tux, the more I want to run my hands over his chest once again, feel every ripple and ridge of his muscles. Despite feeling loose-limbed and warm thanks to the bubbly, I wrap my arms around myself, trying to keep these burgeoning feelings locked down.*

*Everything inside me wishes to have him, show him just how much I want him. Just how wrong I was all those years ago. It doesn't* help when he stares at me the way he always does, as if I'm the only thing he's ever wanted.

Even with our distance, he's looking at me that very way, right now. I love it, and yet I'm at a loss, not knowing what to do with his adoration. I don't deserve it.

I've been blessed with people who love me like I'm their world. Léa and Nick were more than a sister and brother to me. They were like parents and friends. Our parents left us. My father died and my mother…my mother just left us.

My life could have been horrific, nothing like what it is today. I could have had to sell my body like my sister did to put food on the table or run in circles with vicious criminals like Nick did.

They both did what they had to in order to give me everything—a home, food, university, all of it. And now, I look at Kit and he's no different than my siblings. He had no choice.

Guilt and humiliation surge in my stomach, reminding me of all the foolish things I did or didn't do.

He did what he had to do to live, to survive. And what did I do? I blamed him for those tough and unimaginable choices. I left him because of those choices, because he wanted to live.

And he got out, not because I told him he had to but because he wanted to, because he was finally at a point, I guess, when he realized he could be so much more.

Angry at myself and needing to drown my shame, I stride to the cabinet along the wall, figuring it's where he keeps the liquor, or at least hoping that's where it is. A faint smile crosses my lips as I pull out a bottle of Crown Royal. Alcohol isn't how I typically deal with stressful, unpleasant things. Work or exercise are my usual numbing agents, but neither are possible.

And earlier tonight, with the champagne bubbling through my veins, I felt good… no, I felt nothing. And it was fucking glorious. I screw off the cap, and it's when I tip the bottle to my lips that Kit sees what I'm doing.

"Fuck, Caro, don't." He rushes to my side but not fast enough to stop my first gulp.

*The liquor scorches my throat and tingles as it makes its way through my body. One of his hands grips the base of the bottle but he doesn't take it from me.*

*"Why not?" I want to get rip-roaring drunk.*

*Agony and anguish are all around me every time I look at the man I so desperately want, have always wanted.*

*He walks me backward until I hit the wall and raises his arms, bracketing either side of my head. Bending, he brings his face close, so close the tip of his nose nudges mine as he shakes his head back and forth. It can't have been accidental.*

*A kunik, the Inuit's greeting for close relatives, much like Europeans greet others with multiple kisses to the cheek.*

*His dark lashes flutter closed and warm breath rushes from him, bathing over my mouth.*

*Oh, God. Yes.*

*This is us. The intimate way in which we would show each other affection. Love. Our kisses were many and only for each other.*

*A whimper slips from my lips. "Kiss me again."*

*His lips press together and I'm not sure if that's to prevent himself from kissing me or from me reaching up to capture his mouth. He slides a hand down the wall, stopping to brush his fingers through my hair.*

*"You don't want this." It's a murmur in my ear.*

*Yes, I do. My chest pulsates wildly and erratically, like someone's taken a hammer to my heart. I groan, frustrated and greedy with an unleashed desire for him.*

*"Don't tell me what I want." I fist my hand in his shirt. "You're all I want."*

*He cups my cheek, thumb rubbing back and forth along my skin. "I know you better than you know yourself. I'm not good enough for you. You're everything good in this world and you'll regret this in the morning."*

*I've done such a good job of pushing him away, denying myself and him, that he can't believe I want him. He believes he isn't good enough. God, what have I done?*

"Don't say that." I tug at his shirt, heart thumping painfully in my chest.

Everything he's saying is some variation of what I said to him when we broke up. I'm such an idiot and a horrible person too.

"You're more than good enough for me. I'm the one who doesn't deserve you." I press onto my toes, teeth capturing his bottom lip.

His eyes flutter closed and he groans when I lick at his lips. But as soon as I release his flesh, he pulls back, pain lacing his soul-deep eyes. "Caro, you're drunk."

The anguish in his voice lances my chest and I suck in a breath, regretting what I said and did to him many years ago. Can he ever forgive me?

"I'm not drunk. I know exactly what I'm doing. I'm sorry for what I said years ago. I was wrong. An idiot… There's no explanation that will make what I did all right. I'm sorry."

Inadequate. My apology is inadequate. Nothing will ever make up for what I did. I'm the one who is less than. Am I too late to make this right? Our time apart was unbearable and futile, and I deserve his rejection or punishment.

His hands cradle my head, fingers digging into my curls, and I lift once more onto my toes. Buoyed by his touch that I've dreamed of over the years, I reach for his lips with mine.

My insides quake, nausea at the ready…he could reject me…and I'd deserve it.

Then he slants his head, bringing me closer and giving me his mouth. An agonizing cry tumbles from my lips and my breath catches. We're all tongues and teeth, probing, hungry, reckless.

His throaty groan slides down my throat, grabbing at my hips and lifting my feet off the floor. Thank you, Willow, for the dress. The full front slit makes it easy for my legs to wrap around his waist.

My pulse quickens, toes curl, and tears prick at my eyes. His need is like an effervescent warmth blanketing me. He wants me.

One hand clutches at his shoulder, the other wrestles with the buttons at the front of his shirt, a needy moan building deep inside me. I need to feel his skin, have him as close to me as is possible.

*"God, I've missed you," I mumble against his lips when he breaks the kiss for air.*

*"Caro." The reverence in his tone weakens my knees, and I'm glad he's holding me up as his lips capture mine again.*

*This is Kit. I can't believe I'm in his arms. I truly thought this would never happen again. We'd never touch, kiss, and just be together.*

*His strong confident strides carry us closer to his room and he's everywhere. Hands, lips, and everything in between wander all of my body. The solace and ecstasy of being this close to him is dizzying.*

*My desire for this man, bone-deep and neglected for far too long, is finally unleashed and consuming, something I can't control and no longer wish to.*

# KIT

She nuzzles her nose into my neck and her soft lips linger there, hot and wet. Can she taste the salt of my skin mingling with my growing hunger for her?

"Caro...we shouldn't." My words are in stark contrast to my true feelings.

I don't want to fucking stop but I can't...I can't stand to have her look at me the way she once did, with only pain and something close to disgust. It would kill me.

We're on the bed and she straddles my lap, and it takes everything in me to wrap my hands around her biceps and gently draw her away from me.

Espresso-brown depths glimmer. "I love you, Kit."

A painful groan slips past my clenched jaw. "Fuck, you can't say that."

She may still be tipsy and definitely horny, and all of that feels like she isn't in her right mind. This can't happen. Yet for someone under the influence, she's quick to unbutton the first five on my shirt.

Long slender fingers slide under the open fabric, roaming the expanse of my heated chest. Her touch is lethal. A quiver runs along my spine and heat pools low in my groin.

This is both heaven and hell. I've dreamed of this, of having Caro, for so long, and I'm torn between right and wrong, hunger and honor.

At the same time, a voice in my head shouts for her to keep going and another, for her to stop. Damn, I'm going to hell.

"Kit, I want you. Always have, always will. I was cruel and wrong to say what I did. Can you ever forgive me?" Her warm lips roam my chest, indulgent and adoring.

*Every kiss, every touch is amplified by her words, her acceptance. My throat clogs, still processing the words I'd wanted to hear for so long. The words I'll never tire of her saying—she wants me.*

*A wet, hot tongue flicks at one hardening nipple and then the other. She licks and laves at the sensitive skin and then almost like a flipped switch, she pops up, sitting up straight upon me.*

*A distressing prick of doubt rises in my gut—is this when she comes to her senses? When she realizes the alcohol has taken over and muddled her brain and I'm not who she wants?*

*She grins from ear to ear, hair a wild mess as she fumbles to take off her dress.*

*No, she hasn't changed her mind. Thank fuck, no.*

*Her clumsy fingers pull a spaghetti strap down her arm and one of her round, perky breasts, her nipple a dark pink, springs free of the gown.*

*I watch it pebble and pucker into a hard little nub. Fuck.*

*My cock pulses with the need to be inside her, and like a kid who can't resist licking the cake batter, my mouth and tongue shower her chest with open-mouthed kisses.*

*I start from where her neck meets her collarbone, moving downward. My mouth draws in a nipple, and she shudders and gasps for breath. Her head drops backward and she grabs at my hair in a frenzy, trying to keep me in place.*

*I'm not going anywhere.*

*Suddenly, she wants her dress off and pulls back from me, struggling with the side zipper, grunting and cursing. If I wasn't so turned on and desperate for her, I might find it funny.*

*Putting us both out of our misery, I lift her off me, placing her feet firmly on the floor. I sit up and drop my feet onto the carpet, widening my legs to pull her in between them.*

*Warm chocolate-brown eyes lock onto mine, and my fingers find the zipper, shaking with anticipation as I leisurely drag it down the dress. Mesmerized, she follows the languid trail of my fingers along the side of her body.*

*I've craved Caro for so long, heart, mind, body, and soul, I can hardly believe this is happening.*

*Once loose enough, the gown falls, pooling at her feet, and she stands before me in nothing but white lace panties. Dark hair tumbles around her in riotous waves, obscuring her face.*

*My heart contracts and swells in equal measure, breath moving too fast through my lungs. She's everything, the only thing, I've ever wanted. And now, standing before me, she's giving herself to me. Utterly beautiful. Utterly cherished. Utterly mine.*

*My hands brush back her hair and I'm struck with the undying need to spill everything with three little words. "I love you."*

*Her fingers wrap around my wrists and she bends to bring her mouth to mine, hovering, barely a breath away. "I love you."*

*The force of those three words nearly sends me to my knees. I've loved her to the ends of the earth even when I didn't have her.*

*Now, hearing her say she loves me only intensifies how much I would do anything for this woman. I would kill for her. I would die for her.*

*And finally, she is mine once again. And this time, I'm never letting her go.*

*She pushes my upper body onto the bed and straddles me once more, pressing her naked chest into mine. My hands run lazily up and down her back, and her teeth latch onto my earlobe.*

*Hot air from her mouth sends a shiver down my spine into my balls, and I buck my hips up into her sex.*

*A moan sails past her lips. "Kit, fuck me."*

*My cock is rock hard, pre-cum beading on the crown, and I'm so ready to take her. I tug at my pants and she lifts slightly so I can slide them down my legs, taking my boxers with them. At full mast, my stiff cock slaps onto my stomach and her fingers grip the base.*

*At her touch, a low grunt comes from deep within me, and she lowers herself onto my erection. Fingers pierce my chest and she slides herself up and down. She feels fucking amazing and I'm dazed with pleasure.*

*The sounds she makes, her shameless whimpers and moans, send shudders sweeping through me, and if I don't get a grip on my control, I'll come like some pubescent teenager.*

But she's close, so I grit my teeth and drink in her climax. She tenses, muscles rock hard, arching her back and thrusting her tits into the air.

She releases, screaming my name, then collapses onto my chest, hair covering part of my face and head burrowed under my neck. Boneless and euphoric, I tighten my grip on her. This woman is impossible not to love.

A light sheen of perspiration coats her chest, and her quick, shallow breaths, more like pants, even out in only a few seconds until they slow and steady. We lie like that for more than a minute and she doesn't stir.

"Caro." My hand brushes the tousled waves from her face, and my fingers cradle the back of her head, gently lifting her from my chest.

Her smile is lazy, eyes hazy and heavy-lidded but no longer from desire and more from sleepy satisfaction. Long, thick ebony eyelashes flutter closed.

"Kit, I'm so glad you're here with me." Her head snuggles back onto my chest, settling immediately, and I stifle a chuckle.

In a few short beats, she's asleep. Smiling despite blue balls, I'm happy, so happy to have her next to me. My arm snakes around her back and I turn onto my side, pulling the blankets over her.

I slip from the bed and pad through the loft to turn off the light and check the door is locked before getting back into bed.

Caro immediately rolls into me like a magnet, and I secure her in the crook of my arm and shut my eyes. I sleep soundlessly that night with a smile on my face, I'm sure.

Loud, persistent banging causes me to wake from a deep sleep. The drumming of my pulse is deafening and my adrenaline spikes. Who the fuck is that? I jump out of bed and shove on my jeans.

"Oh God, what is that?" Caro's face is in the pillow, her voice muffled.

"Go back to sleep, I've got it." I stride to the front door, finger-combing my bedhead.

My hand reaches for the door and pauses on second thought as I come out of my sleep-induced fog. I'm no longer in a hurry to open the door.

148

No one called to get buzzed in and it can't be Logan. He usually doesn't rise before noon, which is still a few hours away. And it isn't Nick—he'd have called first.

I open the closet and wrap a hand around my gun, resting on the top shelf. "Who is it?"

"Police," says a deep male voice from the other side of the door. "Open up."

I curse under my breath and shut the closet, leaving the weapon where it is. Can I keep this quick and quiet so as not to wake Caro? My hand curls around the knob and I release the lock, opening the door.

Detective Holman looks a hell of a lot better than the last time I saw him despite his perpetual scowl. He's shaved, for one, although not today, possibly yesterday. His clothes are different and aren't nearly as wrinkled. And of all miracles, he actually smells okay, like fresh laundry instead of a greasy spoon and stale breath.

"Where's Caro Archer?" He brushes past me as if he owns the place.

"Doctor Archer, you mean." I just can't play nice with this guy and especially when he acts like a dick.

Over his shoulder, he looks at me, and it's meant to be nonchalant but his glare gives him away. He doesn't like me either. Satisfaction blooms inside me and plays on my lips.

"She's sleeping. If you'd called..."

"I'm right here," croaks Caro from the bedroom door.

She's in sweatpants and an oversized sweatshirt with her hair in a messy bun on top of her head. She doesn't look so good. Still beautiful, but I can tell from her pale complexion, hand resting on her stomach, and squinting that she's hurting.

"What can I do for you, Detective Holman?" She shuffles into the room, her steps slow and measured.

"Are you all right, Dr. Archer?" He emphasizes the doctor and makes a point to throw a scowl in my direction.

He's quick to return his attention to Caro, examining her closely. What does he see? Does he guess she's hungover? Or is he thinking something more nefarious, like she's coming off drugs? If he's aware of the Elliot connection, then that's the logical conclusion.

"I'm fine, thank you." She lowers herself onto the sofa way too carefully for someone who is okay. "What do you want?"

"You left out a few things in your statement." The staccato taps of his pen against the notebook in his hand, slow and calculated, only make his sardonic tone blunter.

"What are you talking about?" Her elbow rests on her thigh, holding up her head.

"Aren't you using the Jane Clinic to supply drugs to the street?"

I open and close my fists, battling to keep my calm. This bastard.

"What? Are you out of your mind?" She straightens, face twisted in fury followed by a wince at what looks like a stabbing pain in her head. "Where the hell did you come up with this crazy story?"

He chuckles, wanting us to believe he finds this conversation amusing, and I'm getting bored with him and his games.

"Do you know a Dr. Elliot Foley?" He ignores the question, and Caro doesn't call him on it, rather she goes with him.

"Yes. He used to work at the clinic." She opens her mouth, most probably to say more but I shake my head no. He's going to have to work for more information.

"And weren't you two dating at one point? Living together?"

I shudder and my stomach clenches. Were they living together? Fuck, were things more serious between those two than Nick led me to believe?

"We never lived together. We did date, but it was nothing serious."

My gut settles and I exhale a long breath, relieved.

"You were in a relationship for more than a year, were you not? And you call that not serious?"

"It wasn't quite a year and no, we weren't serious. Weeks would go by before we'd spend any time alone together." She looks at me, maybe for some kind of reaction, but I keep my expression blank.

The thought of her with him isn't something I like to dwell on, and it's over. That's what matters. Elliot isn't a threat to us, no matter how much I dislike the jerk.

"A year is still a long time. But nowadays, no one dates anymore. It's just sex, or what's it called now? Hooking up?" He scratches at his jaw.

Enough of this bullshit. Holman has yanked her chain long enough.

"Do you have any more questions or are you just sharing your pointless opinions?" I step forward, widening my stance.

"Were you aware that Foley is under suspicion for illegally obtaining prescription drugs and supplying them to known drug dealers?"

"What? No, I don't know anything about that." She isn't quick enough in feigning surprise, and as much as I'd like to think Holman is stupid, he's not that stupid.

He catches her moment of hesitation as captured in the crude slash of his mouth. My heart stutters, feeling like it's physically seizing in my chest. He doesn't have anything on us, on her, but he can make things difficult for us.

"So you're telling me you're not aware of shipments of oxy being sent to the clinic?" He pauses and I'm surprised he revealed the drug to us.

"What? No, I know nothing about that."

"All shipments were in your name."

A wave of panic washes over her face, skin ashen and eyes wide with worry. "I don't oversee deliveries. Who signed for them?"

She's on the ball now, asking all the questions someone would if this was the first time they were hearing this.

"Dr. Archer, you need to come down to the station for further questioning."

If he wasn't a cop, I'd have tossed him out on his ass a while ago. Agitation seeps into my muscles and bones.

"She's not going anywhere. Caro gave her statement and it was thorough and accurate. At this point in time, she has nothing to add."

I glare at him and he scrunches his nose, making his face uglier than it already is. "Your latest development about Elliot Foley and the drugs has nothing to do with Dr. Archer. So unless you have concrete evidence linking her to any of this, we're done here."

# KIT

*I should face-punch this jackass. He's barking up the wrong tree and he knows it. He's just looking to rattle her.*

"You should have been a lawyer." Holman pats at his belt buckle and pulls at the waist of his pants. "Is this how you want to play it, Dr. Archer? You could make things a lot easier on yourself, should charges be brought against you, if you cooperate now."

"Charges?" *Her anxiety is palpable and I squeeze her shoulder, reminding her she isn't alone.* "You can't charge me when I don't know anything Elliot might or might not have been doing."

"Elliot hasn't worked at the clinic for over five months." *I look to Caro and she nods. I want to make this look like we haven't already discussed this.* "Have you looked into where he is now? If he's doing what you say he is, wouldn't there be signs of this at his new place of work?"

"Yeah, we're on it. Do you know where Elliot is?" *Holman points the question at Caro, who shakes her head. He mashes his lips together, flicking his gaze back and forth between us.* "I'll be in touch. I will have more questions for you."

"Goodbye, Detective Holman." *I saunter to the door, holding it open.*

*Grudgingly, he closes the notebook, stuffing it into his jacket pocket, and then leaves.*

"You okay?" *It's a stupid question because it's plain to see she isn't with the way she's worrying her bottom lip.*

"I need water." *She snaps out of her disquieting thoughts and trudges to the kitchen, and I follow, opening a cabinet and handing her some aspirin.* "Thank you."

She guzzles the water with two pills, leaning her head against the cupboard, eyes closed. "Well, Holman has now officially linked me to Elliot."

"Yeah, but remember, he didn't just make that connection." I make coffee.

"True. The cop you called mentioned Holman had wanted in on both our cases—the clinic, Foley's break-in, and of course, there's my house although we called him. So this visit was to see how we reacted? Catch us in a lie?"

I nod, turning to face her, curling my hands over the edge of the counter and leaning back into the cupboards. "Yup. Pretty much. We still need to figure out if he's working for whoever is behind this or if he's trying to find Elliot to use as leverage. Something to barter with for cash? Drugs? We don't know what his motive is. That isn't clear."

"Well, one thing is for sure, he's not doing this because it's his job." Her sarcasm causes me to chuckle.

She takes the milk from the fridge for coffee and I move in behind her to grab the eggs, holding up the carton to her. She nods and I set about making breakfast.

"Or the other possibility is Elliot's been on the cops' radar for a while and if so, they may have been watching him and lost him. Holman is drug enforcement so that part would make sense."

The eggs hit the hot pan with a sizzle and I stir the spatula through the yellow liquid.

"Yes, but like you've said all along, there's more to Holman than meets the eye." She fixes our coffee. "Willow sent me a text with the name of the construction company who did the clinic renovations and Flora's home information."

This is the only lead we have right now. All roads to Elliot are dead ends and we're on the clock. We're losing precious time and Flora better give us something.

"Are you okay to call Flora or should we go by her home?"

"Let me call first." Before I can insist she eat something, the phone is to her ear.

I scramble the eggs and stick several slices of bread in the toaster, setting out plates for us.

"The number isn't in service." She sighs, tapping on her phone. "I'm texting Willow to let her know and see if she can find out anything else."

She then pours two glasses of orange juice and slides into a kitchen chair. I plate our food and join her.

"We should go by her home." I lift the fork to my mouth. "It's Saturday, she might not be working and so we have a good chance of running into her. Worst case, we go to the construction company, but I'd rather focus on Flora first. If anyone is going to know most about Elliot, it will be her."

"Yes, that makes sense."

My eggs go down easy, as well as the toast, whereas she still picks at her food.

I rinse my plate, leaving it in the sink, and pour another cup of coffee. "You need to eat if you want to feel better."

"I'm trying. I just feel sick to my stomach and it's not from drinking." She drops her forehead to her forearm, resting on the table, and speaks into the wood. "How the hell did everything go so wrong? How did I get mixed up in this mess? The police think I'm involved or behind this."

Lifting her head, her bottomless brown eyes glisten with unshed tears. The accusation is huge for her. She's a rule follower and has reluctantly broken the law only a few times to help her brother. And even at that, if charges had ever been brought against her, any decent lawyer would have gotten her off because her actions didn't hurt anyone. Her actions were ultimately to help people and save lives.

"Holman's bluffing, trying to get a reaction out of you, or if we're lying and know where Elliot is, I bet he's hoping we'll go straight to him." Now standing in front of her, my hand curls a few strands of hair behind her ear. "We'll clear your name. I promise."

"To do that, we have to find Elliot. He's the only one who can explain all of this." She pushes back her chair and carries the plate to the sink.

Hesitation tangles my tongue as I'm tempted to discourage her thinking. "I'm not so sure Elliot's going to help."

*At the dishwasher, she places the dish on the wire rack and pauses, gazing up at me. "What do you mean?"*

*"I think you know what I mean. Elliot's the one who put the cops onto you. It looks like he set up his operation at the clinic in such a way that he could implicate you should he ever get caught."*

*I brace myself for the denial or anger. Whether she wants to face it or not, Elliot is the reason she's in this mess. And last night may have felt like progress—no, it was fucking nirvana—but she'd been drinking. I'm not sure anything has changed.*

*On paper, next to me, Elliot Foley is a saint. A fine, upstanding citizen. Intelligent, selfless, and wealthy. Everything she wants in her life.*

*"More and more I realize I never knew him, and I'm not talking about our dating. That was nothing—we never hit it off, really." She shuts the appliance door and nears me. "We should talk about last night."*

*"There's nothing to talk about. You got off and fell asleep." I force a rueful grin even if I'm feeling anything but.*

*Last night was fucking awesome. I can't listen to her talk her way out of the things she said or did. Her declaration of love felt real, all of it did, and I'm not so sure I can keep it together if she destroys it by taking it all back.*

*She doesn't return the sentiment and nibbles on her bottom lip, eyes boring into me. "I—"*

*I cut her off, not ready to have the bottom fall out from under me just yet. "Hey, how things turned out last night…it was for the best." I head for the exit from the kitchen and pause. "We have a lot to do today. I've got something I have to take care of, then there's Flora. I need to take a shower. You can stay here and rest while I'm gone."*

*I'd rather not leave her alone since we haven't gotten another text but today's the day when our time runs out.*

*"No, I want to come." Her gaze is fierce, earnest. "Besides, I know Flora, I can help. What else do you have to do?"*

*I have an appointment with Pinter. I need to get him to sign the purchase agreement for his car. Do I want to get into this with Caro? It's my dream, but will it only be another disappointment to her?*

*"Just something work related. It won't take long, but there's no point in you coming. It's in Oshawa." The drive isn't far, only forty minutes or so east of the city.*

*"I'm coming." She smiles.*

*"Fine. Let me get ready first and then while you take a shower, I'll fill in Nick and Logan."*

*The drive to Earl Pinter's home is easy, and traffic is light since we're leaving the city. Caro spends most of it with her eyes closed, waiting for her stomach to settle, and fortunately, her current condition lessens her probing questions about where we're going.*

*It's stupid really and no big deal. I should just tell her. My reluctance pisses me off. Why do I still care so much about what she thinks? Expanding Maggie's business is legit and a decent goal, something that's good for both me and the Phoenix.*

*So what if Caro doesn't get it? Or approve of it? It's okay. I mean, as much as she hurt me when we broke up, I understood her logic and even agreed with her.*

*We love each other but we don't fit. I'm a high school graduate, barely, who made his living fixing bad people's problems. I can't say what I did was good or that it didn't lead to more violence. We both know that would be a lie.*

*"Why aren't you telling me where we're going?" Her head rests in her hand against the passenger window, eyes still closed, and it's like she's reading my mind.*

*I slow to make a left, waiting for an opening to make the turn into Pinter's impressive late Georgian revival style home.*

*"It's for the Phoenix. I'm closing a sale and the guy is kind of eccentric and a loner. He might react badly to you being here." I swing the vehicle onto the long paved driveway and Caro's head pops up, eyes opening.*

*"Wow, this house is amazing. I promise to keep my mouth shut, or I can stay in the car."*

*I drum my fingers on the steering wheel. It's shitty of me to leave her in the car. What harm can she do? If she says she'll be quiet, she will.*

*"Fine, let's go."*

# CARO

*Kit's ahead of me, disappearing around the corner of the house, and I hurry after him, shivering as a bitter wind slices through me.*

*I round the stone house and abruptly stop. He stands at the entrance to a garage, separate from the main house, and a short, round elderly man, leaning on a black cane, hobbles toward him.*

*Kit advances in the stranger's direction, talking to him, but with the whistling wind and his back to me, I can't make out any words. The shorter, well-dressed man looks up from the snow-covered ground, breaking his intense concentration to stay upright rather than lose his footing.*

*He stills at the sight of me, making a strange rocking motion with his body as if convulsing. Kit stares at me and his told you so gaze blisters my insides. Shit, I don't want to mess up whatever this is for him. He holds out a hand as if calling me to his side.*

*"Mr. Pinter, this is—"*

*"Mr. Jensen, this will not work. The deal is off. Leave." The elderly man's gaze is trained on me, unrelenting.*

*Why do I feel like I've been caught with my hand in the cookie jar? My stomach roils at the thought of my punishment. Kit did say the man was a loner, and it seems like my presence has spooked him.*

*"Mr. Pinter, please..." Something in Kit's voice causes a sharp pang in my chest.*

*He's almost pleading, as if his life depends on this deal. Why?*

*"I'm sorry, I can go wait in the car." I'm also begging the man, if only for Kit's sake.*

*"No. I said I'd only talk to you and you obviously have no regard for my wishes. Get off my property." Mr. Pinter awkwardly turns, giving us his back, and starts his wobbly journey to the house.*

"Wait." Kit rushes to Pinter's side, grabbing his elbow. The old man fires a scathing look at Kit and even I shrink a little, but the big guy doesn't back down.

"This is Caro Archer. Dr. Caro Archer. She's very important to me. The most important person in the world." His broad, striking frame is all I see of him but he might as well be staring into my eyes and cradling my heart. Every one of his words rips me open. "She's in danger and I had to bring her with me."

I suck in a breath, a pressing urgency to fix this crowding my insides. I can't be the reason this deal falls apart. I've already ruined enough for Kit.

"In danger? How?" Pinter asks at the same time, I say, "I'm sorry. I'll go."

"No, stay." The old man stares at me. "Tell me more. Explain yourself."

I swallow hard, unsure of any of this. "I'm Caro and I'm sorry for barging in like this. Kit told me to stay in the car and didn't tell me anything about this meeting. I don't know why he's here or what this is about."

My mitten-covered hand hangs in the air between us, and the man makes no move to shake it.

"I'm Earl Pinter." His inclination to distrust is a neon sign flashing from every one of his pores. "Why are you in danger?"

I'm a rambling mess when I begin answering his question, summarizing as best as is possible without going into great detail. This man doesn't need all the details and once in a while, Kit interjects, redirects, helping me not to divulge too much.

Mr. Pinter gets enough of a picture to understand I'm entangled in something dreadful and Kit is helping me unravel myself.

"Interesting." His eyes are full of life and his sharp features temper. "Now let's talk about the Ford."

He pulls out a small device, similar to a remote, and hits a button. The garage door clickety-clacks its way up the tracks, revealing an old fading-red automobile. A classic—of what era, I'm not sure, but it needs a lot of work.

Kit mouths thank you to me before following the man inside. I keep my distance, close enough to hear most of the conversation but far enough not to get in the way.

Slowly, things start to fit together. Kit wants to buy the car for the Phoenix. Why didn't he just tell me?

The men go back and forth, Pinter being a hardass on many aspects of the deal that it seems they had already agreed on. But Kit's impressive and kind of a hardass himself, and if I had to say, he comes out the victor in the end.

With a pen in one hand and the sale agreement in the other, Kit glances once more at the fine print before lifting his head to Pinter.

"So let me get this straight, you want right of first refusal on the restored car?" His head cocks to the side, brow furrowed.

"That's correct." Earl nods.

"You realize you could just ask us to restore the car and it would be cheaper than selling it and then possibly buying it back at a higher price?" He scratches at his jaw, perhaps at a loss to understand this man's logic.

"I'm fully aware of that and this is how I want it. I'd rather not pay for restoration when I'm not certain I want the vehicle. I'll decide once the work is done." Earl Pinter is best described as eccentric.

Some might think he's crazy and he just might be, but he's also stubborn. I know nothing about cars but the better deal is to have the car restored.

Nonetheless, the old man doesn't budge on this point as Kit probes a bit more, ensuring Pinter understands what he's doing. Finally, Kit relents and Mr. Pinter signs the documents.

When the deal is done, Pinter watches us walk to the car in silence. The purchase agreement is firmly in Kit's hand and his smile splits his face in two.

Snow now falls, blanketing the already hardened wintery white ground, and the sun has dropped as the days are shorter. We're on our way to Flora's, and at the rate the flurries are coming, our drive back into the city may be slow going.

"You were amazing with Mr. Pinter. The way you handled him... You kept your cool and had an answer for all of his objections." I'm giddy, feeding off his high.

To see Kit happy makes me happy. This is important to him and while not fully comprehending the significance, I want him to know he's awesome.

"I almost did call it off, once or twice."

"You're really good at this. Do you like this part of your job?"

We haven't talked about his work at the garage, how he ended up there and if he likes it. There's a lot about him I don't know anymore.

We've both changed, I suppose. I have and I want to know everything about him like I once did. He's always liked cars so the Phoenix fits, but is it all he wanted it to be? What are his plans or dreams for the future? What's it like working with Maggie?

While I shouldn't have, I've asked Maggie about Kit in the past. She loves working with him. Kit's like a big brother and they're tight. I imagine they work well together, but I'd love to hear it in his words.

"Why didn't you tell me to stay in the car?" I blast the heat, no longer able to feel my toes despite the turmoil in my chest. "I could have ruined the deal for you by being there. I'm sensing you didn't want to tell me about it. Why?"

We were outside for over an hour and my extremities are stiff and frozen despite being dressed for the weather.

One hand braces the back of my headrest and he changes lanes. "I...you won't understand."

"Try me." Gloves off, my hands hover over a vent, soaking in the hot air.

"At the Phoenix, the restoration side of the business is solid. Maggie's rep is so good that business is constant."

He pauses again, as if struggling with his tongue to get the words out, and more to rescue him than anything else, I say, "I'm sensing a but."

"Yeah, we aren't proactive. We wait for the customers to come to us."

"Okay."

*Maggie's told me the family history and how she's gotten to where she is, but what it takes to succeed and the ins and outs of restoring cars is a foreign language to me.*

"It could be so much more, and Maggie's done a lot—" His mouth clamps shut and he shakes his head. "You know, forget about it. It's just something I had to do for my job. That's it."

*He's defensive, almost angry, and the weight crushes my chest. His aversion on this topic has everything to do with me and not the garage. I'm not sure why, but everything within me screams to fix this.*

"Hey, talk to me." I rest my hand on his over the gearshift. "Please."

"It isn't a big deal. I asked Maggie if we could expand the restoration part of the business, be proactive in our approach. She supports it, so it's mine to make something of. Her hands are already full."

*He's playing this off as nothing, looking straight ahead at the road, shoulders tense, arms locked, hands gripping the wheel and not willing to spare me a glance.*

*Yeah, it's me. I'm making him this uncomfortable, but why? I should back down but I want to get to the bottom of this, show him he has my support.*

"That's great. Maggie trusts you. She must fully support this and love the idea of you fully partnering with her."

*We're drowning in his reluctance to talk about this, and I'm wary about pushing for too many details but I can't help myself.* "And the restoration end of things, this is what you want to do?"

"Yeah."

"And Pinter, the Ford, is a big deal?"

"Yeah, hopefully the first of many." His tone is more open, even confident, and I'm optimistic that he's coming around. "When we put that baby on the market, we'll be getting our name out there as a business that can not only help source a car but also restore it."

"So if I was looking for a certain older car and model, you'd help do the legwork?"

"Yup."

"That's great, and this means a lot to you, doesn't it?"

"Can we drop it?" He veers into the left lane of highway 401 westbound, back to the city.

"Why? This is a big deal and important to you, so it's important to me."

"Really?" He gifts me with a look, but it's brief and scrutinizing, as if waiting for a caveat or pitfall.

"Yes. You're important to me." Everything I feel for him stirs and rises in my chest like a tsunami. "Tell me more. I want to understand."

"I owe Maggie. She's done a lot for me. When Nick decided to go legit, I had a choice to make. Stay in that life and align myself with another group or get out. Going it alone wasn't a smart option because Nick and I were a team, no one touched us. But if one of us was in it alone, we'd have become vulnerable."

My heart aches and soars at the same time. I'd never looked at his situation like this before, and what he did, leaving that life, took courage. I nod and keep my expression open, surprised he's said as much to me given I've never wanted to talk about that life. I want to change that, make him see he can tell me anything without concern of criticism.

"Nick wasn't the only one. I was tired of always watching my back, and more and more it felt like we were pushing our luck. Maggie and I kind of fell into this working arrangement."

"What do you mean?"

"She didn't offer me a job and I didn't ask. It just kind of happened. And I love it…"

"But?"

"Pulling my own weight is important to me. This is her business, already established and successful. I want to contribute, help it grow, rather than just collect a paycheck."

Of course he does. This is who Kit is at his core, always has been. That's one of the reasons I was drawn to him. His strong sense of decency and drive to help people. How could I have overlooked that all those years ago?

*"I get it. And she's lucky to have you. This proactive approach to growing the restoration side of things is smart. I can tell you'll make it work. No, you'll succeed beyond your wildest dreams."*

*He scoffs, disbelieving, and my chest squeezes, realizing I have my work cut out for me. Once more, my hand covers his. "You don't need to hear this because I hope you know it, but I'm really proud of you. You should be proud of yourself."*

# KIT

*I swallow hard and my eyes burn. Are those tiny pricks at the back of my eyes tears? Fuck, no.*

*Blinking, my head turns away from her, scanning busy Avenue Road, a major north-south street through Toronto. I need to get ahold of myself, steady my breathing.*

*She's got it all wrong. Her views about me do count and I want to hear them even if I shouldn't. Caro matters to me and her pride in me means a lot, yet it's the last thing I expect.*

*"Well, uh, thanks." Clearing my throat, I slow the car to a crawl as we pass the apartment building where Flora Brown lives.*

*I turn onto the side street, and a white Dodge Caravan pulls out in front of me, freeing up a parking spot right out in front of the building.*

*"It's apartment fifteen ten, right?" I parallel park and she nods.*

*"Kit, don't go just yet." She snags my hand, pulling me back from opening the door. "We've got a lot to talk about, and while this doesn't seem like the right place and time, it feels like it is. And truthfully, I doubt there ever is a right time."*

*Do I want to talk? Could I handle another ripping out of my heart? Uh, no. Although she's right, we should talk as much as I'd rather not. Last night was amazing, just the two of us...but she was drunk.*

*"Caro, let's keep the talk until later. We're here." I jut out my chin toward the apartments behind her. "We've got to get some answers from Flora and then we'll go back to my place. We can talk then."*

*"All right." Shutters slide into place, and her face is a mask of indifference.*

With her profession, she's perfected the unaffected, neutral expression and as much as I'd like to rail on her for using it on me, I can't. I'm the one pushing her away.

Is it out of spite? I don't think so. Now isn't the time nor the place for this kind of conversation. And I'm not even convinced there's a conversation to be had. But we both declared our love. That has to count for something.

I'm no longer a career criminal, but I'm still the guy she met in high school. And there's no denying that while I haven't killed someone with my own hands or supplied young kids with pills, molly, or H, my actions have aided both. Worse, of that I've no doubt.

Sure, I'm older and wiser. I may have grown, learned some, and developed a taste for new things, but underneath it all, I'm the same person.

And she is who she is. She doesn't need a brute like me. A high school graduate with a rap sheet. So what if I'm out of that life and fix cars for a living? My hands are stained crimson, and no amount of atoning for my sins will wash off the blood. And no matter what I want or long for, she shouldn't be saddled with the likes of me. She deserves better.

The visit to the building is a bust. Flora Brown no longer lives at this address, and the new tenant doesn't know where she is, nor does the landlord. She moved out five months ago.

"Now what?" I slip the key into the ignition and secure my seat belt, fresh out of ideas and full of the dread of our time coming to an end looming over us. Neither of us have spoken about it but we're going to have to soon.

"Let me see if Willow has anything new. She said she'd ask around." Caro taps a text out on her phone, head down even after she's already sent it.

Tired and hungry, it's time to head home. Maybe Logan's had better luck. The car squeezes into the bumper-to-bumper traffic and I settle into the seat, preparing for a longer than usual drive home.

"Willow says an old college friend told her that Flora is working at another clinic. This one's in Deer Park." Her demeanor's jubilant. We have another lead.

"Deer Park?" It's an affluent neighborhood in North Toronto, close to here, and a far cry from Jane and Finch. "That's great. We should—"

I pause to check the clock on the dashboard and Caro does the same. It's six o'clock. "It's too late now. We'll have to do it tomorrow."

"Yeah, tomorrow." Some of her elation deflates.

"Hey, look on the bright side. Since it's walk-in, they're open on Sundays. We're not losing a day."

"Yeah, but today is the deadline and there've been no texts from that unknown number." She nibbles on her lip and my body tenses. "What do you think that means?"

"Not sure. We'll figure something out." I force a grin and switch our focus. There's no point fixating on something we can't control, although we're going to have to plan for an attack. "You know, Deer Park is close to Elliot's home." In fact, the neighborhoods are side by side.

"You think it's more than a coincidence?"

Nodding, I turn left onto a not so busy east-west street. "I don't believe in coincidences."

"You think Flora is working with Elliot, don't you?" It's beginning to sound that way to me too.

"It looks like it, but I don't know for sure. Judging from what Willow said, there's something going on there. Flora moved jobs and living arrangements around the same time they both left the clinic. It's too convenient."

"Willow says she works Sunday to Thursday at the clinic, on the front desk, and she breaks for lunch at eleven thirty." She's texting on her phone when I glance over.

"Wow, Willow's hired." I chuckle at this new information, impressed with how invaluable her intel has been to moving things along, even if we haven't hit pay dirt yet. "How was she able to find this out so quickly?" I have a sinking thought and ask, "Willow isn't friends with Flora, is she?"

"No way. They don't like each other. Come to think of it, not many people like Flora. But Willow has many connections, not only in the hospitals and clinics. She reached out to a bunch of people who have worked with Flora and finally, someone responded today about her new job."

"Well, now we know what we're doing tomorrow."

We get in a little after seven and order pizza. While Caro makes a call to fill in Nick, I call Logan. It goes straight to voicemail and I leave a message wanting an update. My next call is Maggie, and she's freaking thrilled to hear the news about Pinter.

Caro's on the couch and she ends the call with her brother, staring up at me in frustration. "He thinks things aren't moving fast enough."

"Of course he does. Let me guess, if he was running this, it would all be wrapped up by now." It's unrealistic but I get it. Nick isn't one to sit around and do nothing.

"Pretty much. We talked about the forty-eight hours being up, and he thinks we should text them back and ask for more time. He wanted me to talk it over with you."

"And then what? I think it's best if we don't respond and see what happens. There's nothing to suggest they know you're with me unless they're connected to Holman, but so far nothing indicates that either."

"True." She bites at the inside of her cheek in contemplation. There really isn't a right answer here because we're on the defensive, any way you look at it.

The intercom buzzes. "That's our pizza. I'll go get it."

When I return, she has the table set and she's popping open two Steam Whistle beers.

"I'm starving." She takes the box from me and pulls out a slice of Terroni's Pizza Cosí.

Our favorite, both the restaurant and the pizza. She slides into her chair, biting into the steaming slice of tomato, porcini mushrooms, mozzarella, fontina, and prosciutto di Parma.

With each chew, her whimpering summons a growl from deep in my throat and a blistering jolt of arousal shoots straight to my balls. Fuck. Fuck. Fuck.

Her eyes snap open and a naughtiness flashes in her simmering gaze. She takes another bite, eliciting another deep, throaty moan, and now she's being just plain devilish.

167

"Can you stop?" I rip a slice from the box, ruthlessly chewing, as if that will demolish my desire. We should talk first.

"What can I say? I love this pizza, and it's been way too long since I've last had it." Her tongue licks at her lips and I fight the feeling that she's talking about a lot more than pizza.

"Fine, but eat it in silence." My gaze begs for mercy.

"Fine. I'll do it for you." Even her agreement tumbles out like a tease.

Despite the delicious food and easy banter, my single-minded focus is on her so much that I'm dumbstruck when she climbs onto my lap and straddles me.

"What are you doing?" My voice is gravelly, almost pained as I try to shut down the wicked sensations of her hot heat nestled over my crotch.

"We need to talk."

Dang. Talk is the last thing I have in mind, but this is a good thing. Talk will kill my raging need to claim her, among other raging body parts.

"I don't—" Her fingers rest against my mouth, silencing me.

"Shhh. I'll talk. You listen." Dark soulful eyes fix on me and I stop breathing. "It really meant a lot to me when you told me about Pinter and the Phoenix today. I hope you know this and I need to say this..."

She shifts in my lap and it takes everything in me to ignore the intense heat coiling around the base of my spine and not give in to my base desire. My dick is so hard it might snap in two.

"I'm sorry I ever made you feel less than. Even when things weren't working out between us, I never thought of you as anything but the best man I've ever known."

My chest spasms and I'm at a loss for what to do with her words. I'm not sure I got it right, or if I'm dreaming.

Her hand grazes the side of my stubbled jaw. "You're my equal. I'd even say better than me."

A huff slips past my clenched jaw, barely keeping a grasp on my control, and I shake away her touch. Both hands drop to her thighs and I immediately regret the move, what she's perceived as a rebuff.

"Not possible. You're a doctor, for crying out loud. You help people and do what's right. We're nothing alike and I'm certainly not better than you."

When she ended our relationship, she didn't act superior and she wasn't cruel. Hell no. She may think she was—I see the regret and self-loathing in the way her body sags and features dim when she talks about that time. But no, never cruel. Never.

She was only being honest and brave. In some ways, she did us both a favor. I was a thug and she was so close to becoming a doctor. Our worlds didn't mesh. We'd never talked about it but I understood her internal conflict.

I had the same doubts storming my mind, every day. How could I be so lucky to have a woman like her when I was what I was? And how could she turn a blind eye to our differences? Differences that were as large and as wide as the Atlantic Ocean.

There's no way I could fault her for wanting better, even if it shredded my heart.

And if we'd stayed together, all the amazing memories, those magical moments we'd created...where would they be now? We would have destroyed them with animosity and doubt.

"We don't have to be alike to be together." Her warm delicate fingers trail one of my eyebrows, sending an electric pulse skittering down my spine, bringing me back to the here and now. "And you aren't a bad person, or evil. God, no. And being on the right side of things isn't always an option. I know that now."

She pauses, nibbling on her bottom lip, and her eyes swell with an intimacy I've only ever seen directed at me. Or maybe that's what I tell myself. Either way, I'm losing this battle—the temptation to take her.

"What I'm trying to say is, I never should have left you. Especially for the reason I gave. It was ignorant and insensitive of me." She's so close, her sweet breath bathes my face.

"You had to make difficult choices when you were young and so did Léa and Nick. I was spared all of that. We had no parents or money and neither did you. If I'd been in your shoes, I'm not so sure I would have made different choices."

A knot lodges in my throat and I push past it, not willing to let her excuse the past, my dirty deeds. "But I did—"

She kisses me, really kisses me, swallowing my protest. Her fingers thread my hair and she arches into me.

This part was always easy. We never had any difficulty being close, kissing, holding each other and so much more.

Unable to pass up a chance to touch her, taste her, my hands race along the curve of her back, gripping at her waist. The sensation of her body in my hands is...exhilarating.

She creeps closer. Every inch of her from core to chest presses into me and she deepens the kiss. I lose myself in the sweep of her tongue delving into my mouth, her sexy little sighs tickling at my throat, and the hard points of her tits scraping along my chest.

Then it's over. She pulls away, yet her eagerness and impatience vibrate in her bunched muscles.

"Life isn't neat and tidy, even when I tried to make it so. When we broke up, I was so fixed on this unrealistic ideal of what my life should be that I was so blind to reality. Life isn't easy and we all have to make difficult decisions, and sometimes they aren't what others would see as right. You were doing what was needed to survive. And I—"

"Hey, it's okay." I curl her hair behind her ear. "There's nothing wrong with wanting a good life even if it didn't fit with my choices. We don't need to rehash the past."

My heart is about to tear out of my chest, not wanting to relive our history. I'm a selfish bastard and so close to just taking what she's so willing to give.

I want her. Always do.

But what happens tomorrow when our lust is satiated and the harsh glare of reality rises like the sun, blindingly irrefutable and unforgiving? What then?

"Last night, like everything else, is in the past. I will keep you safe and get to the bottom of this. I will let nothing happen to you. Ever." I cup her face in my hand, staring intently at her. "And then we can go back to our lives."

My last words are sand, gritty and bland on my tongue, and I drop my hands to my sides.

"I don't want to go back to how things were." She runs a hand down my chest, stopping just above where we are joined. "I've missed you. Every day. And I meant everything I said last night. I wasn't drunk." Her hands cup my face and there's a pinch in my chest.

"Why it took me so long to do something about it..." Her head dips and she pauses so close to my mouth. "It isn't easy to admit I'm wrong. You know, all us doctors think we're gods among men."

She laughs, a mixture of melancholy and toying in her gaze. I join her in spite of this mind-altering conversation. I used to joke about her chosen profession and how she had to be careful not to become an egomaniac.

"I don't know what to say to this. Nothing has changed. I can't change my past." My body is too tight, the muscles at the back of my neck as hard as stone, joints stiff and my limbs tingling.

"I don't expect that of you. I'm the one who fucked things up." She grips the sides of my face once more. "I want a second chance."

I want to believe her. Fuck, my heart is all in and so is pretty much every other part of my body, but my head knows better.

She isn't lying. Every word out of her mouth must feel like the truth, but she's scared, her life is on the line. I'm familiar and...we did once love each other. Both believing we'd be together forever.

Fuck.

Reality will crush us. We can hide from it but not forever.

Her face comes close to mine, angling her head to one side and blinking an eye rapidly as she nears my cheek. Shit, no.

Her eyelashes softly graze my cheek.

Ticklish.

Sensuous.

Butterfly kisses.

This was always our thing.

How many times had I imagined this very sensation? Her warm breath caressing my jaw, lashes stroking my skin. A million times. Easily.

Heck, I'd even started it the other night with a kunik, rubbing the tip of my nose against hers. My knees had almost buckled, and the *years apart had almost been erased. It was like nothing had changed. Almost.*

*Her fingers track across my cheekbones and I'm focused solely on the here and now and what she's doing to me. Both inside and outside.*

*Still holding my head in place, her nose rubs back and forth against mine and a warmth stirs deep within my chest, uncurling and spreading. My eyelashes flutter closed at the swoosh sweeping through me, and my fingers sink into her waist.*

*What the hell is she doing to me?*

*Lastly, her lips touch mine. It isn't a long or deep kiss, more a peck, but it's sweet and gentle. And that does it.*

*Whatever sense of self-preservation I have left is gone. Poof, vanishes into thin air. None of my concerns or hesitations are of any importance.*

*All I want is her.*

*Caro. To claim her, to have her.*

*My fingers tangle in her hair and I deepen the kiss. Her lips crinkle into a smile against mine and she opens wider, our kiss shifting from sweet and tentative to vicious and greedy.*

# CARO

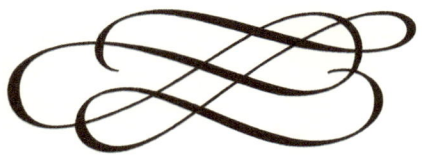

He combs his fingers through my hair, setting my scalp on fire as his lips rove from my jaw to kiss my neck. In one swift move, he turns with me in his arms and places me on my back on the couch, fingers working fast to remove my shirt and bra.

Just as eager to have him naked, I tug at his shirt, exposing his chest, and my fingers linger on his cut muscles. I revel at how his abs ripple and twitch under my touch. His responsiveness sends an electric pulse through my fingertips and straight to my core.

Dark, hooded eyes, corded neck, and the firm set of his jaw intent on me is a heady, overpowering sensation. One arm brackets one side of my head and his body weighs on me. It's glorious and not enough.

He pushes on his one hand, eyes dipping down and between us, and his smoldering gaze nearly scorches my bare breasts. Then his tongue is trailing a path through the center of my chest, lazy and lavish, descending lower and lower.

My nipples bead and tighten, skin on fire, as his hand slips into my panties, and shamelessly, my hips rock against his fingers, rubbing right where I need him the most.

"Fuuuck, Caro." He leans his forehead against mine. "You're so wet. So ready. And it's all for me."

A soft, needy sob pours from the back of my throat, and the noise spurs him on, fingers increasing their tempo. Bright stars dance on the backs of my eyelids and the intensity is blinding.

"Kit," I scream, arching my back, my muscles tense, strung tight like a bow.

My core clenches and I explode. Not a single massive spasm, but many, so many.-My entire body is racked with mind-numbing bliss.

Incoherent sounds and words spill from my lips as my fingers dig into the cushion of the couch, at his back, anywhere I can gain purchase, and through it all, he doesn't let up.

He works his magical fingers deep inside of me, wringing out every last ounce of pleasure. And my orgasm is never-ending.

Finally, I come down and a wide grin runs wild across my face. I wipe a tear from the corner of my eye, blinking up at him. His grin is gorgeous and breath-stealing, dimples as bright as stadium lights.

"God, I missed you." I stretch, delighting in the wonderful afterglow of my climax.

Deep, rough laughter spills from his parted lips and his eyes hold a satisfied sparkle. "Good."

I sit up, meeting his lips with mine, relishing a slow, long kiss before falling back onto the sofa. The back of my hand covers my mouth, stifling a yawn, and he quirks a brow.

"You're not going to fall asleep on me, are you?"

"Oh, God, no." A rush of heat climbs up my neck, embarrassed I passed out on him last night after my toe-curling orgasm. What a fool. "We're only getting started."

My fingers wrestle with the button of his pants, feeling his hard length against the tightly stretched fabric. He helps, quickly discarding his pants, and grabs at my hands, ready to wrap around his hard cock.

"Condom? Or are you still on the pill? I'm clean." Urgency frays his words that come out as heavy pants. "I've never been bare with anyone but you."

His words hit me in waves, intense and drugging. I'm undone. His admission of being skin to skin with only me is so powerful and overwhelming.

I need him now. I ache for him. His love for me fuels my arousal, drenches my sex, and coats my thighs.

"Me neither," I'm quick to answer, pressing my legs together. "I don't want anything between us. I'm on the pill."

I reach for his hips, needing to hold him. To lose myself in his scent, the feel of him inside me. He nods, nudging his erection at my entrance, one hand sliding under my ass for a better angle. Gazes locked, he thrusts into me, setting a deep and steady rhythm.

The feel of him, filling me, setting me on fire, brings more tears to my eyes and our bodies move like one.

His mouth covers mine, drinking my cries, feeding on my pleasure as if he's only now coming to life. This is more than sex, and not just for me but for both of us. Raw and exposed, his soulful eyes gaze into mine. He's seeing me, really seeing me as I see him.

He pumps hard and fast into me, stretching me and hitting the spot, the one that does crazy things to my body, over and over again. Hips gyrating and skin slick with sweat, his hair is now damp and falls over his forehead.

My fingers slide through his locks and I rock into him, lifting my hips to meet every one of his thrusts. His body tenses, muscles as hard as steel, and our gazes are still locked. This man, so utterly perfect.

Tender, savage, protective, and mine. The most incredible feeling of being loved rolls over me in waves.

Then he's kissing me hard and fervently as he slams wildly into me, no longer measured and rhythmic, more frenzied. Then snap. Every inch of him hardens, the veins in his neck bulge and he goes off with a roar, coming inside of me.

I go with him, throwing myself off the cliff as he buries his face in my neck. Goosebumps break out along my spine, my orgasm flowing through me fast and furious, leaving me shattered.

"Christ, Caro." Slanting his head, he seizes my lips in a kiss, both loving and hungry.

Our night is much more of the same. We sleep for a few hours and then wake, one or both of us needing the other, and we make love. The next morning, we wake up later than usual, both lazy and satisfied.

"We should get up, shouldn't we?" Even as I ask it, the answer is obvious.

Still no texts from the unknown number or Elliot, and the silence makes me nervous. I don't know which is worse, another threat or nothing.

We are out of time and if they follow through on their threat, it could be anything. I hate the waiting and not knowing. Flora is our last chance at any indication as to what Elliot is up to or where we can find him.

"Yeah, we should." Kit captures my lips for a kiss. "We're going to get lucky today."

His voice carries optimism, and I wonder if he really believes that or if it's for my benefit.

"Really?" I push up onto my elbows and rest my hands on his warm, solid chest. "I think I already got lucky." I kiss the center where his heart is. "I don't want to push my luck. You're all I need."

I mean it. Even in our current predicament, I wouldn't change a thing if it meant I'd be without Kit. All we've been through, so far, has been worth it. Yes, even the horrifying explosion.

"You've got me. Always." He raises his head to lightly kiss my forehead. "I think we're due some more luck. We've been years apart and we've got to catch a break on this whole nightmare."

Hands wrapping around my arms, he sits up and swings his legs over the side of the bed, bringing me to sitting. "C'mon. Let's get clean. I'll wash your front."

He winks, arching a dark brow, his eyes laser-focused on my breasts. His hazel pupils liquefy.

"I can do my chest but I could use some help with my back." I leap from the bed, running to the bathroom on a giggle.

Large hands capture my waist as I hit the tiled floor and he hoists me over his shoulder. "I tell you what, let me wash all of you."

He smacks my bare ass, and the sting is quickly followed by a warm soothing rub of his palm. The pleasure and pain flood my core and I'm all too happy to let him have his way with me.

After our long and pleasurable shower, we grab breakfast and get ready for the day. Flora is our only task today and we get to the clinic in time for her lunch.

The walk-in clinic in Deer Park is busy, and we're third in line to talk to the nurse at the front desk. This is Flora, and she's talking to a mother with a crying baby. No, the diminutive Filipino woman isn't the child's mother, more like the nanny.

176

*Flora Brown is in her late twenties with bird-like features, straw-colored hair to her shoulders, and is dressed in sky-blue scrubs. She's pixie-like and pretty, how I remember her.*

*At first she's pleasant, an inviting expression for those of us waiting while the nanny maneuvers a top-of-the-line stroller with wheels big enough for off-roading adventures.*

*Flora makes eye contact with Kit and her smile widens, quickly shifting into a scowl at the sight of me at his side.*

"What did you do to her?" *he mumbles, a twinkle in his eyes as he leans into me.*

"What?" *I frown, confused. I never did anything to Flora.*

"She doesn't like you." *His gaze returns to the sprite of a young woman straining to see past the old man leaning over the desk in front of her.*

*Flora no longer looks the least bit attractive even with her delicate features. Daggers shoot from her blue eyes, fixed on me. As we step up to the counter, she straightens in her chair, chin out defiantly. She's staring at Kit and I might as well not be here.*

"Hello, how may I help you?" *Obnoxiously forward like always, she paws at his arm resting on the desktop and my insides seethe at her touching him.*

*To make matters worse, he doesn't blink or pull away. Instead he volleys a flirtatious response while taking her tiny hand in his.*

"Hey, I'm Kit, and it's nice to meet you, Flora."

*She flushes, basking in the attention, and I want to gag.*

"Hi, Kit. Love the name." *She angles away from me as if she can deny my existence. It's quite comical and all Flora. She's a shameless flirt and can be inappropriate if my memory serves me right from when she worked at the Jane Clinic.*

"Thanks." *He winks, now moving his arm closer to his body. She takes the hint and lets her fingers drop to the counter.* "I was hoping you could help us by answering a few questions about Elliot Foley."

"Elliot? Is something wrong?" *Worry skates across her blonde brow and it doesn't seem fake.*

"You worked at the Jane Walk-in Clinic at the same time he did, and you also oversaw the renovations to the supply room, correct?"

177

She nods, less flirty now, and folds her arms over her middle, clearly cautious of this line of questioning.

"Can you tell us what work was done to the room?"

"Caro knows." She's snide with my name. "It was a total overhaul. New cabinets, an island was installed, shelving and better lighting. Just look at the place. She can tell you." She flashes me a look to match her 'you're an idiot' tone.

"We can't." I hadn't planned on saying anything given she was responding so well to Kit, but I can no longer resist. "The clinic burned to the ground."

"What?" Wide-eyed, she tenses.

"Yes. There was an explosion." I'm blunt and want answers.

"Was anyone hurt?" She jumps when a nurse steps in behind her, saying it's time for her break. The nurse takes over and Flora stands back, now more anxious than ever to leave. "Okay, thanks. I have to go, sorry I couldn't be more help."

Undeterred, Kit walks through a door similar to the one at my clinic, and like that one, it leads to a hallway to the examination rooms and staff-only areas.

"You can't come back here." Flora steps into him, putting her palms out in a lame attempt to stop him.

"We just need a few minutes. Is there a break room where we could go to speak privately?"

"I don't have much time for lunch. And you shouldn't be—"

"You asked about the explosion at the clinic—no one was hurt." Kit's tone is low and tender and in turn, her shoulders relax.

"Thank goodness." Relief blankets her features. Kit's doing a great job at putting her at ease. I try to fade into the background and listen.

"Elliot trusted you, didn't he?"

"Yes. A lot." Like a flower blossoming under the sun's rays, she inches toward him, the horrible news about the clinic no longer of significance. "I suppose we could chat in the back room. Follow me."

"Thanks so much. Can you tell me more about what you did while the renovations were underway? Tell us what responsibilities Elliot trusted you with." He's laying it on thick, and she's gobbling it up.

"Well, he asked a lot of me. Let's see, where should I start?" She holds open the door to a small room with a kitchenette and a round table for five.

I keep my mouth shut even with questions tripping over themselves to get out of my mouth.

"Like what?" He leans against a wall while she grabs a container from the fridge.

"Well...I'd rather not say in front of Dr. Archer." She casts her gaze on me, curling her lip.

Her dislike for me never bothered me before and it doesn't now. For some reason, other women intimidated or pissed her off.

"It's okay, Flora. I know Elliot liked you a lot." It's a lie, but I draw on Willow's comments from yesterday because I wasn't observant enough to notice Elliot and Flora were close.

"He did." Her attraction to Elliot is clear, and there's a real possibility something happened between them. And no surprise to me, I feel nothing.

The more I think about it, I really didn't pay much attention to Elliot, and now I wonder why I even dated him. Was I bored? Lonely? Punishing myself?

"Don't worry about my feelings." I try not to come off as uncaring or callous, more offering myself as a target for her bitterness.

It must do the trick because she gives me a smug smile, almost eager to unload in front of me. "My brothers own a renovation company, so you'll have to ask them what exactly they did. My job was to make sure no one interrupted them. Elliot made that very clear."

She moves the fork around the greens but she doesn't eat. "I tried to tell him I could do more, but he said I was a strong leader and the staff liked me, so they'd listen to me. And they did."

I hold back a scoff. The staff didn't argue with her because she's unstable and none of them wanted the hassle of her going off on them.

"Great. Do you know why he had the renovations done and why he didn't tell Caro about it?" Kit's now resting his hands against the back of a chair.

"It was some sort of gift for Dr. Archer. He wanted to surprise her. But that's just what he said—I got the truth out of him." She's triumphant, glowering at me, and I hope my expression is neutral or even wounded if only to encourage her to talk.

"The truth? What does that mean?" Kit quirks a brow, sparing a glance my way.

She places the lid back onto the container, her food untouched. "He wanted the supply room to be better equipped and organized. I mean, the place was small and a mess. He did it for the good of the clinic."

I don't know about Kit, but I call bullshit. Something just changed, and she's no longer maintaining eye contact. This could be about Elliot. Like Willow suspected, there was most probably more going on between those two.

"Do you still see Elliot?" He switches gears, picking up on her sudden caginess. "Would you say you're friends?"

"More than friends. I mean..." Now she bites her lip.

"You're dating?" He cuts to the chase.

"Yes. We've been together since the Jane Clinic." Her shoulders tense as she gives me a sideways glance. "Caro, sorry to have to tell you this way, but he wasn't faithful to you. In fact, he didn't even like you. He wanted to be with me."

Even as she grows uncomfortable, she's enjoying this, unloading the truth about Elliot, but I don't care. Maybe I should act like I do if it would make her talk some more.

"Okay. Did Elliot ask you to do other things?" Kit's trying to get her to focus.

"I think you should go now." She shoves her lunch back into the fridge.

He pulls out his phone, tapping on the screen a few times before turning the screen toward her. "Have you ever seen this before?"

"No." She snorts, refusing to look any longer at the phone. "No, I've never seen the beetle."

He must have shown her the picture of the blue pill with the insect logo.

Her choice of words is both strange and interesting.

The beetle.

She's certain, knowing the kind of insect it is, no guessing. Meanwhile neither of us, nor Nick and Logan, could say for sure what insect it is because the symbol is too small for any kind of detail.

I'm now more suspicious of Flora than ever, and Kit and I share a look. His intense gaze says we're not leaving until she talks.

"You have to go now." She opens the door to the hallway and again, I hold back a laugh, more because I'd like to see her try to get Kit to leave.

"Caro, do all clinics like this have storage rooms?" He doesn't move.

At first, I'm puzzled by his sudden question. Flora is also thrown, forgetting her immediate desire to get rid of us as she quietly looks on.

"Yes, most of them would have a room to store supplies, equipment, drug samples, and stuff like that."

"Great." He brushes past Flora and instead of going left, the way we entered, he turns right. "Now where would it be?"

"Hey, where are you going?" Flora scurries after him.

He opens a door, then just as quickly closes it. The bathroom. The next door he tries is the supply closet and he barges in. Flora and I step into the room and she's making all kinds of demands, telling us to leave, but neither of us move or say a thing.

My legs shake and my mind blanks. I can hardly believe it. The room is near identical to the Jane Clinic but bigger.

Oh my God. There's an island in the middle of the room. Kit squats in front of a large floor mat directly in front of the cupboards.

Before he pulls back the mat, my breath stops, already knowing what he'll uncover. And sure enough, in the floor, hidden under the rubber mat, is a similar door to the one at the Jane Clinic. Elliot renovated this room too.

"You need to go before I call the cops." Flora tugs at his shoulder, but he's a big guy and her efforts are futile.

"Go ahead, call the cops."

Her head snaps to me at my challenging tone.

Kit slides his finger into the metal ring and pulls. It's locked. "Open it." He motions to Flora.

"What?" She backs away from him, eyes as round as saucers. She's panicked and ready to escape. "I've never seen that before in my life. I don't know how to open it."

I'm quick to close the door and press my back against it, blocking exit from the room.

Kit's hands are planted on the countertop, jaw set and an unwavering determination in his eyes. "Start talking or we will call the cops."

Her top teeth sink into her bottom lip, and there's a flash of something wild, almost fearful, in her gaze.

"Don't call the cops. I'll tell you what I know but none of this can come back on me." Her hands rake back and forth through her hair, blonde wisps sticking up in every direction.

"Talk." He folds his arms over his chest.

"Did Elliot have this renovated too?" My question's rhetorical, but I want her to say it, confirming what we all know.

She nods, worrying her hands. "He arranged for my brothers to do the job, but I was the one to suggest it to the higher-ups. Elliot's never set foot in here."

My gaze collides with Kit's. Flora is more involved than I thought, and I feel like an idiot. How did I miss all this going on in front of me at the clinic?

"So you run the operation?" I don't fully understand what the operation is but I'm hoping she'll fill in the gaps.

"No, no, this is Elliot's. I just..." She spins around and around like a hula hoop, finally leaning into a wall. "After you asked him to leave the Jane Clinic, he needed a new set-up and I wanted to help. He was in a jam. I got this job, we built the compartment under the floor, and we started all over again."

"The oxy was shipped here and then what?" Kit's growing impatient, shifting from one foot to the other, and I can't help but feel the urgency. We are out of time, and we need more. We need to find Elliot.

"I would take the shipments to my place and Elliot would get them there."

*For all of Flora's shortcomings, I feel sorry for her. I doubt she sees just how Elliot is using her. There's no way he would have gotten me to do any of this, but he likely knew that.*

"So you're taking all the risks?" He cocks his head to one side, really looking at Flora.

*Why put herself in such jeopardy for a man? A selfish, egotistical man at that. But in some ways, I was also a means to an end.*

*While Elliot served a purpose for me, I did for him. Dating me enabled him to keep an eye on me, make sure my attention was elsewhere. And he succeeded; I never suspected him.*

"No. Elliot's in danger. He's being followed, and that's why he slips in and out of my building unseen, and why I bring the shipments to my place. The more they know about him, the less bargaining power he has."

*A strange buzz of hope courses through me. Elliot is in hiding, as Kit figured.*

"Who are they?" Kit pushes.

"I don't know." Her eyes drop to the floor like a stone sinking to the bottom of a river. *She's lying and I clench my fists, forcing myself not to shake her until she talks.*

"When was the last time you spoke to Elliot or saw him?" *Kit either doesn't pick up on her lie, which I doubt, or he'll come back to it.*

"Two days ago. He slept over."

"So what you're saying is, it's possible that no one knows about you or this clinic?"

"What do you mean, knows about me? Elliot isn't keeping me a secret." *She's too quick and too heated not to reveal it's a sore spot for her. She's definitely a secret.*

"Who are they? And don't lie." *His voice is as sharp as a knife's blade.*

"I swear, I don't know." *She's shaking her head.* "But whoever they are, they're scary, dangerous people. They don't mess around."

"Why'd you say that?"

"After leaving the Jane Clinic, Elliot tried to get out. He'd had enough but they wouldn't let him go. He was beaten to within an inch of his life." She slides her back down the wall until her butt hits the floor. Her worn sneakers squeeze against the tile as she comes to a stop.

Because the jerk is in hiding, they are after me. And what Kit's said all along rings in my ears. Elliot had to have implicated me in some way. Flora is involved in this and they don't know about her, but they know about me.

Fucking Elliot.

"He really wants out. That's why…" Flora stares up at us, tears pooling in her eyes. "He's done something. I don't know what but it isn't good."

"What do you think he did?" My question is a near whisper, unsure if I should even be talking since she doesn't like me.

A reminder of my presence might cause her to clam up. But staying silent is torture. I need to know what those people think I have or know where it's hidden.

"He's in hiding and I can't reach him. The last shipment he picked up… I've heard things… I mean, I don't do drugs but I've made it a point to keep my ear to the ground. There's a shortage of beetle juice on the street."

"Beetle juice?" Kit and I ask at the same time.

"Fuck." She looks like she wants to shove the word back in her mouth and starts pounding her fist into her thigh.

Diving to her level, I grab her arm, stopping her punches before she does any real damage to herself. "It's okay. Stop. What's beetle juice?"

"It's the pill Kit has on his phone. That's what it's called on the street. It's oxy and it's in high demand on the streets. Would you believe it's trending, the 'in' drug? Big at snotty rich kid parties and on university campuses. A shortage would hurt distribution and the dealer."

"Do you know how to get ahold of Elliot?" Kit stands on the other side of Flora now.

"I thought so. I have his number but he isn't answering." She pulls out the phone, showing us his contact information. It's the same number I have. "That isn't like him. I'm afraid he's dead."

# KIT

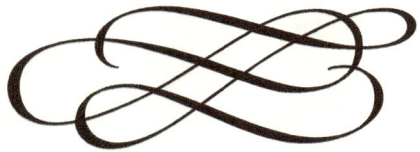

Elliot, the spineless asshole, could be dead, hiding, or worse, out of the country by now, leaving Caro holding the proverbial bag.

"Caro, can I have your phone?" I hold out my hand.

Understanding why I'm asking, she unlocks the phone and taps a few times, bringing up the texts from the unknown caller before giving it to me.

"Do you have any idea what these mean or who could be sending them?"

Flora blanches while she reads, vehemently shaking her head. "I don't know who that is but if I had to guess, they're talking about whatever Elliot did."

"And why are they looking at Caro?" I leave out the "and not you" to my question. Flora's sensitive to other women, and she doesn't need to feel any more on the defensive than she already is. I need to keep her talking.

She's saved from answering when the same nurse who relieved her for lunch opens the door.

"Flora? What are you doing in here?" A deep groove forms between the woman's knitted brows. "All of you out, now. Flora, your lunch is over. We'll talk about this later."

Caro and I share a look, both hightailing it to the front of the clinic as the nurse calls after us. We're not sticking around for any questions as to why we were back in the staff area of the clinic.

The harsh snap of wintry air lashes at my face and Caro ducks her head, pulling her jacket tighter around herself and shoving on her mitts. I grab at her hand, curling mine around her wool mitten.

She peers up at me. "What do you think about all that?"

*We trudge up the street toward the public parking lot, less than a block from the clinic.*

*"We need to find Elliot." I fish the key from my pocket.*

*Everything comes back to this asshole, and while our theories and speculations have been on the money, Elliot has the shipment of drugs that will get Caro out of danger.*

*"What I'm still trying to figure out is why Elliot has brought me into this."*

*I swing her around to face me. Why can't she see what's right in front of her? Is she so deep in denial that she's unable to entertain the possibility of Elliot being a bad motherfucker?*

*"Caro, whoever's in charge has been led to believe you're Flora in Elliot's dealings."*

*"What?"*

*"Think about it. Flora's role in this. She's his partner even if she doesn't know everything." I pause, letting all that Flora just shared with us sink in.*

*"But Elliot made it look like you are. Your name on the shipping labels. The Jane Clinic was a known location to whoever distributes the drugs. And from the sounds of things, the distributor or dealer doesn't know about the Deer Park Clinic. If they did, Flora would have mentioned getting a similar visit to what you did."*

*I squeeze her hand. "He set you up to be his scapegoat. He's missing and they're looking at you."*

*"It's so stupid. Of course. Hearing you say it all out loud." She pulls away, taking her hand from mine.*

*Her mouth opens and closes twice before anything comes out. "Most of what you just laid out, I knew...but a silly part of me didn't want to believe he'd do that."*

*It pisses me off that she can't see her ex is an asshole, and I'm no good at keeping it to myself. "Why? Because he's well educated and a fucking doctor?"*

*"What?" She's taken aback and her posture goes rigid, but it's short-lived. She stands in front of me and softens her expression. "No. Because I didn't think he was smart enough to set up someone and...I'm ticked at myself for not seeing what was right in front of*

me. If I'm being honest, our relationship was kind of like a beard for each of us, hiding something else. I didn't want to date or be hassled or set up on a blind date and he…he was keeping me preoccupied so he could operate out of the clinic undetected."

My lips mash together, forcing the I told you he was a dick down my throat. It's the last thing she needs to hear. I grip her hand once more and we resume walking, this time at a quicker pace, toward the car. It's started to rain, freezing rain.

Once inside the car, she leans over and grips my arm, preventing me from doing any more than starting the SUV.

"Kit, listen. Elliot wasn't anything serious. We didn't really hang out and even when we both worked at the clinic, we…we didn't have much to do with each other." She shrugs, releasing me. "I don't know how to explain it, and when I look back, I wonder why I even dated him. There wasn't any attraction."

She sinks back into the passenger seat, imploring me with her warm gaze to hear every word she utters. Sincerity radiates from her and the lump in my throat loosens.

"He served a purpose for me. I hate to say it like this but I think I used him and he obviously did the same to me."

"Used him? How?" I do not want to hear about her sexual needs and how that fucking asshole…ah, fuck no. My gut roils.

"Colleagues and friends didn't hound me since I was seeing someone. No one pestered me to go out to a club or offered to set me up on a blind date."

"Oh." Flicking on the windshield wipers, I watch the rain splat onto the glass, unsure what to say or how to feel. Each raindrop flattens and freezes upon contact, but just as quickly the frozen snowflake is destroyed with the swipe of a blade.

"You know, I'm not objective when it comes to Elliot and…" I look away for a second, wanting not to sound like a jealous asshole or a pussy. "I really don't like the guy. In fact, it's fair to say I hate him after all he's put you through."

"I don't like him either." She leans closer to me, resting her hand on my thigh.

"Thanks for explaining all of that to me." My lips press to hers and she tastes so sweet, like candy. "We should get a move on."

Groaning, her forehead rests against my chest before she pulls away. "Yes, we should. If this keeps up, the roads are going to be crappy."

She squeezes my arm and pulls the belt over her middle, clicking it into place. I hit the dial pad on the car screen and bring up a number.

"Let's see if Logan's got any new information."

He's supposed to have feelers out on Elliot and the drug, but I haven't heard anything. The car eases into traffic and it's slow going with the change in weather.

Even with winter four to six months of the year, it always amazes me how people suddenly forget how to drive with a little snow or ice.

"Yo, what's up?" Logan's voice filters through the car speakers.

"Hey, Caro and I just talked to Flora Brown."

"Oh yeah? Isn't she the chick who's banging Elliot?" He chuckles and clears his throat. "Shit, Caro's with you, right?"

"Yes, I'm here." Caro rolls her eyes.

"My bad, not cool." The idiot just remembered Caro and Elliot were a thing and I can't help but laugh. It comes easier since Caro's showed me what she had with the doctor was nothing.

"Logan, don't sweat it. Tell us what you found out." Her lopsided I like to see him squirm grin is infectious. "Flora had a lot to say."

"Yeah, I meant to call last night but, uh, I got busy with an old friend."

"You can stop right there." She shakes her head, cutting him off and sparing us the graphic details of his night.

"Logan, this is important. I need you at your best. Remember what Nick said." I hate playing the hardass, but left on his own, Logan will take his sweet time getting answers, or worse, he'll hit the road without a word.

"Hey, relax. I'm on it. Really nothing to report on Elliot. No one's heard of him, but they all know the pill. It's called beetle juice—a high dose of oxy."

My pulse spikes, excited to have confirmation of information from more than one source. "Yeah, that's what Flora said too."

"It's very popular. You can get it pretty much anywhere in the city, but not right now."

"Is that because of supply?" She leans forward in her seat.

"Yeah, there's a shortage on the street. Dealers were promised and have paid for the stuff, but they've been left dry. There's a lot of angry dealers and the supplier's shitting bricks. Tensions are high on the street and some say blood will be spilled."

"Who's the supplier?" I change lanes, keeping an eye on a black SUV, possibly an Escalade, two cars behind that has been on us since I left the parking lot.

It could be nothing, but then again, we're due for a surprise. The forty-eight hours are up and according to Flora, no one knows about her existence in Elliot's operation. In which case, the Deer Park Clinic isn't being watched.

Caro is a different story.

The tail could be on her, although I've seen no sign of anyone following us. Unless they've been lying in wait?

I shudder, tightening my jaw to hold back a curse.

"Don't know who supplies it. They call him the Beetle and he brings the juice."

"Him?" I make a right onto a residential street.

The SUV is right behind me.

Fuck. I grip the wheel and glance to Caro. For now she's unaware.

"Yeah, it's a guy." Logan pauses, making a slurping sound like he's drinking through a straw. "What did you learn from Flora?"

I give him a rundown on the conversation and stress the importance of finding Elliot. The car is still on us. "Do some more digging on who Beetle is and I'll see what Paddy says."

"Sure thing, bro. I'll call you as soon as I get something."

"All right. Talk later."

She hits end call and the black Escalade is practically on our bumper. Yeah, this isn't some coincidence. We have a tail and I'm going to have to lose them.

Even with tinted windows, I can see two muscled WWE rejects in the front seat. Both in black or navy jackets with white button-down

189

shirts and dark ties. It's some kind of uniform, with a crest or emblem embroidered in gold and white on the left breast pocket of their blazers.

One guy's bald and the other's got a thick brown or reddish mustache. Both wear sunglasses.

"Hey, listen to me." My voice is calm, nothing like the battleground inside my head. "There's a car following us."

Caro's safety is my only concern. I rack my brain for some ingenious way to lose these assholes. We're smack in the middle of traffic with congested streets, parked cars, and people everywhere.

We need a miracle.

"What?" Caro whips around to look out the back window.

I squeeze the SUV in between two smaller cars in the next lane and the Escalade lags, no longer on our bumper but not far behind.

What's their goal? Follow us? Harm us? Capture us? Or worse? This must be them making good on their threat, but how the fuck did they find us?

"Three cars back, the left lane. Black Escalade. They've been on us since we left the clinic."

I veer right onto a side street, intending to cut to another main roadway a block over and lose them in the process.

"Do you think those are the same people looking for Elliot? Texting me?" Her voice wavers and I spare a glance; her eyes are wild and her face tight. "Did they find us?"

As if bowled over by a tidal wave, I'm swamped with only one thought. I must keep her safe.

"Maybe." I swing the car left, heading south once again.

No sign of them behind us. Yes, this could be our miracle. I gun the engine, zooming through the intersection on a yellow light as it blinks red.

"Did we lose them?" Hope tinges her tone.

"Shit." I draw my lower lip between my teeth and hiss. "They're running the light."

Not too far behind, there's an eruption of horns blaring and screeching brakes. The bastards aren't losing us. They'll do whatever it takes, even bulldoze pedestrians or smash into other vehicles.

"What are we going to do?" She's panicked.

"It's going to be okay. Just hang on tight." My foot presses on the accelerator, grateful for a patch of thinning traffic.

The street is slick and the salters haven't covered this stretch of road yet. Up ahead is Upper Canada College, a private school for boys in elementary and high school, and I've got a decision to make.

The road forms a Y, with one route bypassing the college whereas the other leads toward the school, coming to a T junction at the outer edge of the school grounds. At that point, it's left or right.

Our SUV is only feet away from the split and if we were to continue this way, there's no doubt the car behind would ram into us. I stay in the right lane, giving the impression we're going straight through.

At the last minute, I spin the wheel left onto the other road. "Fuck."

The Escalade cuts across the road and nearly collides with another car coming in the opposite direction. They are right on us.

They want to do damage.

At the bend in the road, I tap the brakes. The car starts to slide, and with a swift turn of the wheel, I prevent the fishtail. Shit. Black ice.

The Escalade hood takes up the rearview mirror. This is more than tailgating. The SUV rams into us. My neck cracks forward, teeth rattling, and the seat belt tightens on my chest. Tires screech, metal pops and Caro shrieks.

"Fuck, hang on." I white-knuckle the steering wheel, the car gliding across the road as if on skates.

Another blink and another smash. This time harder. So hard, the car takes flight and rolls. Everything outside the car tumbles around and around.

Glass sprays, metal crunches, tires squeal, and the air bags deploy. Tires, black metal, someone's bald head, the flash of steel, gold and red.

The windshield splinters, spiderwebbing, the hood crumples, and Caro's screams pierce my heart.

Thunk. The SUV smashes onto the ground, right side up, bouncing once or twice before coming to a complete stop. My mind spins like I'm in a dryer but I'm alive.

*Caro.*

*Blinking and dizzy, my fingers reach out, brushing at her hair, then her face. "Caro, you okay?"*

*Soft moans come from her side of the car. Blinking furiously, my vision steadies. Head lolling to one side, against the passenger door window, she's in one piece, no blood but eyes closed.*

*I scramble to release my seat belt, inching closer to her, hands holding her face. "Babe, talk to me."*

*She stirs, murmuring and disoriented. Her lashes flutter, and clear brown eyes rest on me.*

*The world stops. She's okay.*

*Whispering her name, I kiss her softly, dragging a calming breath through my body. "Caro."*

*"I'm okay. Are you?" One of her hands grips the side of my face and her touch alone melts away any pain or fear.*

*But not for long.*

*"Yeah, fine. We have to get out of here."*

*Did the guys from the Escalade sit around to make sure the job was done right or did they take off? Are they outside and going to make sure they finish the job?*

*I turn my head, stiff and a little the worse for wear, and scan outside. Cars have stopped on either side of the road and someone's on the sidewalk, cellphone to their ear. Hopefully, they're calling the cops.*

*A couple of people are edging toward our car. There's no sign of the Escalade. The driver side door opens and I tumble from the car. Icy drops of snow lick at my face, coming down fast and slushy, and I shiver.*

*Something warm and sticky trickles past the corner of my eye. My fingers feel along my flesh, looking for the source, and stop at a small gash along the edge of my hairline. Blood covers my digits. Head wounds always bleed like a geyser.*

*A man I've never seen before stands to my side and takes my elbow, guiding me away from the car. His lips are moving and words are coming out of his mouth but I can't make sense of them.*

*"Caro." My desperation impales her name and my heart rate ticks up, needing eyes on her.*

Only when she approaches me, another stranger, a woman, at her side, does my pulse slow. On shaky legs, she grabs my arm and we walk carefully from the median onto the slippery road toward the sidewalk.

She looks okay, no signs on the outside of the crash, but she could be bleeding internally. Hasn't she already been through enough? My body vibrates with anger.

"Are you sure you're okay?" I croak, tightening my hold on her.

She nods and someone reassures us that the police are on the way, and like rubber, my legs buckle and I drop to sitting on the cold, wet curb. I cling to her, careful not to squeeze her too tight in case of injuries.

I scan the area again, looking for those motherfuckers or the Escalade. They have the advantage. They know us, what we look like. I don't know them and there could be others with them.

"Did you see what happened to the car that hit us?" I ask the guy at my side.

"The assholes took off." He's angry, glaring in the direction the SUV likely headed.

"Did you get a look at them?" I hold my breath, hoping for some good news.

"No, I was behind both of you on the road. I couldn't believe what I was seeing. It was like they deliberately ran you off the road."

I've got no words for him. That's exactly what they did.

Police, fire, and ambulance arrive and the freezing rain is now snow, thick and wet, coming down in heavy droves. I put a quick call in to Paddy to fill him in on Flora, beetle juice, and the car crash.

Like before, I'm reluctantly separated from Caro and we're taken to the nearest hospital in two different ambulances, where we're checked out. The doctor gives me three stitches to the head but other than that, I'm fine.

"We'd like to keep you overnight for observation." The ER doctor stares at Caro, trying to muster a stern, authoritative expression despite looking like he's never shaved a day in his life.

"That's not necessary." She's dismissive, bending her legs and digging her heels into the mattress to scooch off the hospital bed.

*Doogie Howser's eyes dart to me, wide and pleading for backup, clearly not capable of standing up to Caro even if she is his patient.*

*"Listen to the doctor." I grip her shoulder, trying to keep her put.*

*"Dr. Archer, you were concussed a few days ago and now a car accident—"*

*"I didn't hit my head in the crash, and I feel fine." She ignores me, planting her feet firmly on the ground and glaring at the ER physician. "I am a doctor and know what to look for. Now get out of my way."*

# CARO

"Get out of my way." I glare at the nervous doctor, brushing the flimsy white curtain skirting the small space when I walk by him.

The kid's just doing his job but I'm not staying overnight. A hospital isn't where I want to be if those men decide to come after me again. It's too easy to get to me.

The doctor stutters and stumbles over his words while I slip on my winter boots. Kit is quiet save for his long drawn-out exhalation, only adding to the mounting disappointment coming off him and directed at me.

"Look." I slip on my coat and hope my expression is more pleasant. "I'll sign an AMA waiver, if you'd like."

Relief blankets the doctor's baby face. "Great. The nurse will bring the papers." He can't get out of here fast enough, only stopping for a moment to look at me over his shoulder. "Take care of yourself, Dr. Archer, and good luck."

Kit's expression is part grimace and part unimpressed. "What's an AMA?"

"Against Medical Advice." I'm sheepish as I near him. "I'm fine. Besides, I think we're safer out there than in here if those guys come for us again."

His nostrils flare and he nods, reluctantly. "Yeah, true, but I want to make sure you're okay. In here, the doctors and nurses know what to do."

"I promise you, I'm okay. No headache, no nausea, no dizziness. And I'll tell you if that changes. I just want to sleep in your arms tonight."

"We can do that here." His arms wrap around my waist, giving me what I want. "You wouldn't be alone. I'd stay with you."

"They might not let you stay the night." I could kick up a stink and the hospital staff would let him stay, but right now, I'm appealing to the side of him that wouldn't go for me being alone in the hospital.

"I'd like to see them try." He tightens his hold and kisses my forehead.

The corners of my mouth quirk up, joy filling my chest. "I want to be at your place."

Wordlessly, he releases an arm, securing the other around my shoulder, and we go in search of the nurse. I want out of here.

It's a little after three in the afternoon when we leave. Outside is a blanket of snow and more is coming down. I pull my jacket hood over my head, and the glass doors rattle open as the wind raps violently against the panes.

Holman steps onto the curb, arms hunched into his body, and he waits for us to come to him. Everything inside me locks up and I curl my lip, wanting to yell at the man. He's the police—we should be able to count on him yet we can't.

"You two okay?" The man doesn't look the least bit concerned with our well-being, more annoyed than anything else.

"I've got a better question for you." Kit leaves my side, getting into Holman's face. "Why is a drug enforcement detective showing up for explosions, break-ins, and a hit and run where no drugs are involved?" he snarls, fists balled at his sides, and the wind whips his hair around his face. I want to join him but don't; he's doing a fine job on his own.

Holman pales although Kit has neither touched nor threatened him and I pause, letting the words—his excellent question—sink in. It's just more proof Holman has his own agenda.

The cop gains his composure. "I'd like to ask you a few questions."

"We already gave our statement to a police officer. Look it up or talk to her." Kit grabs my arm and we shuffle past him. "Do your job."

"What I find extremely interesting is how the two of you can't seem to stay out of trouble."

Every muscle in Kit's body is as rigid as a spinal board when he halts, slowly turning to face the detective, and I'm hyperaware this could get ugly quickly. Familiar feelings of frustration at Holman and concern for Kit stir inside me.

I stand beside Kit, also facing the cop, angling my head in a way to buffer my face from the snow and wind.

Holman holds a hand up in front of his face like a visor, shielding his eyes from the falling snow.

"Tell me what's going on, because we both know you haven't exactly been forthright with what you know." The cop straightens to his full height of five ten or eleven, but even still he's no match for Kit.

This man hasn't provided any support to us since we first met him, and even now, he shows no signs of remorse or worry for us nor is it clear what his angle is.

Is he doing his job? Is he here for information to share with the Beetle? Or is this about Elliot?

"From the night we met you, it was clear Caro was in danger. First the clinic, then her home, and now the crash. I'm at a loss for how much more of a picture we need to paint for you." Kit inches closer to the detective, body at the ready, and as much as I'd like him to hit the man, he can't. Holman's a cop and he could wind up in jail. I prepare to throw myself into the mix if I have to.

"Well, since you're convinced every one of those incidents are connected, care to enlighten me on what evidence you have?" Holman's sarcasm is like bile eating away at an empty stomach.

"Don't insult us," I snap. Policeman or not, this man is infuriating and useless. And the thing is, I can't tell if it's an act or if he really is a horrible cop.

"You wouldn't be popping up all the time if you didn't think what's happened so far is connected. And I'm willing to bet you have a lot more information than we do." It's my turn to get in his face.

While he's trying to keep his expression neutral, even disinterested, his brow twitches and there's a glint of acknowledgement in his eyes that only fires my irritation. "But somehow you're content to leave us hanging and vulnerable. When are you going to do your job? When someone winds up dead?"

Unable to look at him much longer, I look up at Kit, who works his jaw and gnashes his teeth, nodding. Holman finally has a shred of decency and suddenly looks hangdog, shoulders collapsing and head lowered. "Look, why don't we step inside? It's cold and you're getting wet."

Now he's interested in our well-being? He walks a few steps toward the building and the automatic sliding glass doors open. We tense, motionless, neither saying a word, and maybe he isn't so dumb after all.

Clearly sensing our reluctance, he says, "I promise to tell you what I know. It isn't much."

That gets us through the door, and the three of us huddle in the small space between the outside and interior of the hospital. For the most part, it's private, although noisy with the wind, snow, and ice whipping around outside.

Kit and I listen as he shares pretty much everything we already know. He's likely holding back information, and it's hard to say if that's because he's a cop and we're civilians, or if he's dirty.

Either way, the little he shares softens Kit's resolve and his tone is more agreeable when he says, "If you haven't figured it out, Elliot Foley is the key to all of this, and I'd bet he's setting up Caro, making it look like she's involved."

"I'm aware that locating Foley is important and so far, from what we've found, nothing links Dr. Archer to this." Holman leans against the glass wall of the vestibule, and a weight lifts from my shoulders, the nagging burden and fear that the police would come after me even if innocent.

"Our resources are focused on finding Foley. We located his phone using its GPS tracking app." He purses his weathered lips, almost as if regretting what he's said.

"And?" Kit raises one dark brow.

Holman dons a suspicious frown. "It was in a dumpster on Temperance Street and his car was not too far from there, in a parking lot by The Bay on Queen. Nothing unusual or useful in the car."

Both locations aren't too far from the hospital where Elliot works. The last I heard from him was the night of the clinic explosion. What's happened since then? Maybe Flora's right and he is dead?

"The phone?" Kit clenches his jaw and I don't blame him; talking to Holman is like pulling teeth.

"Can't say." His lips thin and whiten to emphasize he's said more than enough.

"Fine. Why don't you pay Flora Brown a visit, Foley's girlfriend. She has a lot to say."

Not waiting for more filler from Holman, Kit grabs my hand and we turn our backs on him. A cab idles at the curb and he opens the back door, ushering me in.

"Should you have mentioned Flora?" I slide into the back seat, shaking some of the snow off my hood, worried Holman still holds more of the pieces to this puzzle than we do. We just gave him one more and he could arrest Flora.

"Why not? She's out for herself, just like Elliot. Neither of them gave a shit about bringing you into this."

He has a point. I snuggle into his side, resting my head on his shoulder, and he gives the driver his address. The cab leaves the hospital.

"I texted Nick and filled him in. He's going out of his mind." The scratchy prickling of tears comes back to my eyes. Nick's not handling his role in all this very well, but Maggie and the baby need to come first.

"I'll call him."

"Have you heard anything from Paddy?" I stare out at the slushy thick snow making the drive treacherous and slow.

"Nothing yet. But hopefully soon."

Neither of us say much during the ride to his place. I try not to focus on the beating my body has taken over the past few days, more grateful to have Kit and that we're both alive and well, for the most part.

We make it to his place in nearly twice the amount of time it would usually take, thanks to the incoming blizzard.

"I was really scared today," I say as the elevator doors close.

"Me too." His warm, callused hand slides around the back of my neck and he gently tugs me to his side.

"I've wasted so much time...and today, at one point, all I could think about was what if we died?"

"We didn't." His grip tightens around my waist and I tremble.

I could have lost him today. I may still. God, that hurts. This isn't over yet. Nuzzling my face into his jacket, I blink away the mounting tears of fear. I'm sick of crying or being afraid.

"I know, but all the time we spent apart because of me... I don't want to waste any more time." I look up at him and it comes to me, what I want most. "When this is over, I want us to move in together. Start our future."

His finger lightly brushes my cheek, at what I'm guessing is a bruise, and the corners of his mouth start to lift as the elevator doors ding open. With his mouth partially open, he stills, staring down the hallway. He closes his mouth and something shifts in his demeanor.

He carefully detaches himself from me and I clamp my lips shut, trapping my whimpering lament at the loss of him. What has his rapt attention?

There's a woman standing outside the door to his loft and everything about this is all too familiar. Talk about déjà vu. I'm taken back to the very first night I stayed at Kit's.

It's that woman, Sally. He releases my hand, murmuring something about one sec or I'll be back. I'm frozen just outside the elevator doors.

Kit is now in front of Sally, talking to her. Again, his back is to me and I don't know what's being said.

As if walking through quicksand, I fight to make my way down the hall. The horrors of today, no, the past couple of days, are finally settling in. I wanted to be alone with Kit, forget for a little while. And even if it's foolish, I pray those men don't know about his place, don't know how to find us.

"Come in." He opens his front door, motioning to Sally, and she casts furtive glances my way, looking about as uncomfortable as me.

He stays at the open door waiting for me to come in. Then he takes my hand, shutting the door behind me, lowering his voice and head toward me. "Could you give us a few minutes?"

# KIT

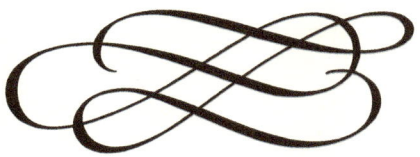

I don't like asking Caro to leave, and when I turn away from her, I falter, nearly tripping over my feet at the sight of Nick in my loft. He's a wreck, dark circles around his eyes, scruff along his jaw and hair sticking up in all directions.

"Nick, how'd you get in?" Caro's moved past me and is now at his side, leaning in to hug him.

My friend closes his eyes, hanging on tight and holding his sister a little longer than usual. The crash must have freaked him out and I can't blame him. I wasn't myself either as we flew through the air. All I could think about was Caro.

"I have a key. Let myself in." He rubs at his jaw, looking to me and then Sally, standing awkwardly near the door. "Hi, Sally. Kit." He dips his chin and looks back at Caro. "We need to talk."

"Yes, sure." She grabs his hand and starts toward the bedroom and stops, peering over her shoulder at me. "We'll just be in here."

I wish I could go with them, to reassure Nick that his sister is okay. I'd sooner die than let anything happen to her. But they need some time alone, and I have to talk to Sally.

"Sure." I nod and force an easy smile, not wanting Caro to worry about anything. "Sally, can I get you something to drink?" I stroll into the kitchen.

"No, I'm good. Thanks." She follows, lingering at the doorway. "I hope it's okay that I just showed up. You weren't saying much with your texts and I wanted to make sure you were okay."

Her tone and body posture indicate she's regretting her decision to be here. She's smart and most probably has figured out the explosion wasn't your run of the mill accident. And I suppose my vague responses don't help either.

"Ah, I wish you'd told me you were coming but it's fine. Um, I actually wanted to talk to you in person, so I'm glad you're here."

"Oh." She slumps against the wall, more resigned than anything else. "Kit, um, I have a pretty good idea what you want to talk about." Her smile is unnatural and doesn't reach her eyes.

"You do?" I throw back two aspirins with water—anything to relieve some of the tension in my neck.

"No surprise to you, I'm sure, but I've been the one pursuing you for some time now and I'm sorry about that."

"What do you mean? You didn't do anything wrong." I rest the empty glass on the counter.

"We're friends, right?" For the first time since entering the kitchen, she looks me in the eye and her gaze is hopeful.

"Of course. You don't need to ask. Sally, I think you've got this wrong."

"No, no, please let me speak. I need to say this." One hand fiddles with the fingers of her other hand. "I wasn't clueless to your reluctance to go on a date but I just thought you were shy. I really like you, Kit, and I think that was partly why I ignored the signs."

"The signs?" I cock my head to the side, wondering where she's going with this.

"Yeah. Usually, if a guy isn't interested, I don't push it. But with you, I did. I really like you and figured you just needed a little encouragement."

"You make me sound like I'm awkward and lacking self-confidence." I chuckle nervously, not recognizing the guy she described.

"No, God, I don't mean it like that at all. It's the opposite. You're confident, easy on the eyes, and a good person. Anyway, I'm getting off topic here." She inhales deeply, forcing herself to look at me once more. "If I didn't see it with my own eyes, I wouldn't have understood."

Now she's staring at the closed bedroom door where Caro and Nick are.

"What?" I rest my hip against the counter, shoving my hands into my pockets and feeling like a jerk.

*She's nervous, and I never should have agreed to that first coffee. I'd been torn about dating. I like Sally and we get along but as for if there was more, I wasn't sure. A part of me wanted there to be more, that it was time for me to move on from Caro.*

*But we never really had a chance. And if I'd declined all her attempts at a date, we wouldn't be here right now. I don't want to lose her friendship over this.*

*"I mean, I finally get it. I should be embarrassed to say this, but I tried for months to get you to go out with me."*

*She already said that but I keep quiet, letting her get it all out.*

*"And I never understood why you weren't interested." Her laugh is nervous. "At first I thought maybe you were gay, but I didn't get that feeling. And then, when you agreed to a date, you kept it really friendly and light. It didn't feel any different than it did when you and the guys would come in and shoot the shit with me."*

*"Shit, Sally, I'm sor—"*

*"No. There's no need to apologize. It's okay. After seeing you with that woman"—her head tilts toward the bedroom—"the other night and again now, I finally understand. You're in love with someone else."*

*"Ah, yeah, we hav—"*

*"Hey, really, you don't need to explain this to me. It's plain to see by the way you look at her. No other woman exists." She steps closer to me, waiting for my permission or something, and whatever it is, she must get it because she slides her arms around my middle, hugging me.*

*Then she pulls away, tipping her head back to look up at me. "She's one lucky woman. You're a great guy."*

*"Sal—"*

*"No hard feelings. We're going to be cool at the diner, I promise. And if you want to bring in your lady friend, I'd love to meet her."*

*She walks toward the front door and the knot loosens in my chest.*

*"I'd like that, Sally. Thank you." A smile rests on my lips.*

*"Take care, Kit, and see you around."*

# CARO

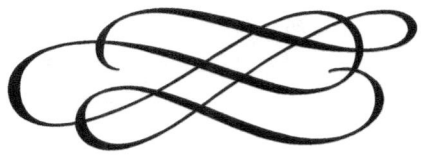

My brother and I sit side by side on the edge of the bed. Worry and guilt mar his usually strong, serene features. Nick is normally great under pressure. He had to be to deal with life or death problems when working with less than law-abiding citizens.

It's funny, our careers are so different and yet we both thrive under fire, balancing life and death daily. Even now, as he runs the Home, the decisions he makes impact the lives of many.

And yet, he's a mess right now and I guess it's more to do with the fact that he's helpless, sitting this out, and it's driving him crazy.

"I want to kill the bastard who ran into you. And Elliot and whoever else is—" He grips at his hair and I pull a hand away from his head, causing him to stop talking.

"Nick, I'm okay. Kit took care of me." I wrap my arms around him and he squeezes me tight.

We sit like that for some time, and I'm comforted by his embrace and also torn up to see him like this. No one is to blame for what's happened but Elliot, and partly me for going out with the jackass to begin with. Yet both Nick and Kit hold themselves responsible.

"How are you two doing?" He pulls back, tilting his head toward the closed door where Kit and Sally are on the other side.

"We're okay. A little shaken and anxious. I don't know if those idiots know to find me here."

He nods, lips thin and tight. "That's not what I meant. Sally's here. What's going on?"

"Kit and I are in a good place. We've been talking and..." A smile springs to my lips.

"More?" Nick raises a brow, smirking, and I nod. Neither of us wants to get into the more.

"Good. Kit still loves you. Always has and always will."

"And I love him too. I've never stopped, even though I did a lot of damage to us." The truth aches and my stomach roils.

Why do I choose now to say my greatest regret out loud? To Nick of all people? We don't do touchy-feely.

I steel my spine, preparing for some insensitive retort, sure to sting and shut down any real talk.

"Yeah, you did." And there it is but he isn't done. "But Kit understood even when I didn't."

"What do you mean?"

"Why didn't you ever let loose on me? Hold it against me?"

"Hold what against you?" I feel like we're playing pin the tail on the donkey and, blindfolded, I've just been spun around several times.

"All that I did. You were practically mute when you found out how I made a buck. Your disapproval and disgust were plain to see but you never said a word."

"You're talking about when we were younger?"

"Uh-huh."

"I don't want to talk about this." My teeth sink into my bottom lip to hold back the angry tears at myself. Since when does Nick want to get deep? "Is the thought of fatherhood making you soft?"

It's meant to be a joke, to lighten the mood, but instead it's a low blow. The hiss coming from him says as much.

"Stop. I hate this shit but it's also long overdue." Now he's playing big brother and there's no room for me to wriggle out of this conversation. "I didn't see it at first, but after you broke up with Kit, I realized what you'd done. You dumped all of your disappointment, anger, and sadness at me onto him. Shit, and what for?"

Shame and regret eat at my insides and make me want to scream and run out of this room. But this is long overdue, and where would I go? I can't live my life in denial, I've done that long enough. I can't outrun the past and my mistakes.

"You know why," I lash out, once again redirecting anger at myself elsewhere. Dammit, Caro.

*My sorry and all the words I want to say, to explain and make it right or at least try to, swell and ball in my throat. I can't bring myself to say anything.*

*"Do you know how shitty I felt, knowing Kit got all that was meant for me?" Frustration tugs at the corners of his mouth and eyes, causing tiny lines of distress.*

*"I-I didn't...I mean, how could I say anything to you?" I close my eyes and hang my head, pressing my fingers into my forehead. "You were my brother, father, and mother rolled into one. Léa died because of me." Something cracks in my chest.*

*My dead sister haunts me daily. Nick's unrelenting commitment to being a better parent to me than our own is both a balm and a plague. I can never repay him.*

*"Don't you dare say that." Nick leaps to his feet, pointing a finger at me like a knife, sharp and cutting. "You didn't kill her."*

*"No, but you both made huge sacrifices, and hers ultimately led to her death. How the hell was I to judge you both? Hold your crimes against you when it meant I got to pursue my dream and become a doctor?"*

*Tears, hot and heavy, stream down my face. My neck aches and head hurts from being battered around in the car, or maybe from facing the ugly truth of it all.*

*Insides bared, ripped wide open, all the hurt, rage, and disappointment spills from me. And most of all, my stupid inability to do anything about it. Even now, freed, the ugliness within me laughs at me at how I closed myself off and pushed those I loved, I needed, away from me. Afraid I didn't deserve their love and their surrender.*

*"You should have said something. I didn't fucking see any of this until you broke it off with Kit. When I pulled away to keep you out of danger and you didn't stop me, things started to fall into place." His cheeks are flushed, eyes wild with finally putting this all on the table.*

*"Seriously, how could I take your money and then in the next breath, tell you your life choices angered me? Troubled me? I never wanted to be part of that life. I didn't want the guns and violence at my door."*

"I get it, but Kit doesn't deserve what you heaped on him. You have a right to feel the way you do and not like his choices, my choices, but—"

"I know." Now I'm on my feet, voice raised. "It never occurred to me what I was doing..." Only now, hearing my brother, does the past rearrange itself, and as much as I don't want to admit it, what he says rings true.

It's nothing to be proud of but it helps make sense of what I did, breaking up with Kit. I loved him even as I was breaking both our hearts.

"I was studying to save lives and yet I worried, what if one day it was his life or yours on the line?"

Back then, I was afraid of so many things. Afraid to lose him to a dangerous and unforgiving life, one I couldn't control.

"Caro—"

"No, let me finish. What if Kit was wheeled into the ER dying? What if I couldn't save his life? And the same goes for you. I'd already lost my sister. Every class I took, learning about the body and how magnificent it was and also how fragile, I was scared of not being able to save your life or his. It became too much and so I pushed him away. It was the only way I knew how to survive."

"Shhh, Caro. It's okay. I get it and Kit does too." He tries to take me in his arms but I'm thrumming, not wanting to be pinned down. I know what I have to do.

"Nick, I need to..." I pull away.

"Go talk to him." He opens the door and Kit is shutting the front door. He's alone.

"What is it?" Kit strides toward the bedroom, concern shrouding his features as his eyes lock with mine.

"Hey, I'm going home. I just needed to see that you're both okay." Nick clamps a hand on Kit's shoulder. "Did anyone follow you?"

"No. I didn't see anyone, but it's getting nasty out there." Kit's gaze never wavers from mine.

"I asked Logan to get his ass over here. He isn't home. He should be here soon." Nick grabs his jacket off the chair and puts it on.

My brother hauls me into his arms and hugs me again, for what feels like the hundredth time tonight. "I'll talk to you soon. Get some sleep."

"I will." He lets me go and turns to leave. "And Nick, I love you."

"Are you all right?" Kit pulls me close and hugs me without any words, knowing I need him.

"I'm so sorry for everything." Pulling back, I stare into his loving gaze that I'm not so sure I deserve but won't ever abandon again. "I ended our relationship and was a fool—"

"Hey, we've been over this." Strong fingers sweep across my face, holding me in place. "Where's this coming from?"

"In talking to Nick, I realized how some—no, most—of what I hated about your life wasn't about you." I worry my lip and he nods, not in the least bit fazed by what I'm saying. "It was about Nick, and to some extent, my sister."

"I know." His tone is understanding. How can he be when I've messed things up for so long?

"What? How can you know when I only just made the connection?" A hot fat tear slips from the corner of my eye.

His thumb gently wipes it away. "I've always known. You and Nick aren't so different when it comes to talking about difficult things." His frank smile matches his tone. "I saw the guilt you wrestled with when it came to how he made medical school a possibility for you. And while you're a driven, smart woman who would have succeeded at anything, you also put a lot of pressure on yourself to be the best...to be deserving of your degree, of being a doctor."

"But I took all of it out on you." My fingers curl around his wrists and his hands still cup my cheek. I don't want to lose his touch. "I'm so sorry. I love you so much and I should never have ended things with you."

"Hey, I forgive you and I love you. You don't need to keep apologizing." He brushes hair away from my face and I'm a ball of emotions. Relieved and overwhelmed with love and joy for his forgiveness as well as upset with myself for the damage I caused.

"I came to terms with this a long time ago. There's no point in getting stuck in the past. We're moving forward." His warm, soft lips press against mine, and I wrap my arms around him, needing him close.

He brings his face to the crook of my neck, lips brushing the shell of my ear, and says, "And yes. I want us to live together when this is all over."

# KIT

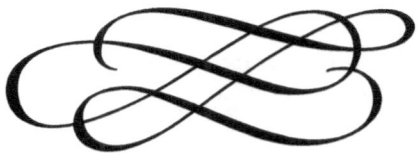

*A knock at the door severs the moment, and I groan into Caro's neck, not wanting to let her go. Before we have a chance to break apart, Logan walks in, key in hand.*

*"Ah, am I interrupting anything?" He pauses at the door, waggling his brows, his smile spreading from ear to ear.*

*"Come in." Not letting go of Caro just yet, my lips brush against hers once more and then I grudgingly put some space between us.*

*"Hey, Logan." She sits on the sofa and I amble to a closet. "We've got work to do. I think we're safe here, for now, but it's only a matter of time before they find us. We need a plan."*

*After tonight's crash, which could have been an attempt to kill us, we've got to go on the offensive, and to do that, we need to go over what we know and figure out our next move.*

*Whiteboard in hand, I use my foot to shut the closet door.*

*"Dude, you have a fucking whiteboard?" Logan snickers, removing his jacket and boots and letting the excess snow fall to the floor. "Who are you, a closet corporate asshole?"*

*"Shut up." I rest the board on a side table and lean the back against the wall. The board is covered in notes and ideas for the business plan for the Phoenix. I've got to capture this before I erase it.*

*On the same wavelength as me, Caro grabs her phone. "Let me take a picture and then you can erase it."*

*"Thanks." I rub my jaw and grab the eraser and markers from the closet.*

*"So what are we doing?" Logan makes himself at home, pulling out a dining room chair, drink in hand.*

*"We need to go over everything we know and see what we're missing…" I look to Caro, who's now cleaning the board. "You know*

me, I'm a visual thinker. I need to see it all laid out. There's got to be something here that we have overlooked."

"Sounds like a good idea." Caro picks up a marker and starts to write the initials of everyone involved, like Elliot and Flora. Logan calls out beetle juice and I make another marking, and off to one side I jot down the locations of various things that have happened, including the clinic locations and where Elliot's phone and car were found.

I step back, standing next to where Logan sits, and take it all in. Caro joins us. This idea is a way of trying to stop things from spinning out of control. So far, we've been scrambling for clues and always behind.

And now, with everything laid out, I'm more frustrated than ever. At first glance, it isn't helping, only adding to the fucking confusion. It's fragmented and nothing jumps out or fits naturally.

"I feel like we're forgetting something." I rub my jaw, combing through the chaos of today and further back, scrutinizing the board.

"Like what?" Logan asks.

"Something to do with the accident." It's an indescribable, niggling sensation but as I say it out loud, the sensation grows and more comes to me. "Or something about the guys in the Escalade."

Then like a bolt of lightning, another memory streaks across my mind and I snap two fingers together. "There was an emblem or logo on the jacket of the guy driving." I squint, trying to picture it as I looked at the guys in the car in the rearview mirror. "And the same logo was on the side of the car."

We're upside down, the car rolling over and over as the shaky, vague logo takes shape in my mind.

Caro leaps from her spot toward the board, her eyes aglow. "One of the witnesses said something similar to one of the officers at the accident scene. They said the Escalade had a logo on the side."

Hope sparks in my belly. This could be the break we need.

"Why don't you try drawing it?" Logan is now standing too. "Even if it's crappy. It might jog your memory or spark something for Caro."

"Sure." I draw a crude shield or crest and shade in parts in red marker. "I think this was red and there was also gold in it." I point to another part of the image.

"Do you remember if there were any words or letters on it?" Caro tilts her head to one side, studying the image.

"Let's see if we can find something similar online." Logan brings a laptop over to the table and opens up the browser.

With a few strokes, hundreds of red and gold logos pop onto the screen. "Let's narrow it down to security or transportation firms." I lean over Logan, scanning the page. This is going to take a while; there are pages and pages of images and my hopes are waning.

Logan types more words into the bar, narrowing the search criteria, and another page of images is displayed. Nothing looks familiar and someone's phone rings.

"It's Paddy. One sec." I hit speaker on my phone and place my finger to my lips, motioning for them to listen but not say a word.

"Hey, Paddy. You got anything for me?"

"I gotta make this quick. Drug Enforcement has been investigating the emergence of beetle juice for some time now. It first hit the streets in Toronto but spread fast. Now you can get it pretty much anywhere from B.C. to Newfoundland."

"What about the supplier? Anything on him?" I scan the computer screen with one ear on the phone call and the rest of my brain intent on finding this logo.

"He's known as the Beetle and Drug Enforcement are trying to identify him. They have a few CIs."

A red and gold shield on the screen screams at me. My finger presses into the screen and all eyes land on me. I mouth 'that's it' and Logan hits the image, taking us to a website for a local security firm.

Paddy continues, "But all they know is he's some wealthy white guy based in Toronto. No name or other details. That's all I got for now. I'll call if I find out more."

"Okay, thanks. We'll call if we need anything else." I hit end on the call and Caro's stunned expression causes me to jolt. "What is it?"

"I've seen that logo before." Her voice is far off, as if she isn't here with us.

"Where?" I ask at the same time Logan asks, "When?"

"I want to say the investor party. It keeps coming to mind when we were standing outside the front entrance...but I'm not sure. I could be wrong." Doubt creeps into her voice.

"Go with it." I rub at the back of her neck to loosen the tension building there. "Don't discount anything. The smallest detail could lead to something."

"SUVs and limos were parked to one side of the entrance and...for some reason, I think one of the cars had this logo on it."

Her head snaps to the whiteboard, and she grabs a blue marker from the table. I want her to tell me what she's thinking but I don't want to break her concentration.

She writes VW on the board close to Elliot and Flora's initials. VW? Who's VW? As I flick through all the names we've come across, nothing and no one comes to mind.

"Outside of Casa Loma, Victor Walsh was standing beside an SUV with that logo on it." Her words come out as a rush and she's just as surprised as I am at that connection. "He was talking to a man wearing a jacket with that logo."

My mind races with the addition of Victor but Caro isn't done. The marker hovers over the letters and she draws a circle around the VW, thickening the lines of the letters until they touch as if they're bleeding into each other, almost as if one.

"It looks like the logo for Volkswagen." Logan's confusion is clear in his tone.

"Yup." I nod in time with Caro and we stare at each other.

All those moments with Victor and his questions about Elliot and his odd behavior, keen interest, come at me in slow motion. Then Paddy's phone call just a few minutes ago—"some wealthy white guy based in Toronto."

"We found the Beetle." I grin as sweat breaks out along my body.

"I think so." Her cheeks are flushed with excitement.

"What?" Logan scratches his jaw, furrowing his brow. "Oh, yeah! They make a car called the beetle, don't they? Or the bug?"

"Yes. Victor's the Beetle." Caro looks a little queasy. "Now what?"

"Are you okay?" I grab her by the elbow, pulling her close.

"Yes. Victor is a donor for the Home and someone Nick and Maggie invested a lot of time in." She's shaking her head in disbelief. "And all this time, he's flooding the streets with drugs."

"Yeah, but we're going to stop him. Do you know where we could find Victor?"

"What? Now?" She takes a couple of steps back, staring at me incredulously. "Why don't we call Holman and get him to arrest Victor?"

"We can't trust Holman. You've said so yourself. If he's working for Victor and we tell him we know Victor's the Beetle, we might as well give him the gun to kill us with."

She gasps, but there's a glint of understanding in her eyes. Holman has proven to be an unknown factor. We don't know where his allegiance lies, and we'd be foolish to trust him now, especially when we have the best lead. Possibly our only chance at ending this before someone gets killed.

"Can't it wait until morning? There's a blizzard out there." She taps a marker in her hand nervously.

"We can't waste time. Look what happened today." My hand reaches out, fingers sliding over the bluish bruise on her cheek from the crash. "Victor may not know about my place, but he will. And soon. They found us today, and my gut tells me they went there looking for Flora and got lucky when we were there too."

It's only now that we've had a chance to take a minute and lay everything out that I figure Elliot's girlfriend and losing time was the reason those guys found us today.

"Flora?" Her eyes widen.

"Of course. That makes sense, man." Logan nods, working through the same information I did to come to the same conclusion. "You said she was snooping around on the streets, and she most probably wasn't discreet."

"Yeah. It wouldn't have taken much for Victor to get her name. A junkie will turn over their mother for a hit, and she may have even used Elliot's name."

"Flora might be in danger." Fear coats her voice.

"Yes, but in case you forgot, we distracted them. They didn't go into the clinic, they came after us. You're the main target right now. And that's why we can't wait."

"Okay, so we can't wait. I get it. But what about Flora?"

"I'll go make sure she's okay. Get her to hiding," Logan says.

Caro's shoulders relax. "Great, thanks."

"Yeah, that's good. Don't scare her, and if she needs help in hiding, we can help with that, okay?" I give Logan a stern tone and look. "You have to be careful. Someone could be watching her too."

"Got it." Logan takes a gun from his jacket, showing me he's got protection.

"How can I help?" She's still hesitant but there's acceptance to her voice.

"We need to know where Victor is right now. Would he be home at this time of night on a Sunday? And if so, where is that, and let's make sure he's there."

"Let me call Willow. I know Victor's wife, but Willow is closer to her. They've worked together."

She makes the call while I get my gun and make sure it's loaded, focusing on what I'm going to say to Victor when I talk to him. This is going to end tonight.

"Willow's calling his wife now. She'll make up some excuse and text me." Her eyes are glued to my gun. "What are you going to do when you see Victor?"

"Kick some ass," Logan chimes in, pumped.

Shaking my head, I hold back a grin. Caro won't find this amusing although I'm also pumped. We finally know who's behind this.

"I'm going to clear your name. Make him understand that you aren't mixed up in any of this. You don't have whatever it is he wants, and you don't know where Elliot is."

"Okay, and I'm coming with you." Caro clings to my shirt, her gaze pleading, and it stabs at my heart.

Securing her to my side, I say in a controlled tone, "Text Logan the details about Flora." Then I look to Logan. "You better get a move on in this weather. Text me once she's secured."

He nods and strides to the door, pausing to take in Caro stuck to my side. She can't come with me. It isn't safe, but I'm waiting for us to be alone before letting her down easy.

Once the door clicks shut, I step back from her. "Please send Logan the details."

She doesn't move, studying me for a beat or two before she picks up her phone. I shrug on my jacket and boots.

"Willow just texted. He's at home. I just sent you his address." She inches closer, eyes red-rimmed and features weary. "She says it's horrible out there, and she was on her way home but our place is closer. She wants to come by, maybe even crash tonight. I said it was okay. And she said she remembered something about Elliot."

My heart rate spikes. Elliot. I still very much want a word with that guy. Or maybe more a fist. "Really? Good. We need to find him too."

She nods solemnly. "Please don't fight me on this. You can't go in alone. What if Victor has those guys at his place?"

"It's his home. Chances are he won't. I can do this on my own. It'll be fine. I need you to stay, please."

"And what about what I need? I need you to be safe." She narrows her gaze and twists her lips.

"I will. I won't do anything foolish, promise. Besides, you have to be here. Willow's coming." I wrap my arms around her and bury my face into her neck. "I can't be worrying about you. Stay, and once Willow is here, don't open the door for anyone. Got it?"

A tiny squeak escapes her. "You better come back to me. We still need to figure out where we're going to live."

"What's there to talk about? My place is best." I force a chuckle, eager to get this over with so we can start our life. I squeeze her tight and pull back.

"What?" She tries to feign offense but worry still etches her features. "See, this is why we need to talk."

My self-control is feeble at best, and I cling to it with an iron grip, briefly pressing my lips to hers. I want to kiss her long and deep but don't trust myself to let go.

*My mouth lingers on hers for a heartbeat, maybe two, before I rip myself from her embrace. "I love you."*

*"I love you. Be careful."*

*One more kiss and I leave. I want a day, a decade, a lifetime to be with her and the sooner I get Victor off our backs, the sooner our time together begins.*

*Victor's home isn't too far and even in this shitty weather, I make it to his Rosedale home in decent time. I park the loaner car, another one from the garage, at the curb.*

*Flurries swirl around, falling and sticking to everything. There's easily a foot of snow and no sign of the weather letting up. This crappy snowstorm doesn't help with getting places; it adds a lot of wasted time and will make it difficult if things go south.*

*Victor Walsh answers the door, a flicker of surprise in his eyes before his features slide into a frown. "Mr. Jensen, I'm surprised to see you at my front door. What can I do for you?"*

*Grunting, elated to see the motherfucker and to finally have the Beetle in my grasp, I push past him into a large, opulent foyer of marble, crystal, and glass. A plump, pleasant looking woman shuffles from an adjoining doorway, pausing at the sight of me.*

*"Victor, is everything okay?" She nears the hall table where a phone sits.*

*Anxiety oozes from her, and calling the cops is likely on her mind. That might not be a bad thing. But I need answers first.*

*"Alma, everything's okay." Victor's tone is calm, and I halt in my tracks. "Mr. Jensen and I are going to my office."*

*He makes a point of saying my name loud and clear. What? So she knows who I am if something happens to him? I don't plan on killing the bastard, although the thought is tempting. Well, at least that's not my intention, but I'm open to whatever is necessary. My only goal is to get him to leave Caro alone. Forever.*

*Walsh leads the way down a carpeted hallway, piloting Alma back into what looks like a family room with a roaring fireplace heating the large space.*

*She's still nervous, and I wonder if she has any idea how much of a scumbag her husband is. I could reassure her that no harm would* come to him, but that's a lie. It's hard to say how things will end; it all depends on Victor. If I have to use other, more unsavory measures, well, I'm prepared.

His office is as I expect, large and pretentious. All the things some men need to feel important. He positions himself in the expensive leather chair behind the desk, interlacing his fingers over his belly.

"Mr. Jensen, I'm trying hard not to be upset with you for coming into my house the way you did. What do you want?"

So far, he's sticking to the friendly hospital administrator persona. The one most believe him to be, and I revel in the ironic lopsided grin I stick on my face. I don't have time for his bullshit and get to the point.

"Beetle juice."

The moment of recognition is so fast, in a blink of an eye, I could have easily missed it. But I didn't and it's all I need.

He cocks his head to one side, wrinkling his graying brow. "I beg your pardon?"

"Cut the crap, Victor. It's just you and me, no audience." I press my flattened palms into his desk, getting closer to him. "Caro doesn't have what you're looking for. She isn't involved in any of this, so back off. Now."

"I'm sorry, but I haven't the faintest idea what you're talking about. Is Caroline okay?"

Like snapping a twig in two, my patience is gone and I bound around the desk, grabbing the lapels of his suit jacket and hauling him out of the chair. It falls backward and he lets out a groan when I slam him into the wall.

"Look here, Beetle, it didn't take us long to figure out who you were once those assholes ran us off the road. With the right info, it won't take the police long either. We're more than happy to fill them in."

With one of my hands, I secure his arms in front of him. I wrap my fingers around his wrists, grateful that with my size, I can easily control him. The forearm of my other arm presses into his neck, holding him in place. His eyes bulge and he gasps, features slack with shock.

"We can prove you were behind the break-in at Caro's house, those texts, and today's crash." It isn't true—I don't have solid proof but with some more digging, I'm confident I could nail him.

I don't need proof for this exchange. He only needs to believe I have what it takes to bring him down and I won't hesitate to do so.

Time is the problem. I don't have all the time in the world, because if this keeps up, Caro could wind up dead. This must stop now.

"Right now, you're anonymous—the police are looking for you but don't have a clue. I can change all of that and I will if you don't stop going after Caro."

It's as if my words release him from his act. His mask clatters to the floor and he sneers. "Give me what is mine and I'll leave her alone. All of you, even Elliot."

"I don't give a fuck about Elliot." I jostle him some more and his teeth clack together. "He set up Caro. Leave her out of this."

"And I'm supposed to just take your word for it that she knows nothing." He pushes on my hold but it's futile. "Elliot disappeared with what's mine, and Caroline knows where it is or how to find Elliot."

"No, she doesn't." I press a little harder on his larynx, hoping it might improve his hearing.

"Well, Flora was a dead end. Pun intended." His expression darkens.

"What does that mean?" My blood runs cold, dizziness dancing around my head.

Why didn't I take action on Flora's safety sooner? I'd only clued in to how they found us at the Deer Park clinic this evening.

Fuck. Fuck. Fuck.

"She's quite the chatty one, but unfortunately she didn't know much, not even where to find Elliot. But she did have lots to say about Caroline. So that leads me to believe Caroline knows more."

My teeth clash, grinding at the thought of what Flora might have said about Caro. I want her to be alive and safe, but my concern only somewhat lessens the burning in my gut at her potential lies.

"If Caro is hurt at all, I will call the police."

*He chuckles but doesn't look me in the eye, suggesting a hint of fear or bluster.*

*"I tell you what." Victor pushes once more against me, and I loosen my hold but stay close. "Caroline is safe...for now. I give you twenty-four hours to find me Elliot."*

*"And if I can't, then what?" As if I can trust this bastard.*

*"Then Caro's fair game."*

*I growl back in his face and my chest bucks against his clavicle. "No."*

*"Take it or leave it. None of this goes away until I get what's mine. You either help me or you're in my way."*

*A strange bristling at the nape of my neck causes me to look toward the door where two bodyguards are poised to attack, both with a hand on a gun in its holster. They are all too eager for Victor's command.*

*"Have we got a deal?" He pushes from me, straightening his jacket and wearing a smug smile.*

*And it isn't like I have a choice, so I nod, snarl, and storm past the gorillas.*

# CARO

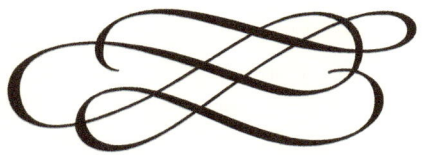

*Alone. Exhausted and also wired, I pace, waiting for a phone call or the buzzer, announcing Willow's arrival. Finally my phone rings and I sprint toward it, hesitating when I don't recognize the number. I can't ignore it, not when Willow's on her way and both Kit and Logan are out there doing dangerous things.*

*"Hello?" Trepidation fills that one word.*

*"Dr. Archer, it's Detective Holman."*

*Great. "Oh, hello, Detective."*

*"I tried calling Kit but it went to voicemail and this...um, it's the kind of thing you...ah, don't leave a message about." He sounds odd, more uncomfortable than usual.*

*"What's wrong?"*

*"There's no easy way to say this but I wanted you both to be aware...Flora Brown is dead."*

*"What?" Bile races up my throat and I bend at the waist, covering my mouth to stifle a cry and the urge to vomit.*

*"Yes. Her body was found an hour ago."*

*"What happened?" I force the words past my queasiness. "Do you know who did it?"*

*Flora...Logan. I switch to speaker phone and text Logan the news, explaining I'm on the phone with the detective.*

*"It's an ongoing investigation—"*

*"Detective Holman, don't give me that garbage." On shaky knees, I drop onto the couch. "You can't call and drop that bomb in my lap without details."*

*I stare at the three little dots, waiting for Logan's reply.*

*"Ah, Doctor, I really can't say much. We don't know a lot."*

"Was it an accident? How did she die?" I blink back my tears, furious with myself. Logan's text comes in—he hadn't even reached her apartment yet in this weather. He's going to turn around and asks for the address to Victor's. He'll join Kit.

Did we get her killed? Oh my God, did our visit today lead the Beetle—no, Victor—straight to her? Or was it Elliot? I'm no longer sure of my ex and what he's capable of.

"We found her in her car just outside her building. It looks like there was some kind of struggle, and while I can't say for sure until we get the medical examiner's report, it looks like asphyxiation."

My hand flies to my throat and breathing becomes difficult. She was strangled. "She was murdered."

"Look, I realize this is horrible news and I have questions for both of you. Kit mentioned Flora earlier today and we'd already questioned her."

"You did?" A flurry of sensations clouds my mind. Were we already too late when Logan left to get her?

"Yes, her number was on Elliot's phone. I need to know what you discussed with Flora."

The sharp buzz of the intercom for entrance to the building startles me. Willow.

Mindlessly, I hit the enter button while still talking with the detective.

"We talked to her briefly, and she basically confirmed she was helping Elliot. He used the clinics, first Jane Street, then Deer Park, as a place to ship the oxy to. At Deer Park, Flora would then get the shipment to him."

"Did she know where Elliot was or how to find him?"

I huff sarcastically, wiping at a stray tear on my cheek. "No. Don't you think if we knew how to find Elliot, we'd have him? Or told you?"

He utters a derisive huff. "Okay, I'll need you both to come down to the station and make this official."

My head shakes from side to side before I even respond. "Not tonight. We can do it in the morning."

"Very well. The weather is crap out there." He sounds beyond tired. "Have a good night, Dr. Archer."

There's a hard knock at the door and I head to open it. "Goodnight, Detective Holman." I swing open the door.

My heart stops.

All the air rushes from my lungs.

Elliot Foley, snow sprinkling his hair and jacket, stands in front of me.

A mad scientist, that's what he looks like, with ill-kempt, dark-brown hair and glassy dark-brown eyes, almost wild. His jaw is covered in a dark beard with a smattering of gray. He doesn't look like the Dr. Foley the police and maybe even Victor are looking for. I've never seen him so disheveled.

Jaw slack and mind reeling, my finger is still on the end call button. Shit. Holman. Could I hit redial? I no sooner think it than his feral gaze darts to the phone in my hand. He lunges and knocks the phone from my grip, where it clatters to the floor.

He kicks the phone farther from me, and I use the chance to get away. I want to push past him out into the hall and scream fire—isn't that what you're supposed to scream instead of help?

But I can't get past him. He'd grab me for sure, and then he slams the door. Retreating into the loft, I try to put as much distance between us as is possible.

"Caro, finally, it's just the two of us." He advances on me.

"Elliot, I've been trying to get ahold of you." My tone is reedy and sounds nothing like me as I try to act normal. "Where have you been?"

"I've been close by. I see you're back with the big guy. What's his name again? Rock?" There's a slight curl to his lip.

"Why are you here?"

He isn't acting like himself. Is he high? His eyes rove around the room, and his posture's wiry, strung tight.

"I've been watching, trying to get to you." His fingers rake through his nest of hair. "I need your help."

"Help? How can I help you?" Maybe if I stall him long enough, Willow will get here and call the police when I don't answer the door.

He's stolen a large shipment of oxy and done who knows what with it. He has Victor Walsh, the cops, and maybe other bad people after him and he wants my help?

"Come with me." His arm shoots out but I'm quick, putting more distance between us.

We're six or seven feet apart and his arms are open as if ready to embrace me but it's more like grab me. I move two steps to the right and he mirrors my movements.

"This doesn't have to be a big deal. Come with me. Put on your coat and let's go."

"Where are we going? Why?" I can't leave with him.

What does he want with me? To kill me? No one knows he's here, and apart from escaping, who knows if I'd ever be found.

I back up farther, closer now to the table with the whiteboard and markers. The kitchen would be good—I could grab a knife—but I can't get there without going closer to him. I need something, a weapon. Something I could throw at him or hit him with.

He edges in my direction, teeth bared and nostrils flaring. "You're going to make me hurt you, aren't you?"

He dives for me, fingers grappling for my shoulder, but I push him hard. He stumbles, falling onto his ass. He's down, but still in my way. I have to go past him to get out of here. Dammit.

I lift my foot to kick him in the groin and he's quick, grabbing my ankle and bringing it down to the floor. Quickly, I roll out of his reach, kicking out my feet and making contact with his body.

He releases a wail and a groan as I ignore the ache in my side and spring to my feet. I'm trapped, with no way out. He's still blocking the path to the exit.

Not one to readily give up, I'll fight him to the end, but in case I fail, I need to leave a message or clue for Willow or Kit, or someone.

He growls from the floor, grabbing at one side of his head and pushing up onto all fours. I grab a dining chair, lifting it over my head and throwing it in his direction. But he's fast, rolling away before the chair crashes to the hardwood.

"Caro, fucking stop," he roars, face dark and menacing.

*Shit.* With a marker in hand, I quickly scribble on the whiteboard, then drop it onto the floor before Elliot realizes what I've done. I whirl around and he's right there.

His hands grip my shoulders so hard it feels as if my bones will crack, and I cry when he tosses me against the wall and my head smacks against the hard surface.

Little white dots dance in my vision, growing bigger and brighter until everything swims and I see nothing.

---

*Someone slaps my cheek and my eyes snap open. Elliot's looming over me and snow pelts my face. I'm bundled in something, arms tight to my body and legs touching. It's like I'm a burrito, and I'm cold and damp. We're...we're outside?*

*He yanks at whatever is around me and rolls me three times, then he pulls on my arm until I'm sitting. It was some kind of sheet he had around me. Is that how he got me out of the loft?*

*My head throbs and I remember hitting my head against the wall. Or more like, Elliot threw me into the wall.*

*Blinking, I try to get my bearings, inhaling deeply to lessen the pain. Where are we? My teeth chatter and my blood is so cold. I'm chilled to the bone with no jacket.*

*Through the gusts of snow and wind, I make out what looks like the deck of a boat. A boat in the middle of a blizzard? Is that even possible?*

*"Where are we?" I stutter through blocks of ice where my lips once were.*

*"Shut up." He wrenches my arms behind my back and heaves me onto my feet.*

*My vision isn't clear, and nausea ebbs and flows in the pit of my stomach. Planting me in front of him, Elliot pushes me across the snow-covered deck into the cockpit.*

Immediately, I welcome the shelter from the elements. He nudges me downstairs, below deck, into a small living space. It's warmer, heated. Thank goodness.

"Stay still." He pushes me onto my knees, tying my hands behind my back. "Why are you always so stubborn? Always thinking you're in charge? You couldn't just make it easy and come with me, could you?"

"Elliot, what do you want with me?" I can't think of one reason why he wants me, of how I could be of use to him. The only thing running through my mind is that he's going to kill me.

I'd never have believed him to be a killer, but it's clear I don't know this man at all.

"I just need to think." He sits on the small sofa across from me, head in his hands. "Why isn't Flora answering?"

"Flora's dead." The words are out before I even have time to think, to consider whether sharing that news with him is a good thing or a bad thing.

His head snaps up and he's pallid, sickly. "Dead? Fuck, no." His hands shake in his lap where they are balled into tight fists.

I don't move or breathe, struggling to keep the pricks at the back of my eyes from turning into tears.

Why did I have to open my mouth? Judging from his reaction, Flora's death is news to him. I had thought it was Victor, one of his men, but Elliot had crossed my mind. But he didn't kill her. Maybe this means he won't kill me?

"When? How? Who did it?" Now in front of me, he clutches the sides of my head, grasping my skull so tight the pressure in my eyes is unbearable. I'm going to throw up.

"You're hurting me. Stop." I wriggle my head and shoulders from side to side and he releases me, sliding back onto his calves. "She was strangled in her car. The cops don't know who did it."

"When?" His voice is so low, I barely hear him over the howling wind above.

"Earlier tonight."

"Fuck!" He gnashes his teeth together and jumps to his feet, once more towering over me. "What the hell am I going to do now?"

"Let me go," I plead, letting him see my fear. If he believes he's got all the power, maybe it'll work to my advantage. "Turn yourself in before whoever is looking for you finds you. They'll kill you." I'm rambling, not even sure if I'm making any sense, but I need to get through to him. "I can help smooth things over with the police. If you untie me, I'll say I came willingly."

At this point, I'll say anything to get away from him. He's unstable and I just want out of here alive.

"No, no, no." He paces in front of me.

"Elliot, give them back the oxy and whatever else you took."

He rolls his eyes with a dramatic, disgusted sigh. "Give them back the oxy? Do you hear yourself? I do that and they'd kill me. There's no forgiveness in this business. Fuck, that's just one reason I wanted out. They're ruthless killers. Besides, the oxy is gone."

"Gone? What?" My heart nearly leaps from my throat, struggling to believe the one thing that could save my life is gone. "What did you do with it?"

"Shut up! I need to think." He stops for a second, then resumes wearing a hole in the floor. I'm getting dizzy watching him tread back and forth.

"I need to leave. Find a country with no extradition to Canada. Somewhere in Africa or the Middle East. Fuck!" Like a child throwing a tantrum, he stomps his feet and I squeeze my eyes shut and focus on my breathing.

I'm not sure what's coming next. Is he taking me with him? Going to kill me? One thing is for sure, it won't be good. I've got to get things under control if I stand a chance of getting away.

His fingers dig into my chin, causing my eyes to spring open and breath to lodge in my throat.

"I knew you'd prove useful." His sinister chuckle surprises me. Who is this man? "I'll leave you for the Beetle. Yes, yes, this could work."

On his feet, he starts his pacing again, talking out loud. "I've already laid the groundwork and planted enough clues to implicate you in all of this." He halts, gazing down at me. I'm a rabbit, trapped, looking into the savage eyes of a wolf.

"He already thinks you're involved, now he needs to find you here. I know, I know." He bounces, eyes and mouth widening like he's just discovered the cure for some infectious disease. "I'll make it look like you killed me."

Is he serious? He's going to frame me for murder? Not only will I have Victor gunning for me, like I already do, I'll have the police. So if I don't die at the hands of a drug lord, I have life in prison to look forward to.

Pointing at me, he rubs at his bearded jaw. "Sorry, I thought about killing you. Sparing you the torture and God knows what else Victor will inflict on you, once he gets a hold of you, but I can't. He won't be satisfied with both of us dead—he needs someone to work out his rage on. And he must believe I'm dead. I can't have him hunting me."

My heart plummets to my toes—Elliot is raving mad.

# KIT

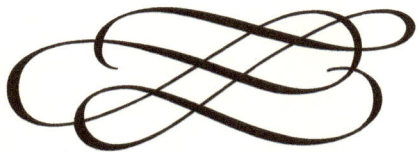

Sleet bites at my cheeks and the wind growls as Victor Walsh's front door slams behind me. This is one hell of a storm.

I tuck my chin into my chest, shielding my face, pausing at the figure trudging up the driveway. The battle is real. It's taking this guy every ounce of energy to push through the thick, wet snow.

He lifts his head and stops. His gloved hands grip the sides of his hood to keep the whistling squall from lashing at his exposed skin. Logan.

"What are you doing here?"

"Ah, Flora is dead." He blinks back the flakes collecting on his lashes.

"Fuck." Not only is it cold outside but now my insides are chilled. I shiver and stop walking. "Does Caro know? Did you find the body? Were the police there?"

"Hey, relax." Logan holds up a hand.

Victor's cryptic comment about Flora careens into my already troubled thoughts. Caro is the only thing on my mind. She's alone. My need to get back to her suddenly overwhelms all my senses.

"I didn't even make it to Flora's. Caro got a call from Holman and texted me. So I turned around and headed here. What did you find out?"

"We gotta get back to Caro." I jog through the drifting snow toward our cars on the road, Logan at my side. "Victor is an asshole."

"Is he the Beetle?"

"Yeah, and he wants Elliot within twenty-four hours. Without him, Victor won't leave Caro alone."

It's going to take at least five to ten minutes to clear off most of the snow from the car.

"Fuck." He smashes his hand through the pile of snow on the hood of my car. "How the hell are we going to do that? That's all we've been doing, looking for Elliot, and we don't have any leads."

"Paddy and Holman may have something more. I'll call them. And Victor doesn't know it yet but if I have to, I'll turn over everything we have to Holman to nail the bastard. Meet you back at my place." Before brushing the snow off the car, I start the engine and crank the heat.

The roads are thick layers of packed snow and ice and growing snow drifts. Even with the plows out, it's slow going. According to the weather report, we're in the thick of a blizzard and it's only just begun. We've got another twelve to eighteen hours of this shit.

Needing to hear Caro's voice, I dial her number. No answer. Shit. I try again and it rings and rings before going to voicemail.

Did something happen? Why the fuck isn't she answering?

Next, I call Paddy, and he has nothing to report. The cop's reluctant to dig any more into Holman's cases. Every time he snoops, he's at risk of getting caught.

I try Caro again, and still nothing. Desperation wheedles its way into my gut, coiling and churning around my insides. Clinging to hope, I dial the detective in search of anything to help us find Elliot.

Holman doesn't bother with greetings. "Mr. Jensen, you heard the news about Flora Brown?"

"Yeah, I did. Have you got anything you can share?" I keep my tone friendly and optimistic.

Holman blows out a heavy breath and with it goes my hope. "No. We found her in her car, strangled. There was some kind of struggle based on the state of the interior of the car, but this weather is a bitch for forensics so we don't have much more."

"Fuck." I press the back of my head into the seat rest and grip the steering wheel so tight that my fingers ache.

That's what Victor meant by his comment. He had Flora killed and he had no qualms in making sure I knew it. Do I share this with Holman?

Do I tell him about Victor being the Beetle? Or do I wait until we regroup? There has to be something we're missing.

*If I tell him about Walsh, Caro could be in even more danger. I'll play it Victor's way for now.*

"I said this to the doctor…we'll need you to give a statement about your conversation with Flora. I'd have preferred it was tonight but this weather…"

"Fine, tomorrow. Any news on Foley?" *The drive is taking way too long. And why the fuck won't Caro pick up the phone?*

"Nope. We're still looking."

"All right."

*The futile conversation with Holman plagues my thoughts, mixing with Victor's threat and my unanswered phone calls to Caro. By the time I finally reach the loft, there's a sharp pain stabbing at my chest, only intensifying with every second without seeing Caro.*

*Logan jogs toward the elevator as the doors start to close and I jab my finger at the open door button and wait for him. I bring him up to speed on the conversations with Paddy and Holman, and still no answer from Caro.*

*Forget an elephant on my chest. I've got a fucking city of dread ready to crush me. I have to see Caro, hear her voice and know she's okay.*

*When the elevator doors slide open on my floor, we need no words. I race to my place and Logan's right behind me.*

"Fuck." *I burst through the open front door, all my worst fears imploding onto me like the demolition of a skyscraper.*

*Something is wrong. She'd never leave the door open like that. A sinking sensation overwhelms me and I'm drowning.*

"Caro." *I don't feel her presence. She isn't here.*

*And despite the open concept and no sign of her in the bedroom, I shout her name over and over.*

"Shit." *Logan laces his fingers behind his head and grabs at the back of his neck.* "I should have stayed with her."

"We don't have time for that." *Guilt eats its way through the room, sucking out all of the oxygen.* "There's plenty of blame to go around. We need to find her."

"Do you think Victor did this?"

231

Shaking my head, I scan the room. "No. He's not above doing something like this, but the way he was talking to me tonight, he hadn't made a move yet. This is someone else. Or something else?"

"We should call Nick." He pulls out his phone and I wrap my hand around his with the device in it.

"No."

How the hell am I going to tell Nick I let someone take his sister? Besides, it isn't like he can help us. He has Maggie and the baby to think about.

"We need to focus on finding her," I growl, ripping the phone from his hand. "Look around, there's got to be something."

My eyes drop to the floor and her phone at one end of the kitchen catches my eye. "Fuck." My hand tightens around the device so hard it pops. We have no way of tracking her, and she's without any way of contacting me or calling for help. "Fuck."

The buzzer sounds and Logan hits the button. "Yeah?"

"Hi, it's Willow." Logan lets her in and I try to clear my mind. I can't think straight.

A few minutes later Willow stands in the doorway. Snow falls from her parka and boots.

"Hello?" She's cautious, rubbing the slick soles of her boots on the mat, but doesn't come in. She must sense the tension or that something isn't right. "Caro?"

"She's missing. We just got here and the door was open and..." I hang my head, unable to continue.

I fucked up big time. If anything happens to her...

"We found her phone on the floor." Logan picks up where I trailed off. "We were hoping you might know something."

"Oh my God." She covers her mouth, eyes darting around the room. "I don't know where she is. I haven't talked to her since earlier. I got stuck behind an accident—that's what took me so long to get here." She's rambling and I'm only picking up pieces of what she's saying. "I remembered something about Elliot..."

"What is it?" I rumble with such intensity she steps back.

*Is this it? The missing bit of information that could change everything? Did Elliot take her? Or someone looking for Elliot other than Victor? Is there another player we're not aware of?*

"I'd been racking my brain for days now, trying to remember anything to do with Elliot or Flora from when they were at the clinic."

*I nod, rolling a hand in front of me, eager for her to get to the point. Logan casts a sharp glare in my direction, as if telling me to quit being an asshole. I don't give a fuck. Caro's life is on the line.*

"Several months ago now, a call came into the clinic for Elliot about marina fees for a sailboat. They left a message, and I had to call them back and let them know Elliot wasn't at the clinic any longer."

"What about the boat?" Logan asks, and I want to yell at her to get to the point. I appreciate the help but every second counts.

"Elliot inherited a boat from a godparent, I think it was his godfather, about eight or ten months ago. The berth had been paid until the end of last year and they were calling for payment for this year. I was thinking—"

"What marina? Do you remember the name?"

*If Elliot has a boat and he hasn't transferred ownership, it would explain why no one knew about it, not even the police. He's got to be hiding on the boat.*

*While finding Elliot is a priority, getting Caro back is more important, and he might not help us with that. If there's another player, we might have to wait for them to contact us and make their demands.*

*Fuck, that's if they have demands. Kidnapping Caro might not be about the drugs or money. It could be for revenge. Teach Elliot a lesson? We're running out of time.*

"Yes. In fact, we log all our calls at the clinic. If you have a computer, I could get the name and even the boat slip number. I remember they left a fairly lengthy voicemail. I'm sure that's where Elliot is staying."

*Willow pushes the hood off her head and her long blonde hair is loose and slightly damp, clinging to the edges of her face. She unzips her jacket and takes off her boots while Logan and I head for the dining room table, toward the laptop.*

233

*That's when I see it. The whiteboard.*

*It's covered in the details from earlier tonight but what catches my eye are black marker rings, too many to count and as if done in haste, circling Elliot Foley's initials.*

*If ever there was a map, those messy black lines would be the X, marking the spot. Or in this case, the who.*

"Look." *I point to the E and F encircled many times.* "It's a clue from Caro. Elliot took her." *My grin splits my face.*

"Damn, I love that girl." *Logan chuckles.*

"She's brilliant!" *Willow's fingers fly over the keyboard.*

"Shit, you weren't kidding. It's got everything here. You entered all this info yourself?" *Logan stares at Willow in awe.*

"No, the software turns voice into text."

*It's all there. The name of a marina just west of Toronto, berth number forty-eight, and even the name of the boat, Destiny.*

*Perfect. We got him. Elliot is about to meet his destiny.*

"Let's go. I'll call Holman on the way. We could use some backup, and I'll let him know about Walsh too."

"Walsh? Victor Walsh?" *Willow slants her head to one side, studying me.*

"Yeah, he's the one Elliot was giving the drugs to." *I grab my heavier jacket with a hood from the closet and start putting it on.*

"Holy…he's the last person I would have suspected. He's well regarded." *She puts on her jacket.*

"Thanks, Willow. This is huge." *Logan steps into his boots.* "You okay to get home in this? If not, you can stay here, or my place is just two floors down."

"I'm going with you." *She puts on her gloves and walks to the door, leaving no room for objection.* "I can help if Caro's hurt…I'm a nurse."

*My stomach spasms, not willing to accept the possibility, but I don't fight her on this.*

*The drive to the marina takes more than twice the usual time, and I curse Mother Nature all the way until I make the call to the detective.*

"Holman, it's Kit. Listen, we've found Elliot Foley."

"What?" *His voice rises several octaves.* "Where is he?"

I tell him about Caro's kidnapping and the information we got from Willow about the boat and the marina, and that we're on our way.

"Wait for me, Jensen. Do not get out of your car or get on that boat. Cruisers are on their way. Wait." Holman's tone is both commanding and frantic.

"I'm not waiting. Elliot has Caro and he's desperate." I don't mention we may already be too late. I can't even let myself think it. "And one more thing. We know who the Beetle is."

He sucks in a breath but quickly gets ahold of himself, coming on strong and authoritative. "Who is it?"

"I'm not saying right now, but I will. Gotta go." I hang up before Holman can say something else.

He'll be pissed at me, and I can't blame him, but withholding all the details on the Beetle is deliberate. It gives him more incentive to get his ass here soon.

We pull into the marina, and with the weather as it is, it's difficult to see your hand in front of your face, much less anything else. From where I park, there are only a handful of boats in the marina, most of which are shrink-wrapped in white plastic.

I never thought it was possible to live on a boat in the winter. How cold would it get? Especially in this storm. Fuck, Caro better be okay. Otherwise, Elliot is going to wish he was dead.

"You see that boat with the lights on?" Logan points ahead of us to a soft yellow glow that stands out in contrast to the stark white snow swirling around.

"Yeah, that has to be Elliot's boat." I turn off the engine and we all get out of the car.

I'm armed, as is Logan, and he thought ahead and brought bolt cutters. Just what we need to get past the locked chain-linked door into the marina.

The walk down to the boat is brutal. Wind and snow nip at my exposed skin, and every step is treacherous. Parts of the dock are slippery as an ice rink and other parts are snow drifts, easily a foot or two high.

*When we finally make it to slip forty-eight, Logan shines a light along the hull of the boat toward the back, scanning for the name. Through the gusting snow, the Destiny comes into view. This sailboat is it, and the lights are on inside.*

*The idiot also doesn't have his boat shrink-wrapped so both the steps and railing used to climb onto the boat are slippery and the deck is covered in snow.*

*The wind batters me about and I cling to the railing, trying to stay upright on the deck of the Destiny. I reach out with my other hand to steady Willow, who is having a hell of a time putting one foot in front of the other.*

*She's a slip of a thing and Logan's behind her, quick to come to her side and hold her by the shoulder. His sharp gaze, even in this blizzard, tells me to let go. He's got her.*

*The cockpit is only a few feet away, and it's where the boat's helm and steering controls are. It's a slim possibility, but what if this is a trap? What if Caro didn't leave that message and it was Elliot or one of Victor's men? And worst of all, even more so than risk of death, what if Caro isn't here?*

*Terror grips my throat and I briefly close my eyes, trying to rein in all emotion. I can't think about that right now. I've got to stay focused. Find Caro. Bring down Elliot. I motion for Logan and Willow to check the deck and I'll go down below.*

*Face angled down to shield my exposed skin from the attacking storm, I make my way inside. It's instantly warmer and although not as deafening as on deck, the boat rattles and shakes, sounding as if it's about to fall apart.*

*Quietly, I descend several steps to below deck and anguish fills my lungs at the streaks of blood on the floor and walls.*

*Caro.*

*My knees lock and my hands press into the walls on either side of me as I try to stay upright. Fuck, it's a lot of blood.*

*Whimpering, barely audible over the uproar outside, snaps my gaze to a corner. Tied up and gagged, Caro's doe-eyes fill with tears, and her dry lips tremble around a rag in her mouth.*

*My muscles taut and primed for a fight, I rush to her and she jerks her head violently from side to side, stare fearful.*

*It's too late.*

*Something hard plows into the side of my head and I stagger backward, gut clenching, and fall to my knees.*

*Everything spins. Caro is there, crying, rocking back and forth, and then she isn't.*

*Black and white, light and dark. Who hit me?*

*Whack. Another strike to my head and my back bows, my legs tremble, and I fall like a redwood cut down, crashing to the forest floor. I curl into myself, head pounding, dizzy.*

*A dark figure looms over me, and the hazy shape of a boot smacks into my side, jarring my ribs, and the air whooshes from me.*

*I can't breathe. It hurts to even try.*

*My vision is a blur and I can't grasp what or who is in front of me.*

*Caro is the first, the last, and only thing on my mind.*

*I must get to her...*

*Black eclipses light.*

*Darkness eats everything around me.*

# CARO

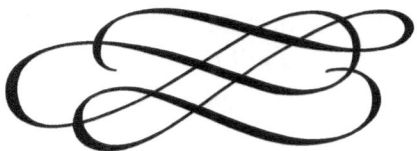

Shards of ice carve into my chest, cracking bones and tearing tissue and organs. A knot builds in my throat with nowhere to go. Kit is motionless on the floor, blood pooling on the rug by his head.

Elliot is enraged, face blotchy, teeth bared, and animalistic sounds come from his mouth. He's kicking Kit in his side and stomach. After a while, Kit no longer moves and my heart stops. Tears sting my eyes, clouding my sight, overflowing and streaming down my cheeks.

I struggle to get off my ass and onto my knees, shuffling toward Elliot with my arms tied in front of me. My body swings into his back and my screams, begging for him to stop, are frantic and garbled.

The monster swings around to face me. "Look what he made me do."

He grips my neck, nails tearing into my skin and fingers squeezing my throat, as he hoists me to standing. "We've got to get out of here. Fuck."

Spittle flies at my face and I flinch, biting into the soggy rag and wrestling for air, unable to take in enough to fill my lungs and steady my heartbeat.

His other hand slides under my arm and he finally releases my throat. Arms around me in a bear hug, my arms stuck to my sides, he lugs me across the floor like a rag doll, leaving Kit unconscious on the ground.

Tears are coming too fast, hair sticks to my face, and I can't tell if he's breathing. What if he has a collapsed lung? Or a concussion. He could choke to death.

I grunt and growl, trying to get Elliot to stop, to not leave Kit like this. I scream and beg for mercy, all stifled by the gag, for Elliot to let me make sure Kit's alive.

He doesn't care. After getting me on my feet, he yanks me upstairs, dragging me through the cockpit and out into the maelstrom of ice, wind, and snow. A blast of icy flakes cut at my exposed skin, nipping at the thin material covering my body, rapidly dampening my clothes. Frosty air rushes at me, chills racing down my arms.

God, I'll get hypothermia if I'm out in this too long. I can't see more than a foot in front of me, and even if Elliot were to release his hold, I'm useless. Hands bound, mouth gagged, and no coat, I'll be lucky to stay alive.

He pulls me along the deck and a man in a dark hooded jacket lunges from the blustering storm. He tackles Elliot and I'm knocked onto the deck. My teeth grind together, causing me to cringe as I'm pulled up by someone behind me.

Oh shit. There are two men? Victor?

He could kill us both right now, no question. I strain, muffled pleas trying to escape from my mouth.

Elliot's on his back, wailing and kicking at the man in the dark jacket, who's now straddling and punching him unconscious. The man on top of Elliot's prone, motionless body looks at me and I expel a muted cry of joy. Logan.

The person at my back turns me to face them and I'm stunned. Willow.

"Oh my God, are you all right?" She pulls the stiff, damp cloth from my mouth and down past my chin.

"Kit's..." The corners of my mouth are cracked and my throat's dry.

"You have no coat, we need to get you inside." Her arms wrap around me but I'm still freezing.

"Willow, Kit...he's downstairs, badly beaten." I quake and my teeth chatter. "I need to go see if he's okay. Can you untie me?"

I push away from her, holding up my bound hands, fingers unmoving, and she works to free me. At my back, Logan leans into me and his warmth is a welcomed relief.

"Are you okay? You can't stay out here." He squints past us, from left to right. "Where's Kit?"

"He's—" I croak, moving my legs in place to keep my core body temperature up.

"Where is he?" At his feet, Elliot's passed out, and Logan takes over from Willow, untying me quickly.

"He's below deck. Elliot knocked him out. I have to check on him." Uncurling my fingers is torture. My bones ache and joints crack, frigid and numb.

Logan squats to secure Elliot's hands with the rope used to bind me. "Is anyone else down there?"

"No."

"Go. Get inside. You'll freeze to death. Willow, go with her."

My body is sluggish and mind foggy from the cold but the warmth of hope glows within me, forcing me to put one foot in front of the other. Once inside and at Kit's side, everything will be all right.

From the bitter, wintry gloom Victor Walsh steps into my path, gun aimed at me, and two muscled men are at his back, each with their own gun.

"Caro, stay where you are," Victor says.

Blood thunders in my ears and sharp fingers of icy terror stab my heart. Kit needs me. I can't get to him.

Logan wraps his hand firmly around my arm, pulling me behind him, now blocking Willow and me from Victor and his men. I'm trembling uncontrollably and I can't tell if it's only from the cold or the raw, frigid fear coursing through my body.

"Who the fuck are you?" Logan snarls, and while he saw Victor at the investor party, it's hard to make out anything or anyone in this weather.

Victor laughs, motioning with his gun for his men to grab Logan and Willow. We couldn't run for it even if we tried, and one of the men grabs Logan's gun and tosses it onto the snowy deck.

We're all captured. The men have Logan and Willow and that leaves Victor and me. All I can think about is Kit.

If he stumbles outside, into this mess, he could get himself killed. But that's if he's even conscious. He took a brutal beating.

What if…no, I can't think about what ifs—I've got to get to him. But first I need to get past Victor.

I swallow thickly, a dry iciness coating my throat. I'm not afraid to die; right now with the way I feel, dying might be a mercy. But what I can't fathom, won't accept, is losing Kit.

He's finally back in my life. I can't lose him. I won't lose him.

"I wanted to thank Mr. Jensen for leading us to Elliot. Where is he?" Victor glances around the boat, straining to see more than a foot in front of him.

"He's hurt. Victor, please let me go to him." My tears sting my cheeks like icy darts.

"Victor, drop the gun." Kit's large frame breaks through the whiteout.

Dried blood sticks to one side of his face and I want to cry tears of joy. Kit is free. He's here. Alive.

An abrupt bark of laughter ruptures from Victor. "You're quite funny, Kit, I'll give you that. In case you haven't noticed, I'm the one with the gun." He waves it around for good measure.

Kit is unarmed, hobbling toward me, and slides an arm around my shoulders. The weight and heat of him...I'm still cold but a little warmer with him at my side. He drops a kiss on my chilled lips, unzips his coat and drapes it around me.

I cling to the warmth of him, biting my lip to keep my sobs from escaping.

"Kit, you work fast, finding Elliot like you did. It's a good thing I had you followed." Victor grimaces.

Elliot, now awake, shivering and glowering from the deck, says, "Victor, we need to talk."

"The time for talking is done." The older man's eyes darken and narrow into thin slits of hate. "Your time is up, Foley. As for you,"—he turns to face Kit and me—"I'm generally a man of my word..."

Despite what he says, I get the sense this will be one of those instances where he won't follow through on a promise. Although I don't know what he's talking about.

"I'd like to say I'd leave you and Caro alone, but this is far messier than anticipated. I recognize my man, Foley, made the mess that it is, but you inserted yourselves into this business."

I tense and my fists curl. He makes it sound like we wanted to be involved. As if reading my mind, Kit says, "No, we did nothing. Elliot framed Caro. He wanted you to believe she was part of the operation and that she took the drugs. She didn't."

"Ah, that may be the case, Kit, but the problem is you now know about the drugs. You all know who I am..." He pauses, pulling his scarf higher up his neck. "I can't have that, and I won't accept your word. In this business, one must deal in absolutes."

Victor glares at us, standing tall and indomitable, oblivious to the storm swallowing us. "It's a shame, but this is how it must be."

His hand does something, the one holding the gun, and what exactly I can't say, but I hear a click, or maybe I imagine it because it's hard to hear anything. All I know for sure is he's going to kill us and I can't let that happen.

There is a long, thin rod, maybe eight feet tall, resting against the boat at my back. Its tip is pointed and sharp.

Slow and muddled, a numbness seeps deep into not only my bones and muscles, but also my thoughts. I fight through the cold heaviness, inching backward ever so slightly. At first Kit tightens his hold, but sensing my intention, he relaxes and I slip from his coat.

In one fluid move, or at least that's what I command my body to do, my fingers coil around the shaft and my arm pulls back and rises. I'm surprised by how light it is. And icy, so very icy.

The skin of my palm sticks to the chilled rod, I think it's aluminum, like a tongue to a cold metal spoon. It's going to hurt when I pry my hand away, but I can't worry about that now.

There is no time to second guess or pause and I bend, arcing my arm forward in one smooth sweep, projecting the javelin-like object at Victor.

Kit's hands latch onto my waist to stop me from falling over. His weight anchors me and also provides extra tension, helping to ensure the spear hits its mark.

The harpoon with its barbed claws tears into Victor's thigh and he falls backward. Impaled, he screams in agony, flinging his gun into the blizzard.

*While I didn't have the clarity of mind or forethought to think about my aim, the spike missed his femoral artery, maybe by a millimeter or two, and I'm grateful. My intention hadn't been to kill even if that's what he had planned for us.*

*One bodyguard flings Willow toward Logan and starts toward Victor. Dark scarlet, almost black, blood soaks the white snow around his leg, and through the din of the storm, a man's voice bellows, "Police. Drop your weapons."*

*I never thought I'd hear those words, and relief comes at me in one fell swoop, weakening my knees. I grab onto Kit and everything goes black.*

# CARO

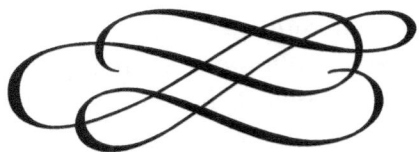

Blinding white lights pierce my skull and I moan, turning to one side. My head aches, pulsating, and a dark figure cuts across the dazzling beam, shielding me from further assault.

Kit hovers over me, expression severe if not for his teasing half grin. His face has fresh bruises and a new butterfly bandage where he'd been stitched after the car rollover. His unruly strands of honey-blond hair tumble over his forehead, and his gaze is tender.

"You're awake." His voice is raspy and low and my stomach somersaults.

"Where am I?"

"The hospital. How do you feel?"

"Okay." I settle farther under the covers. "Warmer. Better now that you're here and okay."

Clumsily, my hands reach for him, needing his touch, to feel him. I curl my hands around the warm, tight skin of his forearms, climbing up his arms to his broad shoulders and settling with my fingers entwined at the nape of his neck.

"Are you okay?" My fingers thread through the curling ends of his hair.

"Yeah. Just a mild concussion and a few more stitches—"

"Stitches." My hands still and I worry. "Where?"

"Just four at the back of the head where Elliot hit me. I'm fine." His confident, calming tone reassures me. "It's nothing my girlfriend can't handle." One corner of his lips tips up and one of his dimples makes an appearance.

"Girlfriend?" My gaze sweeps past him, pretending to look for this woman. "Where is she?"

"I'm looking at her." His thumb strokes across my brow. "Are you sure you're okay? You passed out on the boat, and it took what seemed like forever for the paramedics to arrive. Once they got you on the ambulance, they said you were hypothermic but fortunately your body temperature hadn't dropped too far."

That's good and likely means any impact to my body due to the freezing temperatures won't be lasting.

"I've never been so cold in my life, but I'm good." I pull at his shoulder, bringing his face closer to mine. "Better than good."

Lips brush over mine, causing me to moan and pull him closer to me. The kiss is painstakingly gentle and oh, so slow. Almost too slow for me to keep my sanity.

His mouth sweeps over mine, mapping every ridge and valley of my lips, and it's as if he's imprinting my mouth, the feel and taste of me onto him.

Tiny, sparking shivers of need course through me, not a hint of cold, only heat filling me. My trembling hands curl into the back of his shirt and I'm so relieved he's here, alive and well. And damn, this kiss.

It's everything, as if breathing new life into me. I can't get enough, but flinch when tenderness near one of my hips jars me out of my bliss.

He breaks the kiss, resting his forehead on mine, and his breath heats the lower half of my face and neck.

"You've got a nasty bruise. Not sure if it's from the fall or something else...something Elliot did." His jaw clenches and his gaze is fierce with a hint of something else, dark and brooding, almost mournful.

"What's wrong?" I sink my head into the pillow to get a better look at him.

"Nothing. I just wish I'd stopped Elliot before he took y—"

"Shhh, let's not play this game. We're both okay. Elliot's in jail, isn't he?" I ask, not knowing what happened after I passed out.

"Yeah, both Elliot and Victor were arrested." His gaze brightens. "You need your rest."

My fingers sweep across his forehead, examining the stitches and bruising by his hairline.

"Did you kiss me to get a better look at my injuries?" His tone is stern but features soft.

"No, I wanted to kiss you. And I wish I could do more."

He leans down and cups my face, brushing his long lashes against my cheek, and a hot tingling races down my spine, spreading tiny bumps all over my skin.

Then he pulls back, an amused smile darting across his lips, and then his nose rubs against mine and I can't help but beam as his soft lips find mine in a quick, sweet kiss.

"I have to call Nick. He's going insane and would be here if not for the weather." He stands up and takes out his phone, tapping on the screen before putting it to his ear.

Eyes on him, his features tense and furrow then relax as a smile spreads across this ruggedly handsome face. "Nick, she's awake."

He waits a few more minutes, nodding before he passes the phone to me.

"Hello." My stomach twists and sudden nerves constrict my throat, anxious to hear my brother's voice.

"Caro, thank fuck you're okay. I wish I could be there, we were so worried—" his words are fast and furious and his anxiety palpable even through the device.

"Nick, I'm okay," I reassure in a soft tone that also does wonders for my churning insides. "We got them and I'm doing fine."

"I don't know what I'd have done if I lost you." It's a husky whisper, his voice fading with each word. Is he crying?

My heart spasms at Nick's anguish. I can't fully grasp what he's been going through. It's been a harrowing time for me but for Nick, sitting this out must have been torture.

"Hey, Caro." Maggie's now on the line. "How are you?"

"Hi, I'm good. Actually better than good. So glad to have this all over with."

"We're so happy you're okay and now you can put this behind you. I wish we could be there." Remorse resides in her voice.

"I know but it's better this way. It's horrible out there and you're safer off the road. Maggie…is Nick okay?"

"Yes, he is." She half chuckles, half sniffles. "You know him, he's so happy you're okay but he's a little…" she trails off, likely searching for the right words to convey my brother's emotional state without making him sound weak. As if.

"I get it," I offer, saving her from the hunt.

"Well, I'm going to let you go. You need your rest. But as soon as this weather settles, we're coming to see you."

"I'd like that." I beam even though she can't see how happy the idea of seeing them makes me. "Love you both."

"You too. Take care." She ends the call and I hand the phone back to Kit.

"You all right?" His gaze lingers on my face, studying me.

"Yes. It was good to hear their voices, and Nick can finally relax. Hopefully, stop beating himself up for not being around for this."

He snorts and shoves the phone in his back pocket. "Not possible. That's his specialty."

I chuckle, wincing at the sharp stab to my head.

"You okay?" He bends down once more, getting close to me and I carefully nod. "You have to promise me three things."

"Three things? What?"

"One, you take some time to heal."

I open my mouth, readying the doctor in me to make an entrance but not in a good way. Heal is all I should be doing right now.

Kit's already ahead of me and presses a finger firmly on my lips to silence me. "Hear me out before you go all I know best on me."

I laugh and my cheeks flush. "Fine. Go on."

"Come away with me. If you stick around here, you won't rest. We'll go to the cottage in Quebec or if that sounds too cold, we'll lie on a beach somewhere."

"Either sounds amazing and this is an easy promise. I'm there. I'm yours, just say when."

"When." He gifts me with a sly, lopsided grin.

"Let's go." I grip the covers, preparing to throw them off, when his hand rests on mine and he chuckles.

"Not so fast. Once we've got the okay for you to go home, and that's not happening tonight. You're in here overnight and I'll be right here. They're bringing in a cot."

My lips brush along his stubbled jaw, thrilled to have him with me tonight. Forever. "I promise, as soon as I'm good to travel, we'll go."

I want to steal another kiss and a lot more but we're in a hospital. And even if we weren't, it isn't like Kit would let me take it too far. He's more concerned about my health than anything else right now.

"What's the second promise?"

"This one might not be so easy."

I tense and he notices, an eyebrow rising as one side of his lips hitch up.

"I'm not promising until I hear more," I tease, although I'm a little on edge, not quite sure what to expect.

"Relax." He drags the tips of his fingers in a sensual path along my collarbone.

My eyes flutter closed and a quiver runs through me as I blink, gaze landing on his loving face. I trust him and I'm open to whatever this is.

"I'm moving in with you." He's confident.

"My place?" I'm stunned, not at living together but at the location.

"Yes. And before you say a word, hear me out. The promise I want you to make is not to fight me on this. I'll keep the loft as an investment, but I want to be with you and as for where, I don't care. Your house is bigger."

"Okay." I've got nothing else. He's all I want and like him, I don't care if it's in a shack.

"That's it?" There's a triumphant gleam in his eyes, but it's fleeting, as if he doesn't trust my easy agreement.

"Yes. I want to live with you more than anything, and I'm glad it's my place. It is bigger, but if you insisted on your loft, I'd make the move."

His arms pull me into an embrace and his deep laughter rolls through me. "Oh sure, you say that now that I've agreed to your place."

"I mean it." I slide my arms around him and bury my face into the crook of his neck.

He kisses the top of my head and holds me tight. We stay like that for some time, the strong sense of belonging and security overshadowing everything else. So much so, I almost forget there's one more promise.

"Wait." I reluctantly release my hold, forcing him to move back. "You said three promises, so what's the third?"

"Oh, yeah. This one is also nonnegotiable." His fingers smooth the furrow I'm not aware is forming on my brow. "You really have to stop doing this."

"What?"

"All these trips to the hospital. It's getting old, and I'm not so sure I can take much more. You have to promise me you're done with hospitals."

Laughter tumbles from my mouth and tears spring to my eyes. It isn't all that funny but it hits me. This ordeal is over, and as much as it was terrifying and I'd never want to live through it again, I came out the winner.

I screwed up years ago and pushed the man I loved away. And while at the time, it was what I felt and all I knew, not knowing how to work through the warring emotions inside of me—loving a man with all I am and hating what he did for a living—I cast him aside. I hurt him. I hurt me. We were both adrift and wandering but not happy, not whole. Until now.

"That's a promise I'll readily make." I plant a kiss on him. "I love you."

"I love you too."

My stomach flutters as his fingers find their way to the back of my neck. His mouth covers mine and he tilts his head, deepening the kiss and increasing the pressure. Suddenly, the kiss is savage and demanding, curling my toes, stopping my heart, and leaving me breathless.

# EPILOGUE

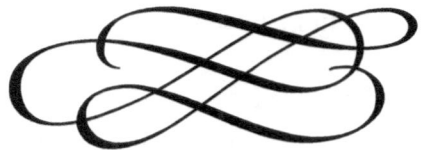

## THREE MONTHS LATER

### *Kit*

*The blackish water and gray soapy bubbles swirl around the sink drain, once, twice, before disappearing. Grease is a bitch to get off your skin, and this is my third attempt to get my hands clean.*

*Tap off, I grab the towel and dry my hands and forearms, dropping it onto the counter. The door opens and Caro enters my garage/workshop. It used to be her mini-hospital, but since her home was vandalized and we then moved in together, she insisted on giving me this space. Now it's my office and garage.*

*The restoration business is doing really well, and we're getting ready to showcase the 1934 Ford 3-Window Coupe I bought from Mr. Pinter. It's hard to believe but that baby is almost done and the old coot wants to buy it back. Yeah, Mr. Pinter, the Ford's original owner, is willing to spend a lot more money to have the car back.*

*On one hand, at the time of the sale, I made it very clear to Pinter that if he wanted the Ford back, he'd have to pay fair price. Now that it's fully restored, the car is worth a lot more and the garage is getting a lot of buzz because of it.*

*I love it. The new business, my new at home working space. All of it.*

*The Phoenix is still my main place of work, but on days when Caro's going into Léa's Home late, I tend to stick around and work from here. Any chance I get to be with her, I take.*

*Gone are the days of the clinic. She finally gave up doing double duty and plans are proceeding well for government funding on the Home so she doesn't have to fret about the salary she now gets.*

*Elliot and Victor are behind us. They're both in jail awaiting trial, and I still smile every time I remember Victor was denied bail. He's a flight risk. Sometimes having money and the means can be a bitch.*

*Dr. Foley is up on serious drug charges, attempted murder and more, with a bleak future in prison. As for Victor, his role in all this has caused quite a stir in the medical community and on the streets. Not only is he facing a string of charges related to the oxy and the damage and torment he caused Caro, he's also charged with Flora's murder and much more. From what Holman says, both cases are solid even if Victor did cover his tracks well.*

*Once things settled down, the shady detective paid us a visit and came clean on his involvement. While he might not be completely aboveboard, it turns out his ex-wife was hooked on beetle juice and almost died. He'd left her because of her drug abuse but still cared.*

*During the time of the clinic explosion and the drug enforcement investigation on beetle juice, his ex-wife was in rehab and he wanted justice. He was vague but basically confirmed he pulled strings to be involved in anything to do with Elliot Foley.*

*The asshole doctor was his only lead. The drive to bring down Foley and ultimately the Beetle was personal for Holman. I can all too easily relate to him.*

*For me, while the whole thing was a nightmare, I can't regret it or say I'd change a thing. It's fucked up to even think it, I know, but I got Caro back.*

*Who knows, I like to think we'd have eventually found our way back to each other, but the ordeal sped things up. And now, I'm one selfish but ecstatic bastard, cherishing every freaking second with her.*

*The past is what it is and we can't change it, but I'm no longer wasting any time.*

*"You ready?" Caro searches my face before dipping her gaze lower, taking in my casual shirt and jeans. "We don't have to do this, you know."*

She's sexy as hell in a plain white shirt stretched over her gorgeous chest and skinny blue jeans hugging her lean, long legs.

"I know, but I want to."

We're having dinner with Maggie, Nick, and Willow. Logan was invited but the dumbass left town a few days ago. Like usual, no goodbye. The guy is haunted, and not even whatever is, or was, going on with Willow was enough to keep him in one place.

"Before we go, I wanted to ask you something." She takes a step toward me, nibbling on her plump bottom lip. It's her tell and usually means she's worried, nervous, or both.

"What's wrong?" I slide my hands around her slender waist, pulling her snug against me.

"Nothing. Why do you think something's wrong?" She brushes a fleeting kiss to my mouth before attempting to step back from my grasp.

"Oh, no. You aren't going anywhere." One hand slides under her chin, tipping her eyes up to meet mine while the other firmly grips her to me. "Maybe you don't want to go to Nick's?"

"No."

"Then what is it? What did you want to ask me?"

"This may seem fast…" She pauses and an amused smile darts across her lips. "Fuck it. I don't know why I'm nervous. I want this more than anything else."

I arch a brow, opening my mouth to speak, when she cuts me off.

"Kit, will you marry me?" Her eyes sparkle and cheeks flush a dainty shade of pink. And instead of waiting for a response, she rushes on, "And I don't mean in the distant future or a big white wedding. I don't want to wait and I don't need our friends or flowers and a gown. All I want is you. We have a few days off in a week. Let's get married in Vegas."

Her hands clutch at my shirt and her need, the overwhelming desire to spend the rest of her life with me, invades every molecule and every ounce of oxygen in the room.

Despite the heady, euphoric sensation rushing through me, I school my features. Surprised isn't the right word, nor is shock. Marrying Caro was always my dream. Our marriage inevitable.

*My chest hurts, but it's the good kind of hurt. The kind where your insides swell to epic proportions, threatening to explode because you're so damn happy.*

*"Say something. Tell me I'm not crazy. Tell me you want this too." She pulls at me as if we aren't close enough, and her eyes are wide and turbulent.*

*"You know, I told myself for years that I had to move on from you." I rake a hand through my hair, brushing away those lonely years.*

*A frown messes with her pretty face. "I'm sor—"*

*"Uh-uh, none of that." I place a finger on her mouth. "I've told you, I don't want your sorrys. You're forgiven, I swear." I pry her hand from my shirt, bringing it to my chest and pressing her palm flat against my heart. "What I'm trying to say is, I would have waited forever for you."*

*"Kit." Her eyes shimmer with unshed tears, and her other hand releases my shirt as her hand rises to my face. She glides her fingers tenderly along the stubble of my jaw. "Is that a yes?"*

*Hope beams from her entire being. She's my beacon of all that's good and beautiful in this world.*

*My lips split into a shit-eating grin, and I slide a hand into the pocket of my jeans, producing a small red box. It sits easily in the palm of my hand and I flip the lid open with my thumb.*

*A sparkling solitaire winks at me from its perch on a red velvet cushion, nestled in a thick gold band. I've had this engagement ring for nearly three months now.*

*The second we were free of the oxy crap, I bought the ring.*

*"Caro, will you spend the rest of your life with me?"*

*Her mouth opens and I bend my head, lips capturing the smallest gasp of surprise from her.*

*She grabs at me, and our kiss isn't gentle or hesitant. I'm possessive, greedy, and determined, taking not only her lips and tongue but also her words and love.*

*My fingers slip into her curls, holding her there as I pull back so there's only a breath between us.*

"So, was that a yes?" I can't stop smiling. Fucking glowing. I never thought it possible but it's me.

Tears tumble down her cheeks, tears of joy, and she nods. "Yes."

My nose rubs against her, warm and soft, before I angle my head and close my eyes, brushing my lashes against hers. She shivers, fingers digging into my sides, and I open my eyes, locking with hers. Her face is flushed and her eyes are glimmering.

"Me too. Yes. I want to marry you." I kiss her once more, warmth spreading throughout my body.

"Were you going to ask me today?" She beams and I nod.

Caro tilts her head back and her body shakes. Her laugh is bright and pretty and the best fucking sound in the world.

Thank you for reading KIT! To continue in the Scarred Hearts universe, grab Logan's race-against-the-click, second chance romance story in Nomad.

**I'm the reason she's a target—and the only one who can keep her alive.**

My mother's locket was supposed to stay lost. Forgotten.
But my uncle won't let it go.
He swears it's the key to the treasure my grandfather died protecting.
And I think he knows I lied.

Truth is, I hid the locket in Willow's home. And when my uncle proves he's willing to kill for it, I know keeping Willow—and the damn locket—close is the only way to keep her breathing.

She hates being trapped with me almost as much as she hates needing me.
And while I try to uncover what this locket truly means, every stolen glance, every accidental touch stirs the ache of what we almost had.

*If I fail to solve this, I risk not only the truth...*
*I'll risk her and any chance we might have.*

### READ NOMAD TODAY!

# OTHER BOOKS BY S.M. WEST

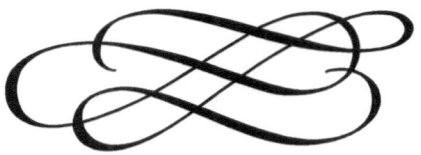

**Scarred Hearts Series**
*All can be read as standalones*
*Prophet*
*Kit*
*Nomad*
*Griffin*
*Zero*

**Winslow Grove Series**
*All can be read as standalones*
*All of You*
*Here with You*
*Fool for You*

**6ix Loves Series**
*All can be read as standalones*
*Kissing the Chef*
*Trusting the Ex*
*Scoring the Player*
*Promising the Billionaire*
*Stealing the Billionaire*
*Falling for the Charmer*

**Trojan Series**
*All can be read as standalones*

# ABOUT THE AUTHOR

*S.M. West is a USA TODAY bestselling and award-winning author of sexy, angsty romances about brave hearts, wild love with a few heart-pounding twists along the way.*

*For new releases, exclusive excerpts, giveaways and more, sign up for her newsletter:*
*https://geni.us/SMWestNL*

*www.smwestauthor.com*